SMALL
FELONIES

SMALL FELONIES

FIFTY MYSTERY SHORT SHORTS

BILL PRONZINI

St. Martin's Press ▪ New York

Design by Glen M. Edelstein

Library of Congress Cataloging-in-Publication Data

Pronzini, Bill.
  Small felonies.

  "A Thomas Dunne book."
  1. Detective and mystery stories, American.
I. Title.
PS3566.R67S6   1988   813'.54   88-15856
ISBN 0-312-02283-2

First Edition

10 9 8 7 6 5 4 3 2 1

CONTENTS

PREFACE

The short-short story is both a difficult and an atrophying literary form. One fact may explain the other: because it isn't easy to concoct a story of two thousand words or less that has a credible plot, deft characterization, suspense, *and* a strong climactic effect, many writers tend to steer clear of that length. Many editors, too—though in the few remaining markets for short genre fiction, good vignettes are still welcome.

Personally, I've always admired the short-short. I find conceiving and writing them to be pleasurable, challenging, stimulating. They're over and done with quickly, too. Novels take *months* to write. You can turn out a finished short-short—the first draft of one, anyhow—in an hour or two. Immediate sense of accomplishment, instant gratification.

I've published close to a hundred vignettes in the past twenty years, in a variety of categories—about the same number (though not, alas, of the same uniform quality) as the master of the category short-short, Fredric Brown. Most of mine, unlike most of Brown's, happen to be in the mystery/suspense field. And that is what led me to the idea for this book.

So far as I know there are only five other single-author collections composed mostly or entirely of popular short-shorts at least some of which are criminous. All fifty-three entries in Octavus Roy Cohen's *Cameos* (1931) are vignettes—mainly of the slice-of-life, slick-magazine variety—but less than a score deal with mystery themes. William MacHarg's 1940 collection, *The Affairs of O'Malley* (reprinted in paperback as *Smart Guy*), contains thirty-three detective tales featuring the tough homicide cop; many are two thousand words or less, but several others are longer. Two superb collections by Gerald Kersh, published only in England, are loaded with short-shorts—thirty-two of thirty-seven stories in *Neither Man Nor Dog* (1946), thirty-one of thirty-five stories in *Sad Road to the Sea* (1947); there are only a few crime tales in each volume, however, and all entries are a remarkable, oddball fusion of the literary story and the genre story, spiced with elements of fantasy, horror, and dark humor. Fewer than half of the forty-seven stories in Fredric Brown's likewise superb *Nightmares and Geezenstacks* (1961) can be classified as crime fiction, and of those, one is five thousand words; the rest are mordant fantasies and science fiction, most but not all of vignette length.

Small Felonies, therefore, is the first single-author collection of exclusively short-short—none is longer than two thousand words—*and* exclusively criminous stories. I make note of this fact with what I hope is pardonable pride. To have a first of *any* kind in the mystery field is a rare treat.

For the most part, the stories in these pages originally appeared in *Ellery Queen's Mystery Magazine*, *Alfred Hitchcock's Mystery Magazine*, and *Mike Shayne Mystery Magazine* between 1968 and 1981. Others were first published in such long-defunct periodicals as *Mystery Magazine* and *Charlie Chan Mystery Magazine*, and in a variety of anthologies. Eight are originals. And there are eight collaborations, five with Jeffrey M. Wallmann and one each with John Lutz, Michael Kurland, and Marcia Muller. A fair number of the reprints, in particular those written and first published early in my career, have been revised to one extent or another, to correct all manner of youthful sins and excesses. Rereading one's early stories can be a *very* humbling experience.

If I may be permitted to coin a collective noun, what you are about to read is a "slumgullion of short-shorts." Lots of disparate ingredients mixed together in the same kettle. Upbeat stories, downbeat stories, offbeat stories. Detection, ratiocination, impossible crime, psychological suspense, satire, farce, horror, light fantasy, apocalyptic fantasy, lady-or-the-tiger dilemmas, the cautionary tale, the biter-bitten, the O. Henry twist, the exercise in *reductio ad absurdum*—even a humorous look at Russian spies (sort of), a shameless "thing" composed mostly of puns, and my candidate for the shortest murder mystery ever written. Plus three brief adventures of the "Nameless Detective," among them a locked-room mystery and a "Nameless"/Sharon McCone collaboration with Marcia Muller told entirely through dialogue. The settings range from San Francisco to New England, Mexico to Montana, the north of England to the Mediterranean island of Majorca. And the styles run the gamut from the Hemingwayesque to Wodehousian whimsy.

You may now begin, if you haven't already, to partake of this slumgullion of mine. I hope you find it a savory blend, up to and including the fiftieth and final morsel.

Bill Pronzini
Sonoma, California
January 1988

ACKNOWLEDGMENTS

"The Facsimile Shop" (as by William Jeffrey), "Once a Thief," "Sweet Fever," "Under the Skin," "A Cold Foggy Day," "Black Wind," "Changes" (as "Times Change"), "The Dispatching of George Ferris," and "The Terrarium Principle" were originally published in *Ellery Queen's Mystery Magazine*. Copyright © 1970, 1975, by Bill Pronzini and Jeffrey Wallmann; copyright © 1976, 1977, 1978, 1979, 1980, 1981 by Bill Pronzini. Revised version of "The Facsimile Shop" copyright © 1988 by Bill Pronzini and Jeffrey M. Wallmann.

"Waiting, Waiting. . . ," "Words Do Not a Book Make," "Don't Spend It All in One Place," "The Clincher" (as by Jack Foxx), "One of Those Days" (as by Jack Foxx), "A Dip in the Poole," "Perfect Timing," "Muggers' Moon," "The Imperfect Crime," "Skeletons" (as "Skeletons Go Forth"), "A Case for Quiet," "The Killing, "Shell Game," "Memento Mori," "Here Lies Another Blackmailer. . . ," "Unchained," "For Love," and "House Call" originally appeared in *Alfred Hitchcock's Mystery Magazine*. Copyright © 1968, 1969, 1970, 1971, 1972, 1974, 1975 by H.S.D. Publications, Inc.; copyright © 1981 by Davis Publications, Inc. Various revised versions copyright © 1988 by Bill Pronzini; copyright © 1988 by Bill Pronzini and Jeffrey Wallmann.

"Retirement," "A Little Larceny" (as "There's One Born Every

SMALL FELONIES

A COLD FOGGY DAY

The two men stepped off the plane from Boston at two o'clock on a cold foggy afternoon in February. The younger of the two by several years had sand-colored hair and a small birthmark on his right cheek; the older man had flat gray eyes and heavy black brows. Both wore topcoats and carried small overnight bags.

They walked through the terminal and down to one of the rental-car agencies on the lower level. The older man paid for the rental of a late-model sedan. When they stepped outside, the wind was blowing and the wall of fog eddied in gray waves across the airport complex. The younger man thrust his hands deep into the pockets of his topcoat as they crossed to the lot where the rental cars were kept. He could not remember when he had been quite so cold.

A boy in a white uniform brought their car around. The older man took the wheel. As he pulled the car out of the lot, the younger man said, "Turn the heater on, will you, Harry? I'm freezing in here."

Harry put on the heater. Warm air rushed against their feet, but it would be a long while before it was warm enough to suit the younger man. He sat blowing on his hands. "Is it always this cold out here?" he asked.

"It's not cold," Harry said.

□ 1 □

"Well, I'm freezing."

"It's just the fog, Vince. You're not used to it."

"There's six inches of snow in Boston," Vince said. "Ice on the streets thick enough to skate on. But I'm damned if it's as cold as it is out here."

"You have to get used to it."

"I don't think I *could* get used to it," Vince said. "It cuts through you like a knife."

"The sun comes out around noon most days and burns off the fog," Harry said. "San Francisco has the mildest winters you've ever seen."

The younger man didn't say anything more. He didn't want to argue with Harry; this was Harry's home town. How could you argue with a man about his home town?

When they reached San Francisco, twenty minutes later, Harry drove a roundabout route to their hotel. It was an old but elegant place on Nob Hill, and the windows in their room had a panoramic view of the bay. Even with the fog, you could see the Golden Gate Bridge and the Bay Bridge and Alcatraz Island. Harry pointed out each of them.

But Vince was still cold and he said he wanted to take a hot shower. He stood under a steaming spray for ten minutes. When he came out again, Harry was still standing at the windows.

"Look at that view," Harry said. "Isn't that some view?"

"Sure," Vince agreed. "Some view."

"San Francisco is a beautiful city, Vince. It's the most beautiful city in the world."

"Then why did you leave it? Why did you come to Boston? You don't seem too happy there."

"Ambition," Harry said. "I had a chance to move up and I took it. But it's been a long time, Vince."

"You could always move back here."

"I'm going to do that," Harry said. "Now that I'm home again, I know I don't want to live anywhere else. I tell you, this is the most beautiful city anywhere on this earth."

Vince was silent. He wished Harry wouldn't keep talking about how beautiful San Francisco was. Vince liked Boston; it was his town just as San Francisco was Harry's. But Vince couldn't see talking about it all the time, the way Harry had ever since they'd left Boston this morning. Not that Vince would say anything about it. Harry had been around a long time and Vince was just a new man. He didn't know Harry that well—had only worked with him a few times—but everybody said you could learn a lot from him. And Vince wanted to learn.

That was not the only reason he wouldn't say anything about it. Vince knew why Harry was talking so much about San Francisco. It was to keep his mind off the job they had come here to do. Still, it probably wasn't doing him much good. The only way to take both their minds off the job was to get it done.

"When are we going after him, Harry?" Vince said.

"Tonight."

"Why not now?"

"Because I say so. We'll wait until tonight."

"Listen, Harry—"

"We're doing this my way, remember?" Harry said. "That was the agreement. *My* way."

"All right," Vince said, though he was beginning to feel more and more nervous about this whole thing with Dominic DiLucci. He wished it was over and finished with and he was back in Boston with his wife. Away from Harry.

After a while Harry suggested they go out to Fisherman's Wharf and get something to eat. Vince wasn't hungry and he didn't want to go to Fisherman's Wharf; all he wanted to do was to get the job over and done with. Harry insisted, so he gave in. It was better to humor Harry than to complicate things by arguing with him.

They took a cable car to Fisherman's Wharf and walked around in the fog and the chill wind. Vince was almost numb by the time Harry picked out a restaurant, but Harry didn't seem to be affected by the weather. He didn't even have his topcoat buttoned.

Harry sat by the window in the restaurant, not eating much, looking out at the fishing boats moored in the Wharf basin. He had his face close to the glass, like a kid.

Vince watched him and thought: He's stalling. Well, Vince could understand that, but understanding it didn't make it any easier. He said finally, "Harry, it's after seven. There's no sense in putting it off any longer."

Harry sighed. "I guess you're right."

"Sure I am."

"All right," Harry said.

He wanted to take the cable car back to their hotel, but Vince said it was too cold riding on one of those things. So they caught a taxi and then picked up their rental car. Vince turned on the heater himself this time, as high as it would go.

Once they had turned out of the hotel garage, Vince said, "Where is he, Harry? You can tell me that now."

"Down the coast. Outside Pacifica."

"How far is that?"

"About twenty miles."

"Suppose he's not there?"

"He'll be there."

"I don't see how you can be so sure."

"He'll be there," Harry said.

"He could be in Mexico by now."

"He's not in Mexico," Harry said. "He's in a little cabin outside Pacifica."

Vince shrugged and decided not to press the point. This was Harry's show; he himself was along only as a back-up.

Harry drove them out to Golden Gate Park and through it and eventually onto the Coast Highway, identifying landmarks that were half hidden in fog. Vince didn't pay much attention; he was trying to forget his own nervousness by thinking about his wife back in Boston.

It took them almost an hour to get where they were going. Harry drove through Pacifica and beyond it several miles. Then he turned right, toward the ocean, onto a narrow dirt road that wound steadily upward through gnarled cypress and eucalyptus trees. That's what Harry said they were, anyway. There was fog here too, thick and gray and roiling. Vince could almost feel the coldness of it, as if it were seeping into the car through the vents.

They passed several cabins, most of them dark. Harry turned onto another road, and after a few hundred yards they rounded a bend. Vince could see another cabin then. It was small and dark, perched on the edge of a cliff that fell away to the ocean. But the water was hidden by the thick fog.

Harry parked the car near the front door of the cabin. He shut off the engine and the headlights.

Vince said, "I don't see any lights."

"That doesn't mean anything."

"It doesn't look like he's here."

"He'll be here."

Vince didn't say anything. He didn't see how Harry could know with that much certainty that Dominic DiLucci was going to be here. You just didn't know anybody that well.

They left the warmth of the car. The wind was sharp and stinging, blowing across the top of the bluff from the sea. Vince shivered.

Harry knocked on the cabin door. After a few moments the door opened and a thin man with haunted eyes looked out. He was dressed in rumpled slacks and a white shirt that was soiled around the collar. He hadn't shaved in several days.

The man stood looking at Harry and didn't seem surprised to see him. At length he said, "Hello, Harry."

"Hello, Dom," Harry said.

They continued to look at each other. Dominic DiLucci said, "Well, it's cold out there." His voice was calm but empty, as if there was no emotion left inside him. "Why don't you come in?"

They entered the cabin. A fire glowed on a brick hearth against one wall. Dom switched on a small lamp in the front room, and Vince saw that the furniture there was old and over-stuffed, a man's furniture. He stood apart from the other two men, thinking that Harry had been right all along. For some reason that didn't make him feel any less nervous.

Harry said, "You don't seem surprised to see me, Dom."

"Surprised?" Dom said. "No, I'm not surprised. Nothing can surprise me any more."

"It's been a long time. You haven't changed much."

"Haven't I?" Dom said, and smiled a cold humorless smile.

"No," Harry said. "You came here. I knew you would. You always came here when you were troubled, when you wanted to get away from something."

Dominic DiLucci was silent.

Harry said, "Why did you do it, Dom?"

"Why? Because of Trudy, that's why."

"I don't follow that. I thought she'd left you, run off with somebody from Los Angeles."

"She did. But I love her, Harry, and I wanted her back. I thought I could buy her back with the money. I thought if I got in touch with her and told her I had a hundred thousand dollars, she'd come back and we could go off to Brazil or someplace."

"But she didn't come back, did she?"

"No. She called me a fool and a loser on the phone and hung up on me. I didn't know what to do. The money didn't mean much without Trudy; nothing means much without her. Maybe I wanted to be caught after that, maybe that's why I stayed around here. And maybe you figured that out along with everything else."

"That's right," Harry said. "Trudy was right, too. You *are* a fool and a loser, Dom."

"Is that all you have to say?"

"What do you want me to say?"

"Nothing, I guess. It's about what I expected from you. You have no feelings, Harry. There's nothing inside of you and there never was or will be."

Dom rubbed a hand across his face; the hand was trembling. Harry just watched him. Vince watched him too, and he thought that Dominic DiLucci was about ready to crack; he was trying to bring it off as if he were in perfect control of himself, but he was ready to crack.

Vince said, "We'd better get going."

Dom glanced at him, the first time he had looked at Vince since they'd come inside. It didn't seem to matter to him who Vince was. "Yes," he said. "I suppose we'd better."

"Where's the money?" Harry asked him.

"In the bedroom. In a suitcase in the closet."

Vince went into the bedroom, found the suitcase, and looked inside. Then he closed it and came out into the front room again. Harry and Dom were no longer looking at each other.

They went outside and got into the rental car. Harry took the wheel again. Vince sat in the back with Dominic DiLucci.

They drove back down to the coast highway and turned north toward San Francisco. They rode in silence. Vince was still cold, but he could feel perspiration under his arms.

When they came into San Francisco, Harry drove them up a winding avenue that led to the top of Twin Peaks. The fog had lifted somewhat, and from up there you could see the lights of the city strung out like misty beads along the bay.

As soon as the lights came into view Harry leaned forward. "Look at those lights. Magnificent. Isn't that the most magnificent sight you ever saw, Vince?"

And Vince understood then. All at once, he understood the truth.

After Dominic DiLucci had stolen the $100,000 from the investment firm where he worked, Harry had told the San Francisco police that he didn't know where Dom could be. But then he had gone to the head of the big insurance company where he and Vince were claims investigators—the same insurance company that handled the policy on Dom's investment firm—and had told the Chief that maybe he did have an idea where Dom was but hadn't said anything to the police because he wanted to come out here himself, wanted to bring Dom in himself. Dom wasn't dangerous, he said; there wouldn't be any trouble.

The Chief hadn't liked the idea much, but he wanted the $100,000 recovered. So he had paid Harry's way to San Francisco, and Vince's way with him as a back-up man. Both Vince and the Chief had figured they knew why Harry wanted to come himself. But they had been wrong. Dead wrong.

Harry DiLucci was still staring out at the lights of San Francisco. And he was smiling.

What kind of man are you? Vince thought. What kind of man sits there with his own brother in the backseat, on the way to jail and ready to crack—his own *brother*—and looks out at the lights of a city and smiles?

Vince shivered. This time it had nothing to do with the cold.

A DIP IN THE POOLE

I was sitting in one of the heavy baroque chairs in the Hotel Poole's lobby, leafing through today's issue of *The Wall Street Journal*, when the young woman in the tweed suit picked Andrew J. Stuyvesant's pockets.

She worked it very neatly. Stuyvesant—a silver-haired old gentleman who had fifteen or twenty million dollars in real-estate holdings—had just stepped out of one of the chrome-and-walnut elevators directly opposite where I was sitting. The woman must have been expecting him; either that, or her timing happened to be perfect. I hadn't noticed her hanging around the elevators, but she'd been somewhere close by; Stuyvesant hadn't taken more than three steps when she walked right into him and almost knocked him down. She caught hold of his arm, brushed at his coat, and offered profuse apologies. Stuyvesant bowed in a gallant way and allowed as how it was quite all right, my dear. She got his wallet and the diamond stickpin from his tie, and he neither felt nor suspected a thing.

The woman apologized again and then hurried off across the lobby toward the hotel's main entrance, slipping wallet and stickpin into her purse as she went. I was out of my chair by then and I moved quickly after her. Even so, she got to within fifty feet of the entrance before I caught up with her.

I let my hand fall on her shoulder, just hard enough to bring her up short. "Just a minute, miss," I said.

She stiffened. And then turned slowly and looked at me as if I had crawled out from under one of the potted plants. "I beg your pardon?" she said in a wintry voice.

"You and I need to have a little chat."

"I am not in the habit of chatting with strange men."

"I think you'll make an exception in my case."

Her eyes flashed angrily. "If you don't let go of me this instant," she said, "I'll call for hotel security."

"Will you? I don't think so."

"I most certainly will."

"All right," I said, "but you'll be wasting your breath. I'm hotel security. Head of it, as a matter of fact. What used to be known as the house detective."

She went pale. But she didn't lose her composure. "Well? What do you want with me?"

"That little chat I mentioned."

I steered her toward the hotel lounge, not far away. She didn't resist. It was early enough so that the lounge was mostly deserted; I sat her down in a booth away from the bar and then crowded in alongside her. One of the waiters started our way but I waved him off.

The woman sat glaring at me with enough chill to freeze a side of beef. She was in her mid-twenties, I judged, and very attractive: slim, regal-looking, with brown eyes and seal-brown hair worn short and on the frizzy side. I said appreciatively, "Without a doubt you're the most beautiful dip I've ever encountered."

"I don't know what you're talking about."

"No?"

"Certainly not."

"*Dip* is underworld slang for pickpocket."

She tried to affect indignation. "Are you insinuating that I. . . ?"

"Oh, come on," I said. "I saw you lift Andrew Stuyvesant's wallet and diamond stickpin. I was about fifteen feet away at the time."

Her gaze slid away from mine. Long, slender fingers toyed with the catch on her purse. Then her shoulders slumped and she sighed—a deep, tragic sigh.

"There's no point in denying it," she said. "Yes, I stole those things."

I took the bag from her and snapped it open. Stuyvesant's wallet, with the needle point of the stickpin now imbedded in the leather, lay on top of the various feminine articles inside. I removed both items, looked at her identification to get her name and address, and then reclosed the bag and gave it back to her.

She said, "Please understand. I'm not really a thief—not the kind you think, anyway. I have a . . . *compulsion* to take things. From people, from stores, wherever I happen to be when the urge comes over me. And I'm powerless to stop myself."

"Kleptomania?"

"Yes. I've been to three different psychiatrists during the past two years, but they've been unable to cure me."

I shook my head sympathetically. "It must be terrible for you."

"Terrible," she agreed. "When . . . when my father learns of this latest episode, he'll have me put into a sanatorium." Her voice quavered on the last word, and kept on quavering as she said, "He threatened to do just that if I ever stole anything again, and he doesn't make idle threats."

I studied her for a time. Then I said, "Your father doesn't have to know what happened here today."

"He . . . he doesn't?"

"No," I said. "No real harm has been done. Mr. Stuyvesant will get his wallet and stickpin back. And I see no reason to cause the hotel, or you, any public embarrassment."

A hopeful look brightened her eyes. "Then . . . you'll let me go?"

"I guess I'm too soft-hearted for the kind of job I have," I said. "Yes, I'll let you go. If you promise me you'll never set foot inside the Hotel Poole again."

"Oh, I promise!"

"You'd better keep it. If I catch you here again I'll turn you over to the police."

"You'll never see me again," she assured me. "I . . . have an appointment with another psychiatrist tomorrow morning, one who specializes in my sort of problem. I feel sure he'll be able to help me."

"Let's hope so."

I slid out of the booth and put my back to her long enough to light a cigarette. When I turned around, the street door to the lounge was just closing and the young woman was gone.

On my way back into the lobby, I thought wryly: If she's a kleptomaniac, I'm Mary, Queen of Scots. What she was, of course, was an accomplished professional pickpocket; her technique was much too polished, her hands much too skilled, for her to be anything else. She was also a fairly adept spontaneous liar.

But then, so am I.

As I walked out through the hotel's front entrance, my right hand resting on the fat leather wallet and diamond stickpin in my coat pocket, I found myself feeling a little sorry for her. But only a little.

After all, I had been working the Hotel Poole for years and that made Andrew J. Stuyvesant *my* mark by right of territorial prerogative. After two days of waiting for an opportunity, I had been within fifteen seconds of dipping him myself when she appeared out of nowhere.

Wouldn't you say I was entitled to the swag?

SOMETHING WRONG

A "Nameless Detective" Story

The instant I walked into my flat, I knew something was wrong.

I stopped a couple of paces through the door, with the hairs pulling at the nape of my neck. Kerry had entered ahead of me and she was halfway across the room before she realized I wasn't following. She turned, saw me standing rigid, and said immediately, "What's the matter?"

I didn't answer. I kept searching the room with my eyes: the old mismatched furniture, the shelves containing my collection of more than six thousand pulp magazines, the bay window beyond which a thick San Francisco fog crawled sinuously across the night. There were no signs of disturbance. Nor was there anything unusual to hear. And yet the feeling of wrongness remained sharp and urgent. When you've been a detective as long as I have, you develop a kind of protective sixth sense and you learn to trust it.

Somebody had gotten in here while Kerry and I were out to dinner and a North Beach movie.

Somebody who was still here now?

Kerry came back toward me, saying again, "What's the matter?"

"Go out into the hall," I said.

"What for?"

"Just do it."

We had been together long enough and she knew me well enough not to argue. Frowning now, worry-eyed, she moved past me and out into the hall.

I shut the door after her and turned back to face the room. Nothing out of place in here . . . or was there? Something didn't seem quite right, but I couldn't identify it—couldn't focus on anything right now except the possibility of the intruder still being on the premises.

This was one of the few times I regretted my fundamental distaste for guns; unlike some licensed PIs, I do not carry or even own one. I picked up a heavy alabaster bookend, not much of a weapon but the only one handy, and went across to the half-closed bedroom door.

Nobody in there; I opened the closet and looked under the bed to make sure. No evidence of invasion or forced entry, either—not that anybody could get in through the bedroom window, or any of the other windows, without using a tall ladder. The bathroom was also empty and undisturbed. So were the kitchen and the rear porch. The back door, accessible by a set of outside stairs from an alley off Laguna Street, was still secured by its spring lock and chain lock.

I returned to the bedroom, opened the middle dresser drawer. The leather case in which I keep my few items of jewelry and a small amount of spare cash was still in place under my clean shirts. The jewelry and money were likewise untouched.

But all of that reassured me only a little. The feeling of wrongness, of a violation of my private space, would not go away. As unlikely as it seemed, somebody *had* gotten in during our absence. I was as sure of it as you can be of something unproven.

In the front room again, I opened the door and motioned for Kerry to come back inside. Just in time, too. She is not the sort of woman to stand by passively for very long, danger or no danger.

She said as she entered, "What is it? Burglars?"

"Something like that."

I got down on one knee and examined the two dead-bolt

locks on the front door. A professional burglar can get past the best dead-bolt made, but he can't do it without leaving marks; there were none on either of these locks. Nobody could have come in this way, then, without a key . . .

I asked Kerry if she had lost or misplaced her key recently; she said she hadn't. Mine hadn't been out of my possession either. And ours were the only two keys to the flat. Not even the landlord had one: I had lived here for more than twenty years and had had the locks changed more than once at my own expense.

Kerry asked, "Is anything missing?"

"Doesn't seem to be. Nothing disturbed, no sign of forced entry. But I can't shake the feeling someone was in here."

"For what reason, if not to steal something?"

"I don't know yet."

"How could somebody get in, with everything locked up tight?"

"I don't know that either."

We prowled the flat together, room to room and back again. There was absolutely nothing missing. I checked the locks on the windows and on the back door; all were secure and had not been tampered with as far as I could tell. I did find a half-inch sliver of metal on the floor of the utility porch, the same sort of brass as the chain lock. But it hadn't come from the lock because I checked to make sure. It could have been splintered off just about anything made of brass, then; could have lain there for days.

We were in the front room again when Kerry said, with an edge of exasperation in her voice, "You must be wrong. There *couldn't* have been an intruder."

"I'm not wrong," I said.

"Even great detectives have hot flashes sometimes."

"This isn't funny, Kerry."

"Did I say it was?" She sighed elaborately, the way she does when her patience is being tried. "I'm going to make some coffee," she said. "You want a cup?"

"Yes. All right."

She went out into the kitchen. I stayed in the middle of the room and kept looking around—turning my eyes and my body both in slow quadrants. Couch, end tables, coffee table, leather recliner Kerry had given me on my last birthday, shelves full of gaudy-spined pulps, old secretary desk. All just as we'd left it. Yet *something* wasn't as it should be. I made another slow circuit: couch, end tables, coffee table, recliner, bookshelves, desk. And a third circuit: couch, tables, recliner—

The recliner.

The chair's footrest was pushed in, out of sight.

It was a small thing, but that didn't make it any less wrong. The chair is a good one, comfortable, but the footrest has never worked quite right. To get it folded all the way back under on its metal hinges, you have to give it a kick; and when you sit down again later, you have to struggle to work it free so you can recline. So I don't bother anymore to boot it all the way under. I *always* leave the footrest part way out, with its metal hinges showing.

Why would an intruder bother to kick it out of sight? Only one conceivable reason: he thought it was supposed to be that way and wanted the chair to look completely natural. But why would he be messing around my chair in the first place. . . ?

"Jesus," I said aloud, and the hair pulled again along my neck. I moved over to the recliner, gingerly eased the seat cushion out so I could see under it.

What I was looking at then was a bomb.

Two sticks of dynamite wired together with some kind of detonator plate on top, set into a slit in the fabric so that it was resting on the chair's inner springs. The weight of a person settling onto the cushion would depress the plate and explode the dynamite—

"My God!"

Kerry was standing behind me, staring open-mouthed at the thing in the chair. I hadn't even heard her come in.

"Not a burglar after all," I said grimly. "Somebody who came in to *leave* something. This."

"I . . . don't hear any ticking," she said.

"It's a pressure-activated bomb, not a time bomb. Nothing to worry about as long as we stay away from it."

"But who . . . why. . . ?"

I caught her arm and steered her into the bedroom, where I keep my phone. I rang up the Hall of Justice, got through to a cop I knew named Jordan, and explained the situation. He said he'd be right over with the bomb squad.

When I hung up, Kerry said in a shaky voice, "I just don't understand. All the doors and windows were locked—they're *still* locked. How did whoever it was get in and back out again?"

I had no answer for her then. But by the time the police arrived, I had done some hard thinking and I did have an answer—the only possible answer. And along with it, I had the who and the why.

"His name is Howard Lynch," I said to Jordan. He and Kerry and I were in the hallway, waiting for the bomb squad to finish up inside. "Owns a hardware store out on Clement. He hired me about a month ago to find his wife; said she'd run off with another man. She had, too, but nobody could blame her. I found out later Lynch had been abusing her for years."

"So why would he want to kill you?"

"He blames me for his wife's death," I said. "I found her, all right, but when I told her Lynch was my employer she panicked and took off in her boyfriend's car. She didn't get far—a tree stopped her three blocks away."

"Pretty story."

"That's the kind of business we're in, Mack."

"Don't I know it. Did Lynch threaten you?"

"No. He's the kind who nurses his hatred in silence."

"Then what makes you so sure he's the one who planted the bomb?"

"He showed up here one night a week after the accident. Said it was to give me a check for my services and to tell me there were no hard feelings. I knew about the wife abuse by then, but I still felt sorry for him—sorry enough not to be suspicious and to let him in. He wasn't here long, just long enough to sneak a look around."

Kerry said, "I don't see why the bomber has to be somebody who was here before tonight."

"That's the only way it makes sense. To begin with, he *had* to have gotten in tonight through one of the doors, front or back. The windows are all secure and there's nothing but empty space below them. There are no marks of any kind on the front-door locks, no way he could have gotten a key, and he would have had a hard time even getting into the building because of the security lock on the main entrance downstairs. That leaves the alley staircase and the back door."

"But that one was—*is*—double-locked too."

"Right. But one of the locks is a spring type, the kind any-body can pick with a small tool or a credit card."

"You can't pick a chain lock with a tool or a credit card," Jordan said.

"No, but once the spring lock is free, the door will open a few inches—wide enough to reach through with a pair of bolt cutters and snip the chain. That explains the brass sliver I found on the porch floor. Easy work for a man who owns a hardware store, and so is the rest of it: When he was here the first time he noted the type of chain lock on the rear door; among the other things he brought with him tonight was *an exact duplicate* of that lock. After he was inside, he unscrewed the old chain-lock plates from the door and jamb and installed the new ones using the same holes—a job that wouldn't have taken more than a few minutes. Then he reset the spring lock, put the new chain on, and took the pieces of the old lock away with him when he was done planting the bomb."

"If he relocked the door," Jordan said, "how did he get out of the flat?"

"Walked out through the *front* door. The locks there are dead bolts, but you can open them from inside by hand, with-out a key; and you can reset them the same way to lock auto-matically when you leave. Simple as that."

There were a few seconds of ruminative silence. Then Kerry shuddered and said, "Thank God you felt something was wrong. If you'd sat down in that chair . . ."

"Don't even think about it," I said.

THE IMPERFECT CRIME

I t was a balmy early summer night, pungent with wood smoke and the sweetness of honeysuckle. In the willow garden behind the small frame house, crickets sang sonorously and tree frogs were in full-throated voice.

On the porch, in the deep shadows at the far end, Ellen and George Granger sat in silence without touching, without looking at each other. They had been sitting there for some time, listening to the night sounds.

George said finally, "What're you thinking about, Ellen?"

"You really want to know?"

"I asked, didn't I?"

"I was thinking about our perfect crime," she said. "I was thinking about Tom."

He was silent again for a time. Then, "What for?"

"T'was an evening just like this one when we murdered him."

"Don't use that word!"

"There's no one around to hear."

"Just don't use it. We agreed never to use that word."

"T'was an evening just like this one," she said again. "You remember, George?"

"Am I likely to've forgotten?"

"We shouldn't have come together so often," Ellen said.

"If we'd been more careful he wouldn't have caught us. But it was such a beautiful night . . ."

"Listen," George said, "if it hadn't been that night it would've been some other soon after. We couldn't of hidden it from him much longer."

"No, I suppose not."

"Worked out fine as it was," he said. "Wasn't no one else around that night. Worked out just fine."

"George, why didn't we run off together? Before that night? Why didn't we just run off somewhere?"

"Don't be silly. I had no money, you know that. Where would we of gone?"

"I don't know."

"No, course you don't."

"If only Tom hadn't been so jealous," Ellen said. "I could have asked him for a divorce. Things would've been so simple, then; we wouldn't have done what we did."

"Well, he *was* jealous," George said. "He was a jealous fool. I'm not sorry for what we done."

"I wasn't either, at the time. But now . . ."

"What's the matter with you tonight, Ellen? You're acting damned peculiar, you ask me."

"T'was a night just like this one," she said for the third time. "The honeysuckle, the wood smoke, the crickets and tree frogs. It could've been *this* night."

"Don't talk silly."

Ellen sighed in the darkness. "Why'd we kill him, George? Why did we do it?"

"Chrissake. Because he caught us together, that's why."

"At the time we said it was because we were in love."

"Well, there was that too."

"That too," Ellen repeated. "At the time *that* was *everything*. It was what made it all right, what we did."

"Why in hell are you talking this way?" George said in exasperation. "We committed the perfect crime—you said so yourself, then and just a couple of minutes ago. Nobody ever suspected. They all thought it was an accident."

"Yes. An accident."

"Well then? What's the matter with you?"

Ellen said, "Was it worth it, George?"

"What?"

"What we did. Was it worth it?"

"Sure it was worth it. We got married, didn't we?"

"Yes."

"We been happy together, ain't we?"

"I suppose we have."

"You always said you weren't sorry."

"So did you. Did you really mean it?"

"Sure I did. Didn't you?"

Ellen was quiet. From somewhere down the block, a dog bayed mournfully at the pale moon—or maybe at something in the dark. The crickets created a symphony all around them.

At length she said, "I wish we hadn't done it. Before God, I wish we hadn't done it."

"Ellen, it was the perfect crime!"

"Was it? Was it really?"

"You know it was."

"I don't know it. Not any more."

"Damn you, woman, stop talking that way."

"I can't help it," she said. "I'm afraid. I been afraid for a long time."

"Of what?" George said. "We weren't caught, were we? Won't never be caught now."

"Not by the law."

"Now what's that supposed to mean?"

"There's no such thing as the perfect crime, George," she said. "I know that and so do you."

"I don't know any such thing."

"Yes you do. Down deep, we've both known it all along. We haven't gone unpunished for what we did—but we haven't paid the full price, either. Won't be long now before we do. Not much longer at all."

They sat once more in silence, with nothing left to say, with the cloying fragrance of the honeysuckle in their nostrils and the songs of the crickets and tree frogs swelling in their ears. Sat without touching, without looking at each other on the deep-shadowed porch . . . remembering . . . waiting.

Ellen and George Granger, seventy-nine and eighty-one years of age, who had committed the perfect crime in the year 1931.

SHELL GAME

(With Jeffrey M. Wallmann)

Gloved hands thrust into the pockets of his heavy tweed overcoat, Steve Blanchard entered the Midwestern National Exchange Bank a few minutes before three P.M. on a snowy Thursday in December. A uniformed guard stood near the main entrance doors with a ring of keys in his hand, his eyes cast upward to the clock on the side wall. Blanchard's steps echoed hollowly as he crossed the almost-deserted lobby to the teller at window four, the only one open at this late hour. He waited until a stout, gray-haired man had finished his transaction, then moved up to the window.

A small nameplate indicated that the teller's name was James Cox. He was a thin young man with dark eyes and sand-colored hair. He smiled at Blanchard, said, "Yes, sir, may I help you?"

Blanchard took the folded piece of paper from his coat pocket and slid it across the counter. The second hand on the wall clock made two full sweeps, half of a third, and then Blanchard turned and strode quickly away without looking back.

He had just passed through the entrance doors, was letting them swing closed behind him, when Cox shouted, "Stop that man! He just robbed me, Sam. Stop him!"

Blanchard halted on the snow-covered sidewalk outside and turned, his angular face a mask of surprise. The guard, a florid man with mild blue eyes, remained motionless for a moment; then, like an activated robot, he pulled the doors open, stepped out, and grasped Blanchard by the coat with his left hand, his right fumbling the service revolver off his hip.

"What the hell is going on?" Blanchard demanded.

The guard drew him roughly inside, holding the revolver pressed against Blanchard's ribs. The near-funereal silence of three o'clock closing had dissolved now into excited murmurings, the scrape of chairs, the slap of shoes on the marble floor as the bank's employees surged away from their desks. Cox ran out from behind his teller's window, the president of Midwestern National Exchange Bank, Allard Hoffman, at his heels. The teller's eyes were wide and excited; he held a piece of paper clenched in his right hand. Hoffman looked angrily officious.

"He held me up," Cox said as they reached Blanchard and the guard. "Every bill I had over a ten."

Blanchard gave his head a small, numb shake. "I don't believe this," he said. He stared at Cox. "What's the matter with you? You know I didn't try to hold you up."

"Look in his overcoat pockets, Sam," Cox said. "That's where he put the money."

"You're *crazy*—"

"Go ahead, Sam, look in his pockets," Hoffman said.

The guard instructed Blanchard to turn around and keep his hands upraised. When Blanchard obeyed, the guard patted his pockets, frowned, and then made a thorough one-handed search. After which he looked as bewildered as Blanchard. In his hand he held a thin pigskin wallet and seven rolls of pennies, nickels and dimes.

"This is all he's got on him," he said.

"What?" Cox burst out. "Sam, I *saw* him put that money into his overcoat pockets."

"Well, it's not there now."

"Of course it's not there," Blanchard said angrily. "I told you I didn't commit any robbery."

Cox opened the folded piece of paper he held. "This is the note he gave me, Mr. Hoffman. Read it for yourself."

Hoffman took the note. It had been fashioned of letters cut

from a newspaper and glued to a sheet of plain paper, and it said: *Give me all your big bills, I have a gun. If you try any heroics I'll kill you. I'm not kidding.* The bank president put voice to the message as he read it.

"He's not carrying any weapon, either," Sam said positively.

"I believed the note about that," Cox said, "but I made up my mind to shout nonetheless. I just couldn't stand by and watch him get away with the bank's money."

"I don't know where you got that note," Blanchard said to Cox, "but I didn't give it to you. I handed you a slip of paper, that's true, but it was just a list of those rolls of coins and you know it."

"You claim Mr. Cox gave them to you?" Hoffman asked him.

"Certainly he did. In exchange for twenty-eight dollars in fives and ones."

"I did not give him any coin rolls," Cox said with mounting exasperation. "I did exactly what it says in that note. I gave him every large bill I had in the cash drawer. The vault cart happened to be behind me at the time, since my cage was the only one open, and he told me to give him what was on that too. He must have gotten sixty-five or seventy thousand altogether."

"You're a liar," Blanchard snapped.

"*You're* the one who's lying!"

"I don't have your damned money. You've searched me, haven't you? All I've got is about twenty dollars in my wallet."

"Well," Hoffman said darkly, "*somebody* has it."

At that moment two plainclothes detectives entered the bank, having been summoned by a hurried call from one of the other Midwestern officials. The one in charge, a lumbering and disheveled man with small, bright eyes, was named Freiberg. He instructed the guard to lock the doors, and when that was done he said, "All right, let's hear what happened."

Cox related his version of the affair. Freiberg, writing laboriously in a notebook, didn't interrupt. When the teller had finished, Freiberg turned to Blanchard. "Now what's your story?"

Blanchard told him about the rolls of coins. "I wanted them for a poker game some friends of mine and I set up for tonight." He made a wry mouth. "I'm supposed to be the banker."

"He also claims to have given Mr. Cox a list of what he wanted in the way of coins," Hoffman said.

"The only note he gave me is that holdup note," Cox insisted. "He must have gotten those coins elsewhere, had them in his pocket when he came in here."

"Why don't you check his cage?" Blanchard countered. "That list of mine has to be around here somewhere." He glared at Cox. "Maybe you'll even find your missing cash."

"Are you suggesting I stole that money?" Cox shouted.

Hoffman said stiffly, "Mr. Cox has been a trusted employee of Midwestern National for four years."

"Well, I've been a trusted employee of Curtis Tool and Die for a hell of a lot longer," Blanchard said. "What does any of that prove?"

"All right, that's enough." Freiberg looked at the bank president. "Mr. Hoffman, detail someone to find out exactly how much money is missing." Then he turned to the other plainclothesman. "Flynn, question the rest of the employees; maybe one of them saw or heard something. You might as well go through Mr. Cox's cage and personal possessions, too."

Cox was incredulous. "You mean you're taking this thief's word over mine?"

"I'm not taking anybody's word, Mr. Cox. I'm just trying to find out what happened here today." He paused. "Would you mind emptying all your pockets for me?"

"Of course I mind," Cox said in an icily controlled voice. "But I'll do it just the same. I have nothing to hide."

It appeared that he hadn't, as far as his person went. He did not have either a list of coins or any appreciable amount of money.

Freiberg sighed. "Okay," he said, "let's go over it again . . ."

Some time later, Hoffman and Flynn tendered their reports. A check of receipts and records revealed that a total of $65,100 was missing. No list of coins had been found in or about Cox's cage or among his possessions, and there were exactly as many coin rolls in his cash drawer as he was supposed to have. None of the other employees could shed any light on the matter; no one had been near Cox's cage at the time. Nor did any of them have the missing money on his person, among his belongings, or at his work station.

"Neither the money nor this alleged note of yours seems to be anywhere in the bank," Freiberg said to Blanchard. "How do you explain that?"

"I can't explain it. I can only tell you the truth. I did not steal that money."

Freiberg asked the guard, Sam, "How far outside did he get before you collared him?"

"No more than a couple of steps."

"Did he have time to pass the money to an accomplice?"

"I doubt it. But I wasn't paying any attention to him until Mr. Cox yelled."

"I don't know much about large sums of cash," Blanchard said coldly, "but sixty-five thousand must be a lot of bills. I couldn't have passed that much to somebody in the couple of seconds I was outside."

"He's got a point," Sam admitted.

"Why don't you search *him?*" Blanchard's voice was heavy with frustration and sarcasm. "Maybe *he's* my accomplice."

"I was expecting this," Sam said. "Go ahead, search me. That'll get the idea I had anything to do with this out of everybody's mind."

Flynn searched him. No large amount of cash, nothing incriminating.

Hoffman was beside himself. "That money didn't disappear by itself. I still say this man Blanchard is responsible."

Freiberg nodded. "We'll take him downtown and see what we can do there about shaking his story."

"Go ahead," Blanchard growled, "but I want a lawyer before I answer any more questions. And if charges are pressed against me, I'll sue the police department and the bank for false arrest, defamation of character, and anything else the lawyer can think up."

He was taken to police headquarters, allowed to call in a public defender, and then interrogated at great length. Not once did he waver from the story he had told in the bank.

Finally, he was taken to Freiberg's office. The detective looked tired, and his voice was grim when he said, "All right, you're free to go."

"You mean you finally believe I'm telling the truth?"

"No," Freiberg said, "I don't. I'm inclined to believe Cox. But we've got nothing to hold you on. Those three poker buddies of yours confirmed your story about a game tonight and you being the banker. We can't find anything to implicate you and you've got no criminal record. It's Cox's word against yours—two respectable citizens—and without the money or some kind of hard evidence, there's not a damned thing we can do." He leaned forward suddenly, his eyes cold and hard. "But understand this, Blanchard: we're not giving up. We'll be watching you—watching you every minute."

"Watch all you like," Blanchard said. "I'm innocent."

On a night three weeks later, Blanchard knocked on the door of unit nine, the Beaverwood Motel, in a city sixteen miles away. As soon as he had identified himself, the door opened and he was admitted. He took off his coat and grinned at the sandy-haired man who had let him in.

"Hello, Cox," he said.

"Blanchard," the bank teller acknowledged. "You made sure you weren't followed?"

"Of course."

"But the police *are* still watching you?"

"Not as closely as they were in the beginning. Stop worrying, will you? The whole thing worked beautifully."

"Yes, it did, didn't it?"

"Sure," Blanchard said. "Freiberg still thinks I passed the money to an accomplice somehow, but he can't prove it. Like he told me, it's your word against mine. They don't have any idea that it was actually *you* who passed the money, much less how it was done."

The room's third occupant—the stout, gray-haired man who had been at Cox's window when Blanchard entered the bank that day—looked up from where he was pouring drinks at a sideboard. "Or that the money was already out of the bank, safely tucked into my briefcase, when the two of you went into your little act."

Blanchard took one of the drinks the gray-haired man offered and raised the glass high. "Well, here's to crime," he said.

They laughed and drank, and then they sat down to split the $65,100 into three equal shares . . .

SWEET FEVER

Quarter before midnight, like on every evening except the Sabbath or when it's storming or when my rheumatism gets to paining too bad, me and Billy Bob went down to the Chigger Mountain railroad tunnel to wait for the night freight from St. Louis. This here was a fine summer evening, with a big old fat yellow moon hung above the pines on Hankers Ridge and mockingbirds and cicadas and toads making a soft ruckus. Nights like this, I have me a good feeling, hopeful, and I know Billy Bob does too.

They's a bog hollow on the near side of the tunnel opening, and beside it a woody slope, not too steep. Halfway down the slope is a big catalpa tree, and that was where we always set, side by side with our backs up against the trunk.

So we come on down to there, me hobbling some with my cane and Billy Bob holding onto my arm. That moon was so bright you could see the melons lying in Ferdie Johnson's patch over on the left, and the rail tracks had a sleek oiled look coming out of the tunnel mouth and leading off toward the Sabreville yards a mile up the line. On the far side of the tracks, the woods and the rundown shacks that used to be a hobo jungle before the county sheriff closed it off thirty years back had them a silvery cast, like they was all coated in winter frost.

We set down under the catalpa tree and I leaned my head

back to catch my wind. Billy Bob said, "Granpa, you feeling right?"

"Fine, boy."

"Rheumatism ain't started paining you?"

"Not a bit."

He give me a grin. "Got a little surprise for you."

"The hell you do."

"Fresh plug of blackstrap," he said. He come out of his pocket with it. "Mr. Cotter got him in a shipment just today down at his store."

I was some pleased. But I said, "Now you hadn't ought to go spending your money on me, Billy Bob."

"Got nobody else I'd rather spend it on."

I took the plug and unwrapped it and had me a chew. Old man like me ain't got many pleasures left, but fresh blackstrap's one; good corn's another. Billy Bob gets us all the corn we need from Ben Logan's boys. They got a pretty good sized still up on Hankers Ridge, and their corn is the best in this part of the hills. Not that either of us is a drinking man, now. A little touch after supper and on special days is all. I never did hold with drinking too much, or doing anything too much, and I taught Billy Bob the same.

He's a good boy. Man couldn't ask for a better grandson. But I raised him that way—in my own image, you might say—after both my own son Rufus and Billy Bob's ma got taken from us in 1947. I reckon I done a right job of it, and I couldn't be less proud of him than I was of his pa, or love him no less, either.

Well, we set there and I worked on the chew of blackstrap and had a spit every now and then, and neither of us said much. Pretty soon the first whistle come, way off on the other side of Chigger Mountain. Billy Bob cocked his head and said, "She's right on schedule."

"Mostly is," I said, "this time of year."

That sad lonesome hungry ache started up in me again—what my daddy used to call the "sweet fever." He was a railroad man, and I grew up around trains and spent a goodly part of my early years at the roundhouse in the Sabreville yards. Once, when I was ten, he let me take the throttle of the big 2-8-0 Mogul steam locomotive on his highballing run to Eulalia, and I can't recollect no more finer experience in my whole life. Later on I worked as a callboy, and then as a fireman on a 2-10-4, and put in some time as a yard tender engineer, and I expect I'd have gone on in railroading if it hadn't been for the Depression and getting myself married and having Rufus. My daddy's short-line company folded up in 1931, and half a dozen others too, and wasn't no work for either of us in Sabreville or Eulalia or anywheres else on the iron. That squeezed the will right out of him, and he took to ailing, and I had to accept a job on Mr. John Barnett's truck farm to support him and the rest of my family. Was my intention to go back into railroading, but the Depression dragged on, and my daddy died, and a year later my wife Amanda took sick and passed on, and by the time the war come it was just too late.

But Rufus got him the sweet fever too, and took a switchman's job in the Sabreville yards, and worked there right up until the night he died. Billy Bob was only three then; his own sweet fever comes most purely from me and what I taught him. Ain't no doubt trains been a major part of all our lives, good and bad, and ain't no doubt neither they get into a man's blood and maybe change him, too, in one way and another. I reckon they do.

The whistle come again, closer now, and I judged the St. Louis freight was just about to enter the tunnel on the other side of the mountain. You could hear the big wheels singing on the track, and if you listened close you could just about hear the banging of couplings and the hiss of air brakes as the engineer throttled down for the curve. The tunnel don't run straight through Chigger Mountain; she comes in from the north and angles to the east, so that a big freight like the St. Louis got to cut back to quarter speed coming through.

When she entered the tunnel, the tracks down below seemed to shimmy, and you could feel the vibration clear up where we was sitting under the catalpa tree. Billy Bob stood himself up and peered down toward the black tunnel mouth like a bird dog on a point. The whistle come again, and once more, from inside the tunnel, sounding hollow and miseried now. Every time I heard it like that, I thought of a body trapped and hurting and crying out for help that wouldn't come in the empty hours of the night. I swallowed and shifted the cud of blackstrap and worked up a spit to keep my mouth from drying. The sweet fever feeling was strong in my stomach.

The blackness around the tunnel opening commenced to lighten, and got brighter and brighter until the long white glow from the locomotive's headlamp spilled out onto the tracks beyond. Then she come through into my sight, her light shining like a giant's eye, and the engineer give another tug on the whistle, and the sound of her was a clattering rumble as loud to my ears as a mountain rock slide. But she wasn't moving fast, just kind of easing along, pulling herself out of that tunnel like a night crawler out of a mound of earth.

The locomotive clacked on past, and me and Billy Bob watched her string slide along in front of us. Flats, boxcars, three tankers in a row, more flats loaded down with pine logs big around as a privy, a refrigerator car, five coal gondolas, another link of boxcars. Fifty in the string already, I thought. She won't be dragging more than sixty, sixty-five. . . .

Billy Bob said suddenly, "Granpa, look yonder!"

He had his arm up, pointing. My eyes ain't so good no more, and it took me a couple of seconds to follow his point, over on our left and down at the door of the third boxcar in the last link. It was sliding open, and clear in the moonlight I saw a man's head come out, then his shoulders.

"It's a floater, Granpa," Billy Bob said, excited. "He's gonna jump. Look at him holding there—he's gonna jump."

I spit into the grass. "Help me up, boy."

He got a hand under my arm and lifted me up and held me until I was steady on my cane. Down there at the door of the boxcar, the floater was looking both ways along the string of cars and down at the ground beside the tracks. That ground was soft loam, and the train was going slow enough that there wasn't much chance he would hurt himself jumping off. He come to that same idea, and as soon as he did he flung himself off the car with his arms spread out and his hair and coattails flying in the slipstream. I saw him land solid and go down and roll over once. Then he knelt there, shaking his head a little, looking around.

Well, he was the first floater we'd seen in seven months. The yard crews seal up the cars nowadays, and they ain't many ride the rails anyhow, even down in our part of the country. But every now and then a floater wants to ride bad enough to break a seal, or hides himself in a gondola or on a loaded flat. Kids, oldtime hoboes, wanted men. They's still a few.

And some of 'em get off right down where this one had, because they know the St. Louis freight stops in Sabreville and they's yardmen there that check the string, or because they see the rundown shacks of the old hobo jungle or Ferdie Johnson's melon patch. Man rides a freight long enough, no provisions, he gets mighty hungry; the sight of a melon patch like Ferdie's is plenty enough to make him jump off.

"Billy Bob," I said.

"Yes, Granpa. You wait easy now."

He went off along the slope, running. I watched the floater, and he come up on his feet and got himself into a clump of bushes alongside the tracks to wait for the caboose to pass so's he wouldn't be seen. Pretty soon the last of the cars left the tunnel, and then the caboose with a signalman holding a red-eye lantern out on the platform. When she was down the tracks and just about beyond my sight, the floater showed himself again and had him another look around. Then, sure enough, he made straight for the melon patch.

Once he got into it I couldn't see him, because he was in close to the woods at the edge of the slope. I couldn't see Billy Bob neither. The whistle sounded one final time, mournful, as the lights of the caboose disappeared, and a chill come to my neck and set there like a cold dead hand. I closed my eyes and listened to the last singing of the wheels fade away.

It weren't long before I heard footfalls on the slope coming near, then the angry sound of a stranger's voice, but I kept my eyes shut until they walked up close and Billy Bob said, "Granpa." When I opened 'em the floater was standing three feet in front of me, white face shining in the moonlight—scared face, angry face, evil face.

"What the hell is this?" he said. "What you want with me?"

"Give me your gun, Billy Bob," I said.

He did it, and I held her tight and lifted the barrel. The ache in my stomach was so strong my knees felt weak and I could scarcely breathe. But my hand was steady.

The floater's eyes come wide open and he backed off a step. "Hey," he said, "hey, you can't—"

I shot him twice.

He fell over and rolled some and come up on his back. They wasn't no doubt he was dead, so I give the gun back to Billy Bob and he put it away in his belt. "All right, boy," I said.

Billy Bob nodded and went over and hoisted the dead floater onto his shoulder. I watched him trudge off toward the bog hollow, and in my mind I could hear the train whistle as she'd sounded from inside the tunnel. I thought again, as I had so many times, that it was the way my boy Rufus and Billy Bob's ma must have sounded that night in 1947, when the two floaters from the hobo jungle broke into their home and raped her and shot Rufus to death. She lived just long enough to tell us about the floaters, but they was never caught. So it was up to me, and then up to me and Billy Bob when he come of age.

Well, it ain't like it once was, and that saddens me. But they's still a few that ride the rails, still a few take it into their heads to jump off down there when the St. Louis freight slows coming through the Chigger Mountain tunnel.

Oh my yes, they'll *always* be a few for me and Billy Bob and the sweet fever inside us both.

PERFECT TIMING

The first call came at ten o'clock Saturday morning.

Carmody had just returned to San Francisco from Barstow, over which Angela's Cessna had exploded at noon on Thursday. A solemn representative of the Federal Aviation Administration had shown up Thursday evening to give him word of the mishap and of Angela's death. He'd flown directly to Barstow with the representative, even though there was really nothing for him to do there.

He had had a bad time in Barstow with Angela's brother, Russ Halpern. Halpern was one of these dim-witted high-school dropouts, a heavy construction worker; once he got an idea in his head you couldn't get it out. He hadn't liked Carmody from the moment Angela first introduced them, had even tried to keep them from getting married. He thought Carmody was after the stocks and securities she'd inherited from her first husband, a Montgomery Street broker whose passion for handball had netted him a fatal coronary one afternoon on the courts. And now he thought Carmody also wanted the $200,000 double-indemnity insurance on her life; that that was another reason Carmody had decided to murder her.

Halpern had flown to Barstow, too, after getting word of the accident, and made a scene in front of a dozen witnesses. Claimed Carmody had talked Angela into flying alone to Tucson to visit her sister; claimed he must have put a bomb of some kind on board the Cessna. He'd been ranting like a lunatic and they'd had to restrain him from attacking Carmody. Later, the FAA people had thrown some hard questions at Carmody— questions that had finally ended when their preliminary investigation uncovered no evidence in the wreckage to indicate sabotage. He'd stayed over an extra day, at the FAA's request, and gotten a flight back early this morning.

So he had been home less than ten minutes when the telephone rang. He was making coffee in the kitchen; he finished spooning freshly ground Vienna roast into the Mr. Coffee before going into the front room and catching up the receiver.

"Hello?"

At first there was silence. Carmody frowned and opened his mouth to say hello again. And that was when the ticking started.

. . . *tick* . . . *tick* . . . *tick* . . .

He said, "Who is this? What's the idea?" But there was only the steady rhythm of what sounded like a clock.

. . . *tick* . . . *tick* . . . *tick* . . .

A chill moved along Carmody's neck. He dropped the receiver into its cradle, stood moistening his lips. One of those crank calls everybody gets now and then? He didn't think so, not after what had happened in Barstow yesterday with Russ Halpern.

A clock ticking. Well, you didn't have to be any brighter than Halpern to figure out the connection. Halpern had it in his head that Carmody was responsible for Angela's death, that he had used an alarm-clock timing device to trigger a bomb; so . . . tick, tick, tick. But what was he trying to prove? Trying to scare Carmody into an admission of guilt? No, that didn't make sense. Putting the finger of guilt on him, then, telling him *he* knew what had happened? But he'd already done that in Barstow, in front of witnesses . . .

Forget it, Carmody decided. Let Halpern play his foolish games. If he made any direct threats, he would find himself in a hell of a lot of trouble, grieving brother or not.

Carmody went into the kitchen to see if the coffee was ready.

The second call came at ten-forty.

Carmody was in the den, going through his and Angela's papers and drinking his second cup of coffee. The hair prickled on his neck when he heard the bell; then he shrugged and moved over to the phone on the desk.

"Yes?"

. . . tick . . . tick . . . tick . . .

The sound of the clock was louder than it had been before. The muscles in Carmody's neck tightened; his lips pulled into a thin line. He listened to the ticking, trying to make out the sound of breathing behind it, but there was nothing else to hear. At length he said, "All right, Halpern, I know it's you. What do you think this nonsense is going to get you?"

. . . tick . . . tick . . . tick . . .

Carmody hung up.

The third call came at eleven-fifteen.

He had gone into the garage, gotten several cardboard boxes, and begun to pack away some of Angela's things— clothes, cosmetics, other personal items. He was taking down the hatboxes from the shelf in her closet when the telephone began its jangling summons.

Startled, he lost his grip on one of the boxes and the others came tumbling down all around him. The phone kept on ringing; the bell seemed unnaturally loud in the stillness of the big house. Carmody kicked one of the hatboxes out of his way, stalked to the nightstand and caught up the receiver on the bedroom extension. Put it to his ear without speaking into the mouthpiece.

. . . tick . . . tick . . . tick . . .

"All right, Halpern, that's it," he said angrily, "that's all I'm going to take. If you call again I'll report you to the police. This is a trying enough time for me without having to put up with you and your psychotic tricks. Have a little respect for your sister's memory!"

. . . tick . . . tick . . . tick . . .

Carmody slammed the receiver down.

When he looked at his hand he saw that it was trembling slightly. He shouldn't let this upset him, but there was something unnerving about the calls and that damned ticking. Well, Halpern had better heed his last warning. Carmody *would* report him to the police if he kept it up.

He went to where the hatboxes lay strewn across the carpet and began to gather them up.

The fourth call came just before noon.

The shrillness of the bell brought Carmody out of the recliner in a convulsive jump. He had been too nervous to continue with the packing, had made himself a drink and sat down here in the den to try to relax. He listened to the phone ringing, ringing. Why the hell hadn't he taken it off the hook? But then if he had, Halpern would only have called back later. And if he didn't answer it now, Halpern would just keep the line open so the bell went on ringing . . .

He half-ran to the desk, jerked up the receiver.

. . . tick . . . tick . . . tick . . .

Louder, now, it seemed; even louder than the last time. Sweat sheened Carmody's face and neck. Wait him out, he thought, don't say anything. Make him commit himself, wait him out . . .

. . . tick . . . tick . . . tick . . .
. . . wait . . . wait . . . wait . . .
. . . tick . . . tick . . . tick . . .

It got to Carmody finally; he just couldn't stand it any more. He shouted, "Goddamn you, Halpern, I've had enough! When I hang up I'm going to call the police *and* my lawyer. You hear me?"

. . . tick . . . tick . . . tick . . .

"I mean it! I'm not making idle threats here!"

. . . tick . . . tick . . . tick . . .

Get control of yourself, Carmody thought shakily. This is what he wants you to do, blow your cool. He wiped away sweat with his free hand. As he did so, his gaze fell on the antique

Seth Thomas clock on one wall. One minute to noon. Was that all? It seemed like half a day since Halpern's first call, but it had only been two hours . . .

Two hours. Ten o'clock to noon.

Carmody's hand spasmed into a clawlike tightness around the receiver. His heart began to race, his brain to whirl furiously.

Two hours, ten until noon—Angela had taken off from SFO at ten on Thursday morning and he had set the tiny travel-clock timer on the bomb for exactly noon—Halpern had returned to San Francisco yesterday and this house had been deserted and there were a hundred nooks and crannies, a hundred potential hiding places in an old house like this one—and Halpern was a heavy construction worker, and that meant he had access to—

"No!" Carmody screamed. He dropped the receiver and turned wildly to run, just as the clock on the wall was about to strike noon.

. . . *tick* . . . *tick* . . . *ti—*

DEAR POISONER

Dear Poisoner,

That's right, Fentress, I know you're the one who poisoned my goldfish pond. There's nobody else in this neighborhood as mean, nasty, and black-hearted. I know why you did it, too—just because I plowed under your damned ugly rhododendron bushes that were growing on *my* property. I had every right to do them in with my roto-tiller and you know it.

We've had our disputes in the past, you and I, most of them on account of you being so pig-headed about the boundary line and Rex's barking and Blanche sun-bathing in the nude. (Don't think I've forgotten you telling people she resembles the Great White Whale, because I haven't.) But this time you've gone too far. You're not going to get away with what you did to my poor little innocent goldfish.

I can't prove you did it, can't turn you in to the police or the SPCA, so you think you're untouchable. Right? Well, you're not. There are other ways to make you answer for murdering my fish.

You're *not* going to get away with it.

Frank Coombs

Dear Poisoner,

Too bad about the fire that destroyed part of your garage
last night. I wondered about those fire engines I heard in the
wee hours, and now I know. Jones, the accountant over on your
block, told me a little while ago.

Spontaneous combustion, eh, Fentress? Well, maybe now
you'll clean out what's left of that rat's nest inside your garage so
nothing like last night ever happens again. Next time, you
know, it could be even worse.

Frank Coombs

Dear Poisoner,

So now it's dogs, is it? It wasn't enough to poison my poor
defenseless fish, now you had to go and murder my dog.

You're a lunatic, that's what you are. A lunatic and a
menace and something has to be done about you before you go
berserk and start poisoning *everybody's* pets in the whole damn
neighborhood.

You mark my words: Rex will not go unavenged.

Coombs

Dear Poisoner,

You don't scare me, Fentress. It's not *my* fault somebody in
your house was stupid enough to accidentally shut off the pilot
light on the water heater. Maybe you did it yourself. I wouldn't
be surprised. If you almost died of asphyxiation, if the whole
house *had* blown up because a spark touched off the gas, you'd
have nobody to blame but yourself.

So if you know what's good for you, you'll keep your veiled
threats to yourself and stay on your side of the fence from now
on. I don't have any more pets for you to poison anyway.
There's nobody left over here, thanks to you, except me and my
wife.

Coombs

Dear Poisoner,

I've just come from Blanche's funeral.

After the service I talked to one of the cops investigating her sudden death, and he said the coroner couldn't find any trace of poison in her body. He said she *must* have died of a heart attack. But you and I know better, don't we? You and I know a pharmacist like you has access to all sorts of undetectable poisons that can kill a poor woman just as easily as goldfish and dogs.

Blanche and I weren't what you'd call close these past few years but I was used to having her around. Besides, she was my wife. When a man's wife is killed he's supposed to do something about it.

I intend to do something, all right. And soon, real soon. I'm working on the problem right now.

Coombs

Dear *Dead* Poisoner,

Hah! They say revenge is sweet, and are they ever right! I never had a sweeter taste in my mouth than I do at this moment.

I wish you could read this, Fentress. I wish there was a way to get it to you. But then, down where you are the flames would burn up the paper before you had a chance to read it. Hah!

I saw the whole thing happen, you know. I was hiding in the bushes in my front yard, at a safe distance, when you came out and got into your car to drive to that drugstore of yours. I watched you buckle your seat belt, I watched you insert the key in the ignition, I watched you turn the key . . . boom! It really was a terrific explosion. In more ways than one.

You didn't know I worked one summer using dynamite to blast tree stumps, did you?

Oh, the police suspect me, of course. But they can't prove a thing. Any more than I could prove you were responsible for what happened to my fish and my dog and my wife.

Perfect irony, eh, Fentress?

Yes indeed, revenge is *so* sweet. He who laughs last really does laugh best.

I believe I'll drink a toast to that. And to you, my never-dear departed neighbor. Some of my twenty-year-old Scotch, I think. I've been saving it for just such a special occasion as this.

Ahh! Smooth as silk going down.

That's funny. It's burning in my throat, my chest . . .

No! No, you couldn't have, it isn't possible—

Poison? In my best Scotch?

Fentress, you damned *lunatic*—

THIRST

March said, "We're going to die out here, Flake."

"Don't talk like that."

"I don't want to die this way."

"You're not going to die."

"I don't want to die of thirst, Flake!"

"There are worse ways."

"No, no, there's no worse way."

"Quit thinking about it."

"How much water is left?"

"A couple of swallows apiece, that's all."

"Let me have my share. My throat's on fire!"

Flake stopped slogging forward and squinted at March for a few seconds. He took the last of the canteens from his shoulder, unscrewed the cap, and drank two mouthfuls to make sure he got them. Then he handed the canteen to March.

March took it with nerveless fingers. He sank to his knees in the reddish desert sand, his throat working spasmodically as he drank. When he had licked away the last drop he cradled the canteen to his chest and knelt there rocking with it.

Flake watched him dispassionately. "Come on, get up."

"What's the use? There's no more water. We're going to die of thirst."

"I told you to shut up about that."

March looked up at him with eyes like a wounded animal's. "You think he made it, Flake?"

"Who, Brennan?"

"Yes, Brennan."

"What do you want to think about him for?"

"He didn't take all the gasoline for the jeep."

"He had enough."

March whimpered, "Why, Flake? Why'd he do it?"

"Why the hell you think he did it?"

"Those deposits we found are rich, the ore samples proved that—sure. But there's more than enough for all of us."

"Brennan's got the fever. He wants it all."

"But he was our friend, our partner!"

"Forget about him," Flake said. "We'll worry about Brennan when we get out of this desert."

March began to laugh. "That's a good one, by God. That's rich."

"What's the matter with you?"

"*When* we get out of this desert, you said. *When*. Oh, that's a funny one—"

Flake slapped him. March grew silent, his dusty fingers moving like reddish spiders on the surfaces of the canteen. "You're around my neck like a goddamn albatross," Flake said. "You haven't let up for three days now. I don't know why I don't leave you and go on alone."

"No, Flake, please . . ."

"Get up, then."

"I can't. I can't move."

Flake caught March by the shoulders and lifted him to his feet. March stood there swaying. Flake began shuffling forward again, pulling March along by one arm. The reddish sand burned beneath their booted feet. Stillness, heat, nothing moving, hidden eyes watching them, waiting. Time passed, but they were in a state of timelessness.

"Flake."

"What is it now?"

"Can't we rest?"

Flake shaded his eyes to look skyward. The sun was falling

now, shot through with blood-colored streaks; it had the look of a maniac's eye.

"It'll be dark in a few hours," he said. "We'll rest then."

To ease the pressure of its weight against his spine, Flake adjusted the canvas knapsack of dry foodstuff. March seemed to want to cry, watching him, but there was no moisture left in him for tears. He stumbled after Flake.

They had covered another quarter of a mile when Flake came to a sudden standstill. "There's something out there," he said.

"I don't see anything."

"There," Flake said, pointing.

"What is it?"

"I don't know. We're too far away."

They moved closer, eyes straining against swollen, peeling lids. "Flake!" March cried. "Oh Jesus, Flake, it's the jeep!"

Flake began to run, stumbling, falling once in his haste. The jeep lay on its side near a shallow dry wash choked with mesquite and smoke trees. Three of its tires had blown out, the windshield was shattered, and its body was dented and scored in a dozen places.

Flake staggered up to it and looked inside, looked around it and down into the dry wash. There was no sign of Brennan, no sign of the four canteens Brennan had taken from their camp in the Red Hills.

March came lurching up. "Brennan?"

"Gone."

"On foot, like us?"

"Yeah."

"What happened? How'd he wreck the jeep?"

"Blowout, probably. He lost control and rolled it over."

"Can we fix it? Make it run?"

"No."

"Why not? Christ, Flake!"

"Radiator's busted, three tires blown, engine and steering probably screwed up too. How far you think we'd get even if we could get it started?"

"Radiator," March said. "Flake, the *radiator* . . ."

"I already checked. If there was any water left after the smash-up, Brennan got it."

March made another whimpering sound. He sank to his knees, hugging himself, and began the rocking motion again.

"Get up," Flake said.

"It's no good, we're going to die of thirst—"

"You son of a bitch, get up! Brennan's out there somewhere with the canteens. Maybe we can find him."

"How? He could be anywhere . . ."

"Maybe he was banged up in the crash, too. If he's hurt he couldn't have gotten far. We might still catch him."

"He's had three days on us, Flake. This must have happened the first day out."

Flake said nothing. He turned away from the jeep and followed the rim of the dry wash to the west. March remained kneeling on the ground, watching him, until Flake was almost out of sight; then he got to his feet and began to lurch spindle-legged after him.

It was almost dusk when Flake found the first canteen.

He had been following a trail that had become visible not far from the wrecked jeep. At that point there had been broken clumps of mesquite, other signs to indicate Brennan was hurt and crawling more than he was walking. The trail led through the arroyo where it hooked sharply to the south, then continued into the sun-baked wastes due west—toward the town of Sandoval, the starting point of their mining expedition two months ago.

The canteen lay in the shadow of a clump of rabbit brush. Flake picked it up, shook it. Empty. He glanced over his shoulder, saw March a hundred yards away shambling like a drunk, and then struck out again at a quickened pace.

Five minutes later he found the second canteen, empty, and his urgency grew and soared. He summoned reserves of strength and plunged onward in a loose trot.

He had gone less than a hundred and fifty yards when he saw the third canteen—and then, some distance beyond it, the vulture. The bird had glided down through the graying sky, was about to settle near something in the shade of a natural stone bridge. Flake ran faster, waving his arms, shouting hoarsely. The vulture slapped the air with its heavy wings and lifted off again. But it stayed nearby, circling slowly, as Flake reached the motionless figure beneath the bridge and dropped down beside it.

Brennan was still alive, but by the look of him and by the faint irregularity of his pulse he wouldn't be alive for long. His right leg was twisted at a grotesque angle. As badly hurt as he was, he had managed to crawl the better part of a mile in three days.

The fourth canteen was gripped in Brennan's fingers. Flake pried it loose, upended it over his mouth. Empty. He cast it away and shook Brennan savagely by the shoulders, but the bastard had already gone into a coma. Flake released him, worked the straps on the knapsack on Brennan's back. Inside were the ore samples and nothing else.

Flake struggled to his feet when he heard March approaching, but he didn't turn. He kept staring down at Brennan from between the blistered slits of his eyes.

"Flake! You found Brennan!"

"Yeah, I found him."

"Is he dead?"

"Almost."

"What about water? Is there—?"

"No. Not a drop."

"Oh God, Flake!"

"Shut up and let me think."

"That's it, we're finished, there's no hope now . . ."

"Goddamn you, quit your whining."

"We're going to end up like him," March said. "We're going to die, Flake, die of thirst—"

Flake backhanded him viciously, knocked him to his knees. "No, we're not," he said. "Do you hear me? We're not."

"We are, we are, we are . . ."

"We're *not* going to die," Flake said.

They came out of the desert four days later—burnt, shriveled, caked head to foot with red dust like human figures molded from soft stone.

Their appearance and the subsequent story of their ordeal caused considerable excitement in Sandoval, much more so than the rich ore samples in Flake's knapsack. They received the best of care. They were celebrities as well as rich men; they had survived the plains of hell, and that set them apart, in the eyes of the people of Sandoval, from ordinary mortals.

It took more than a week before their burns and infirmities healed enough so that they could resume normal activity. In all that time March was strangely uncommunicative. At first the doctors had been afraid that he might have to be committed to an asylum; his eyes glittered and he made sounds deep in his throat that were not human sounds. But then he began to get better, even if he still didn't have much to say. Flake thought that March would be his old self again in time. When you were a rich man, all your problems were solved in time.

Flake spent his first full day out of bed in renting them a fancy hacienda and organizing mining operations on their claim in the Red Hills. That night, when he returned to their temporary quarters, he found March sitting in the darkened kitchen. He told him all about the arrangements. March didn't seem interested. Shrugging, Flake got down a bottle of tequila and poured himself a drink.

Behind him, March said, "I've been thinking, Flake."

"Good for you. What about?"

"About Brennan."

Flake licked the back of his hand, salted it, licked off the salt, and drank the shot of tequila. "You'd better forget about Brennan," he said.

"I can't forget about him," March said. His eyes were bright. "What do you suppose people would say if we told them the whole story? Everything that happened out there in the desert."

"Don't be a damned fool."

March smiled. "We were thirsty, weren't we? So thirsty."

"That's right. And we did what we had to do to survive."

"Yes," March said. "We did what we had to do."

He stood up slowly and lifted a folded square of linen from the table. Under it was a long, thin carving knife. March picked up the knife and held it in his hand. Sweat shone on his skin; his eyes glittered now like bits of phosphorous. He took a step toward Flake.

Flake felt sudden fear. He opened his mouth to tell March to put the knife down, to ask him what the hell he thought he was doing. But the words caught in his throat.

"You know what we are, Flake? You know what we—what I—became out there the night we cut Brennan open and drained his blood into those four big canteens?"

Flake knew, then, and he tried desperately to run—too late. March tripped him and knocked him down and straddled him, the knife held high.

"I'm still thirsty," March said.

SKELETONS

I had put Katchaturian's *Masquerade Suite* on the stereo and was pouring myself a tulip glass of port when the doorbell rang at a few minutes past seven.

Reluctantly I crossed to the foyer, asking myself why it was that whenever a man plans a relaxing evening at home alone, he is invariably beset by interruptions of one kind or another. Sighing, I opened the door.

The man standing on the porch was tall and thin, with eyebrows so thick they formed an almost solid black bar across his forehead. He wore a navy-blue business suit and a dark tie; his narrow mouth was turned into a smile that did not reach eyes as slick as polished black stones. He reminded me of an undertaker.

He said, "Mr. Thorpe? Mr. Emmett Thorpe?"

"Yes?"

"A pleasure, sir, a distinct pleasure." He proffered his hand. "My name is Buchanan, Ian Buchanan."

His grip was cool and moist. I took my own hand away quickly. "What can I do for you, Mr. Buchanan?"

"A business matter, sir."

"Oh," I said. "Well, I'm sorry, but I never discuss business except at my office. Perhaps if you—"

"This is a matter of no little import, Mr. Thorpe, no little import."

"Yes?"

"Oh, very much so."

"Concerning what?"

"Lysander Pharmaceuticals."

"I gathered that much," I said. *"Precisely* why are you here, Mr. Buchanan?"

His smile widened. "May I come in? It's a bit chilly out here—decidedly nippy, in fact."

"I see no reason to let you into my house until you state the nature of your business," I said. I was beginning to grow irritated.

"I don't blame you for that. No, no, not at all. It pays to be careful these days, eh? Well, Mr. Thorpe, to put it quite simply, I am here to blackmail you."

I stared at him. "What did you say?"

"I think you heard me, sir. Now may I come in?"

I hesitated for a moment, and then stood aside wordlessly. We went into the living room. The *Masquerade Suite* was in its closing segments now; Buchanan paused to listen. "Ah, Katchaturian," he said. "A genius, sir, a monumental talent. Perhaps one day he will be given his due as one of the great composers."

I said nothing, standing with my hands closed into fists. My chest felt constricted, my mouth dry and coppery.

When the music ended, Buchanan seated himself in one of the overstuffed chairs and took in the contents of the room in a sweeping glance: the heavy mahogany-and-leather furniture, the fieldstone fireplace flanked by staggered shelves of good, well-thumbed books, the stereo components built into the paneled wall opposite. "A most impressive room, Mr. Thorpe, most impressive indeed," he said appreciatively. "I must compliment you on your taste."

"Suppose you get to the point, Buchanan."

"And the point is blackmail, eh?"

"So you said."

"So I did. An unfortunate word, blackmail, but there you are. I could have said I dealt in silence but I dislike euphemisms. I prefer to call a spade a spade."

"Damn you, what do you think you know about me?"

"Enough, Mr. Thorpe, to ask—and receive—the inconsequential sum of fifteen hundred dollars a month."

"That's an outrageous demand!"

"Not under the circumstances."

"What circumstances?"

"The rather substantial skeleton in your closet, sir. Yes, *very* substantial. Need I remind you of the unpleasant details?"

I said stiffly, "Lay your damned cards on the table."

"As you wish." Buchanan leaned back in his chair and made a steeple of his hands. "In April of 1977, you and a Mr. Arthur Powell, a speculator of shady background, contrived to steal, by fraudulent misrepresentation of certain real estate properties, the sum of five hundred thousand dollars. You were successful in this scheme and equally divided the, ah, spoils."

He paused for a moment, watching me. When I said nothing he smiled and went on. "Mr. Powell squandered his share on a variety of wildcat speculations. He died of a heart attack in Los Angeles in 1982—for all practical purposes, a pauper. You, on the other hand, used your share to finance a power play to gain control of Lysander Pharmaceuticals. The power play was successful, with the result that today you are not only head of the company but a well-respected member of this community and a leading candidate for public office. A senatorial seat, isn't it?"

I remained silent.

"And that is why, Mr. Thorpe," Buchanan said, "I believe you will pay me a fifteen-hundred-dollar honorarium each month. If this skeleton of yours were made public . . . well, I shudder to think of its effects on your reputation and your political aspirations. Don't you?"

"How did you find out all this?"

He smiled. "Come now, you really don't expect me to tell you that. There are ways—many ways to find out many things. Shall we leave it at that?"

"I . . . suppose you have proof?"

"Oh yes. Quite enough."

I drew a deep breath, held it, let it out slowly. "All right," I said. "All right, Buchanan, I'll pay."

"Wise decision, Mr. Thorpe! No hedging, no bluff or bluster; exactly what I expected of you, sir."

"You'll want the first payment now, I suppose?"

"If you have the ready cash, that would be most satisfactory. Indeed it would."

I crossed to the bookshelves and removed several volumes of Tolstoy. A small button on the wall behind them slid one of the panels back, revealing my safe. In a few seconds I had it open. A .32 revolver and a sheaf of vital documents were the only contents.

I let my fingers close around the gun, shutting my eyes for a moment to think. Did I have another choice? No, I decided wearily, this was the only way. I lifted the weapon and turned to point it at Buchanan.

His slick black eyes widened in disbelief. He clutched at the arms of the chair, started to rise convulsively.

"Stay right where you are," I said.

He sank back. Fear had turned his face a stark white and completely destroyed his unctuous, patronizing manner. "Have you gone mad, Thorpe? Put that gun away!"

"No, I don't think I will."

"You . . . you can't kill me!" He almost screamed the words. "The evidence I have . . . it's in the hands of a confederate. If I'm found dead, everything will go the authorities—"

"Shut up," I said without rancor. I felt old in that moment, very old. "I'm not going to kill you. Whatever else I may be, I'm not a murderer. But if you move out of that chair, I'll shoot you in the leg, or hip, or shoulder—someplace crippling. I *am* a good pistol shot."

"Then what. . . ?"

"The police," I said.

"The police! Don't be a fool, Thorpe! If you turn me in, I'll have to tell them about you. I won't have any choice."

"I'll save you the trouble." I moved over to the telephone.

"I intend to tell them myself. Everything, down to the last detail."

"Think what you're doing, man!" he cried desperately. "You'll be disgraced, ruined! And for what? A paltry fifteen hundred dollars a month? For God's sake, Thorpe, you can afford fifteen hundred dollars a month!"

"Can I?" I said. "I am now paying two thousand a month to a man whose uncle was taken in the real-estate swindle and who somehow found out I was involved, twelve hundred to a minor accountant who happened to dig up and correctly interpret some old records, and a thousand to the woman who was Arthur Powell's mistress just before he died—all for *their* continued silence."

I sighed resignedly. "No, Buchanan, I can't afford to pay you fifteen hundred dollars a month. And even if I could, I wouldn't. A man can take only so much pressure and so much guilt before he reaches the limit of his endurance. A fourth blackmailer is my limit, Buchanan; you're the straw that broke this camel's back."

I picked up the receiver with my free hand and dialed the police.

THE SAME OLD GRIND

There were no customers in the Vienna Delicatessen when Mitchell came in at two on a Thursday afternoon. But that wasn't anything unusual. He'd been going there a couple of times a week since he'd discovered the place two months ago, and he hadn't seen more than a dozen people shopping there in all that time.

It wasn't much of a place. Just a hole-in-the wall deli tucked down at the end of a side street, in an old neighborhood that was sliding downhill. Which was exactly the opposite of what he himself was doing, Mitchell thought. He was heading *uphill*—out of the slums he'd been raised in and into this section of the city for a few months, until he had enough money and enough connections, and then uptown where you drank champagne instead of cheap bourbon and ate in fancy restaurants instead of dusty old delis.

But he had to admit that he got a boot out of coming to the Vienna Delicatessen. For one thing, the food was good and didn't cost much. And for another the owner, Giftholz, amused him. Giftholz was a frail old bird who talked with an accent and said a lot of humorous things because he didn't understand half of what you rapped to him about. He was from Austria or someplace like that, had been in this country for thirty years, but damned if he didn't talk like he'd just come off the boat.

What Giftholz was doing right now was standing behind the deli counter and staring off into space. Daydreaming about Austria, maybe. Or about the customers he wished he had. He didn't hear Mitchell open the door, but as soon as the little bell overhead started tinkling, he swung around and smiled in a sad hopeful way that always made Mitchell think of an old mutt waiting for somebody to throw him a bone.

"Mr. Mitchell, good afternoon."

Mitchell shut the door and went over to the counter. "How's it going, Giftholz?"

"It goes," Giftholz said sadly. "But not so well."

"The same old grind, huh?"

"Same old grind?"

"Sure. Day in, day out. Rutsville, you dig?"

"Dig?" Giftholz said. He blinked like he was confused and smoothed his hands over the front of his clean white apron. "What will you have today, Mr. Mitchell?"

"The usual. Sausage hero and an order of cole slaw. Might as well lay a brew on me too."

"Lay a brew?"

Mitchell grinned. "Beer, Giftholz. I want a beer."

"Ah. One beer, one sausage hero, one cole slaw. Yes."

Giftholz got busy. He didn't move too fast—hell, he was so frail he'd probably keel over if he *tried* to move fast—but that was all right. He knew what he was doing and he did it right: lots of meat on the sandwich, lots of slaw. You had to give him that.

Mitchell watched him for a time. Then he said, "Tell me something, Giftholz. How do you hang in like this?"

"Please?"

"Hang in," Mitchell said. "Stay in business. You don't have many customers and your prices are already dirt cheap."

"I charge what is fair."

"Yeah, right. But you can't make any bread that way."

"Bread?" Giftholz said. "No, my bread is purchased from the bakery on Union Avenue."

Mitchell got a laugh out of that. "I mean money, Giftholz. You can't make any *money*."

"Ah. Yes, it is sometimes difficult."

"So how do you pay the bills? You got a little something going on the side?"

"Something going?"

"A sideline. A little numbers action, maybe?"

"No, I have no sideline."

"Come on, everybody's got some kind of scam. I mean, it's a dog-eat-dog world, right? Everybody's got to make ends meet any way he can."

"That is true," Giftholz said. "But I have no scam. I do not even know the word."

Mitchell shook his head. Giftholz probably *didn't* have a scam; it figured that way. One of these old-fashioned merchant types who were dead honest. And poor as hell because they didn't believe in screwing their customers and grabbing a little gravy where they could. But still, the way things were these days, how did he stand up to the grind? Even with his cheap prices, he couldn't compete with the big chain outfits that had specials and drawings and gave away stamps; and he had to pay higher and higher wholesale prices himself for the stuff he sold. Yet here he was, still in business. Mitchell just couldn't figure out how guys like him did it.

Giftholz finished making the sandwich, put it on a paper plate, laid a big cup of slaw beside it, opened a beer from his small refrigerator, and put everything down on the counter. He was smiling as he did it—a kind of proud smile, like he'd done something fine.

"It is two dollars, please, Mr. Mitchell."

Two dollars. Man. The same meal would have cost him four or five at one of the places uptown. Mitchell shook his head again, reached into his pocket, and flipped his wallet out.

When he opened it and fingered through the thick roll of bills inside, Giftholz's eyes got round. Probably because he'd never seen more than fifty bucks at one time in his life. Hell, Mitchell thought, give him a thrill. He opened the wallet wider and waved it under Giftholz's nose.

"That's what real money looks like, Giftholz," he said.

"Five bills here, five hundred aces. And plenty more where that came from."

"Where did you earn so much money, Mr. Mitchell?"

Mitchell laughed. "I got a few connections, that's how. I do little jobs for people and they pay me big money."

"Little jobs?"

"You don't want me to tell you what they are. They're private jobs, if you get my drift."

"Ah," Giftholz said, and nodded slowly. "Yes, I see."

Mitchell peeled out the smallest of the bills, a fiver, and laid it on the counter. "Keep the change, Giftholz. I feel generous today."

"Thank you," Giftholz said. "Thank you so much."

Mitchell laughed again and took a bite of his hero. Damned good. Giftholz made the best sandwiches in the city, all right. How could you *figure* a guy like him?

He ate standing up at the counter; there was one little table against the back wall, but from here he could watch Giftholz putter around in slow motion. Nobody else came into the deli; he would have been surprised if somebody had. When he finished the last of the hero and the last of the beer, he belched in satisfaction and wiped his hands on a napkin. Giftholz came over to take the paper plate away; then he reached under the counter and came up with a bowl of mints and a small tray of toothpicks.

"Please," he said.

"Free mints? Since when, Giftholz?"

"It is because you are a good customer."

It is because I gave you a three-buck tip, Mitchell thought. He grinned at Giftholz, helped himself to a handful of mints, and dropped them into his coat pocket. Then he took a toothpick and worked at a piece of sausage that was stuck between two of his teeth.

Giftholz said, "You would do me a small favor, Mr. Mitchell?"

"Favor? Depends on what it is."

"Come with me into the kitchen for a moment."

"What for?"

"There is something I would show you. Please, it will only take a short time."

Mitchell finished excavating his teeth, tucked the toothpick into a corner of his mouth, and shrugged. What the hell, he might as well humor the old guy. He had time; he didn't have any more little jobs to do today. And there wouldn't be any gambling or lady action until tonight.

"Sure," he said. "Why not."

"Good," Giftholz said. "*Wunderbar.*"

He gestured for Mitchell to come around behind the counter and then doddered through a door into the kitchen. When Mitchell went through after him he didn't see anything particularly interesting. Just a lot of kitchen equipment, a butcher's block table, a couple of cases of beer, and some kind of large contraption in the far corner.

"So what do you want to show me?" he asked.

"Nothing," Giftholz said.

"Huh?"

"Really I would ask you a question."

"What question?"

"If you speak German."

"German? You putting me on?"

"Putting you on?"

For some reason Mitchell was beginning to feel short of breath. "Listen," he said, "what do you want to know a thing like that for?"

"It is because of my name. If you were to speak German, you see, you would understand what it means in English translation."

Short of breath and a little dizzy, too. He blinked a couple of times and ran a hand over his face. "What do I care what your damned name means."

"You should care, Mr. Mitchell," Giftholz said. "It means 'poison wood.'"

"Poison—?" Mitchell's mouth dropped open, and the toothpick fell out of it and fluttered to the floor. He stared at it stupidly for a second.

Poison wood.

Then he stopped feeling dizzy and short of breath; he stopped feeling anything. He didn't even feel the floor when he fell over and hit it with his face.

Giftholz stood looking down at the body. Too bad, he thought sadly. Ah, but then, Mr. Mitchell had been a *strolch*, a hoodlum; such men were not to be mourned. And as he had said himself in his curious idiom, it was a dog-eat-dog world today. Everything cost so much; everything was so difficult for a man of honesty. One truly did have to make ends meet any way one could.

He bent and felt for a pulse. But of course there was none. The poison paralyzed the muscles of the heart and brought certain death within minutes. It also became neutralized in the body after a short period of time, leaving no toxic traces.

Giftholz picked up the special toothpick from the floor, carried it over to the garbage pail. After which he returned and took Mr. Mitchell's wallet and put it away inside his apron.

One had to make ends meet any way one could. Such a perfect phrase that was. But there was another of Mr. Mitchell's many phases which still puzzled him. The same old grind. It was *not* the same old grind; it had not been the same old grind for some time.

No doubt Mr. Mitchell meant something else, Giftholz decided.

And then he began to drag the body toward the large gleaming sausage grinder in the far corner.

HIS NAME WAS LEGION

His name was Legion.

No, sir, I mean that literal—Jimmy Legion, that was his name. He knew about the Biblical connection, though. Used to say, *"My name is Legion,"* like he was Christ Himself quoting Scripture.

Religious man? No, sir! Furthest thing from it. Jimmy Legion was a liar, a blasphemer, a thief, a fornicator, and just about anything else you can name. A pure hellion—a devil's son if ever there was one. Some folks in Wayville said that after he ran off with Amanda Sykes that September of 1931, he sure must have crossed afoul of the law and come to a violent end. But nobody rightly knew for sure. Not about him, nor about Amanda Sykes either.

He came to Wayville in the summer of that year, 1931. Came in out of nowhere in a fancy new Ford car, seemed to have plenty of money in his pockets; claimed he was a magazine writer. Wayville wasn't much in those days—just a small farm town with a population of around five hundred. Hardly the kind of place you'd expect a man like Legion to gravitate to. Unless he was hiding out from the law right then, which is the way some folks figured it—but only after he was gone. While he lived in Wayville he was a charmer.

First day I laid eyes on him, I was riding out from town with saddlebags and a pack all loaded up with small hardware—

Yes, that's right—saddlebags. I was only nineteen that summer, and my family was too poor to afford an automobile. But my father gave me a horse of my own when I was sixteen— a fine light-colored gelding that I called Silverboy—and after I was graduated from high school I went to work for Mr. Hazlitt at Wayville Hardware.

Depression had hit everybody pretty hard in our area, and not many small farmers could afford the gasoline for truck trips into town every time they needed something. Small merchants like Mr. Hazlitt couldn't afford it either. So what I did for him, I used Silverboy to deliver small things like farm tools and plumbing supplies and carpentry items. Rode him most of the time, hitched him to a wagon once in a while when the load was too large to carry on horseback. Mr. Hazlitt called me Ben Boone the Pony Express Deliveryman, and I liked that fine. I was full of spirit and adventure back then.

Anyhow, this afternoon I'm talking about I was riding Silverboy out to the Baker farm when I heard a roar on the road behind me. Then a car shot by so fast and so close that Silverboy spooked and spilled both of us down a ten-foot embankment.

Wasn't either of us hurt, but we could have been—we could have been killed. I only got a glimpse of the car, but it was enough for me to identify it when I got back to Wayville. I went hunting for the owner and found him straightaway inside Chancellor's Cafe.

First thing he said to me was, "*My* name is Legion."

Well, we had words. Or rather, I had the words; he just stood there and grinned at me, all wise and superior, like a professor talking to a bumpkin. Handsome brute, he was, few years older than me, with slicked-down hair and big brown eyes and teeth so white they glistened like mica rocks in the sun.

He shamed me, is what he did, in front of a dozen of my friends and neighbors. Said what happened on the road was my fault, and why didn't I go somewhere and curry my horse, *he* had better things to do than argue road right-of-ways.

Every time I saw him after that he'd make some remark to me. Polite, but with brimstone in it—I guess you know what I mean. I tried to fight him once, but he wouldn't fight. Just stood grinning at me like the first time, hands down at his sides, daring me. I couldn't hit him that way, when he wouldn't defend himself. I wanted to, but I was raised better than that.

If me and some of the other young fellows disliked him, most of the girls took to him like flies to honey. All they saw were his smile and his big brown eyes and his city charm. And his lies about being a magazine writer.

Just about every day I'd see him with a different girl, some I'd dated myself on occasion, such as Bobbie Jones and Dulcea Wade. Oh, he was smooth and evil, all right. He ruined more than one of those girls, no doubt of that. Got Dulcea Wade pregnant, for one, although none of us found out about it until after he ran off with Amanda Sykes.

Falsehoods and fornication were only two of his sins. Like I said before, he was guilty of much more than that. Including plain thievery.

He wasn't in town more than a month before folks started missing things. Small amounts of cash money, valuables of one kind or another. Mrs. Cooley, who owned the boardinghouse where Legion took a room, lost a solid gold ring her late husband gave her. But she never suspected Legion, and hardly anybody else did either until it was too late.

All this went on for close to three months—the lying and the fornicating and the stealing. It couldn't have lasted much longer than that without the truth coming out, and I guess Legion knew that best of all. It was a Friday in late September that he and Amanda Sykes disappeared together. And when folks did learn the truth about him, all they could say was good riddance to him and her both—the Sykeses among them because they were decent God-fearing people.

I reckon I was one of the last to see either of them. Fact is, in a way I was responsible for them leaving as sudden as they did.

At about two o'clock that Friday afternoon I left Mr. Hazlitt's store with a scythe and some other tools George Pickett needed on his farm and rode out the north road. It was a burning hot day, no wind at all—I remember that clear. When I was two miles outside Wayville, and about two more from the Pickett farm, I took Silverboy over to a stream that meandered through a stand of cottonwoods. He was blowing pretty hard because of the heat, and I wanted to give him a cool drink. Give myself a cool drink too.

But no sooner did I rein him up to the stream than I spied two people lying together in the tall grass. And I mean "lying together" in the biblical sense—no need to explain further. It was Legion and Amanda Sykes.

Well, they were so involved in their sinning that they didn't notice me until I was right up to them. Before I could turn Silverboy and set him running, Legion jumped up and grabbed hold of me and dragged me down to the ground. He cursed me like a crazy man; I never saw anybody that wild and possessed before or since.

"I'll teach you to spy on me, Ben Boone!" he shouted, and he hit me a full right-hand wallop on the face. Knocked me down in the grass and bloodied my nose, bloodied it so bad I couldn't stop the flow until a long while later.

Then he jumped on me and pounded me two more blows until I was half senseless. And after that he reached in my pocket and took my wallet—stole my wallet and all the money I had.

Amanda Sykes just sat there covering herself with her dress and watching. She never said a word the whole time.

It wasn't a minute later they were gone. I saw them get into this Ford that was hidden in the cottonwoods nearby and roar away. I couldn't have stopped them with a rifle, weak as I was.

When my strength finally came back I washed the blood off me as best I could, and rode Silverboy straight back to Wayville to report to the local constable. He called in the state police and they put out a warrant for the arrest of Legion and Amanda Sykes, but nothing came of it. Police didn't find them; nobody ever heard of them again.

Yes, sir, I know the story doesn't seem to have much point right now. But it will in just a minute. I wanted you to hear it first the way I told it back in 1931—the way I been telling it over and over in my own mind ever since then so I could keep on living with myself.

A good part of it's lies you see. Lies worse than Jimmy Legion's.

That's why I asked you to come, Reverend. Doctors here at the hospital tell me my heart's about ready to give out. They don't figure I'll last the week. I can't die with sin on my soul. Time's long past due for me to make peace with myself and with God.

The lies? Mostly what happened on that last afternoon, after I came riding up to the stream on my way to the Pickett farm. About Legion attacking me and bloodying me and stealing my wallet. About him and Amanda Sykes running off together. About not telling of the sinkhole near the stream that was big enough and deep enough to swallow anything smaller than a house.

Those things, and the names of two of the three of us that were there.

No, I didn't mean *him*. Everything I told you about him is the truth as far as I know it, including his name.

His name was Legion.

But Amanda's name wasn't Sykes. Not anymore it wasn't, not for five months prior to that day.

Her name was Amanda Boone.

Yes, Reverend, that's right—she was my wife. I'd dated those other girls, but I'd long *courted* Amanda; we eloped over the state line before Legion arrived and got married by a justice of the peace. We did it that way because her folks and mine were dead-set against either of us marrying so young—not that they knew we were at such a stage. We kept that part of our relationship a secret too, I guess because it was an adventure for the both of us, at least in the beginning.

My name? Yes, it's really Ben Boone. Yet it *wasn't* on that afternoon. The one who chanced on Legion and Amanda out there by the stream, who caught them sinning and listened to them laugh all shameless and say they were running off together . . . he wasn't Ben Boone at all.

His name, Reverend, that one who sat grim on his pale horse with Farmer Pickett's long, new-honed scythe in one hand . . .

His name was Death.

THE DISPATCHING OF GEORGE FERRIS

Mrs. Beresford and Mrs. Lenhart were sitting together in the parlor, knitting and discussing recipes for fruit cobbler, when Mr. Pascotti came hurrying in. "There's big news," he said. "Mr. Ferris is dead."

A gleam came into Mrs. Beresford's eyes. She looked at Mrs. Lenhart, noted a similar gleam, and said to Mr. Pascotti, "You did say dead, didn't you?"

"Dead. Murdered."

"Murdered? Are you sure?"

"Well," Mr. Pascotti said, "he's lying on the floor of his room all over blood, with a big knife sticking in his chest. What else would you call it?"

"Oh, yes," Mrs. Lenhart agreed. "Definitely murder."

Mrs. Beresford laid down her knitting and folded her hands across her shelflike bosom. "How did you happen to find him. Mr. Pascotti?"

"By accident. I was on my way down to the john—"

"Lavatory," Mrs. Lenhart said.

"—and I noticed his door was open. He never leaves his door open, not when he's here and not when he's not here. So I'm a good neighbor. I peeked inside to see if something was wrong, and there he was, all over blood."

Mrs. Beresford did some reflecting. George Ferris had been

a resident of their roominghouse for six months, during which time he had managed to create havoc in what had formerly been a peaceful and pleasant environment. She and the other residents had complained to the landlord, but the landlord lived elsewhere and chose not to give credence to what he termed "petty differences among neighbors." He also seemed to like Mr. Ferris, with whom he had had minor business dealings before Ferris' retirement and who he considered to possess a sparkling sense of humor. This flaw in his judgment of human nature made him a minority of one, but in this case the minority's opinion was law.

The problem with Mr. Ferris was that he had been a practical joker. Not just an occasional practical joker; oh, no. A constant, unending, remorseless practical joker. A *Practical Joker* with capitals and in italics. Sugar in the salt shaker; ground black pepper in the tea. Softboiled eggs substituted for hardboiled eggs. Kitchen cleanser substituted for denture powder. Four white rats let loose in the dining room during supper. Photographs of naked ladies pasted inside old Mr. Tipton's *Natural History* magazine. Whoopee cushions, water glasses that dribbled, fuzzy spiders and rubber-legged centipedes all over the walls and furniture. These and a hundred other indignities—a deluge, an avalanche of witless and childish pranks.

Was it any wonder, Mrs. Beresford thought, that somebody had finally done him in? No, it was not. The dispatching of George Ferris, the joker, was in fact an act of great mercy.

"Who could have done it?" Mrs. Lenhart asked after a time.

"Anybody who lives here," Mr. Pascotti said. "Anybody who ever spent ten minutes with that lunatic."

"You don't suppose it was an intruder?"

"Who would want to intrude in this place? No, my guess is it was one of us."

"You don't mean one of *us*?"

"What, you or Mrs. Beresford? Nice widow ladies like you? The thought never crossed my mind, believe me."

"Why, thank you, Mr. Pascotti."

"For what?"

"The compliment. You said we were nice widow ladies."

Mr. Pascotti, who had been a bachelor for nearly seven decades, looked somewhat uncomfortable. "You don't have to worry—the police won't suspect you, either. They'd have to be crazy. Policemen today are funny, but they're not crazy."

"They might suspect you, though," Mrs. Beresford said.

"Me? That's ridiculous. All I did was find him on my way to the john—"

"Lavatory," Mrs. Lenhart said.

"All I did was find him. I didn't make him all over blood."

"But they might think you did," Mrs. Beresford said.

"Not a chance. Ferris was ten years younger than me and I've got arthritis so bad I can't even knock loud on a door. So how could I stick a big knife in his chest?"

Mrs. Lenhart adjusted the drape of her shawl. "You know, I really can't imagine anybody here doing such a thing. Can you, Irma?"

"As a matter of fact," Mrs. Beresford said, "I can. We all have hidden strengths and capacities, but we don't realize it until we're driven to the point of having to use them."

"That's very profound."

"Sure it is," Mr. Pascotti said. "It's also true."

"Oh, I'm sure it is. But I still prefer to think it was an intruder who sent Mr. Ferris on to his reward, whatever that may be."

Mr. Pascotti gestured toward the parlor windows and the sunshine streaming in through them. "It's broad daylight," he said. "Do intruders intrude in broad daylight?"

"Sometimes they do," Mrs. Lenhart said. "Remember last year, when the police questioned everybody about strangers in the neighborhood? There was a series of daylight burglaries right over on Hawthorn Boulevard."

"So it could have been an intruder, I'll admit it. We'll tell the police that's what we think. Why should any of us have to suffer for making that lunatic dead?"

"Isn't it time we did?" Mrs. Beresford asked.

"Did? Did what?"

"Tell the police what we think. After we tell them Mr. Ferris is lying up in his room with a knife in his chest."

"You're right," Mr. Pascotti said, "it is time. Past time. A warm day like this, things happen to dead bodies after a while."

He turned and started over to the telephone. But before he got to it there was a sudden eruption of noise from out in the front hallway. At first it sounded to Mrs. Beresford like a series of odd snorts, wheezes, coughs, and gasps. When all these sounds coalesced into a recognizable bellow, however, she realized that what she was hearing was wild laughter.

Then George Ferris walked into the room.

He was wearing an old sweatshirt and a pair of old dungarees, both of which were, as Mr. Pascotti had said, all over blood. In his left hand he carried a wicked-looking and also very bloody knife. His chubby face was contorted into an expression of mirth bordering on ecstasy and he was laughing so hard that tears flowed down both cheeks.

Mrs. Beresford stared at him with her mouth open. So did Mrs. Lenhart and Mr. Pascotti. Ferris looked back at each of them and what he saw sent him into even greater convulsions.

The noise lasted for fifteen seconds or so, subsided into more snorts, wheezes, and gasps, and finally ceased altogether. Ferris wiped his damp face and got his breathing under control. Then he pointed to the crimson stains on his clothing. "Chicken blood," he said. He pointed to the weapon clutched in his left hand. "Trick knife," he said.

"A joke," Mr. Pascotti said. "It was all a joke."

"Another joke," Mrs. Lenhart said.

"Another indignity," Mrs. Beresford said.

"And you fell for it," Ferris reminded them. "Oh, boy, did you fall for it! You should have seen your faces when I walked in." He began to cackle again. "My best one yet," he said, "no question about it. My best one *ever*. Why, by golly, I don't think I'll live to pull off a better one."

Mrs. Beresford looked at Mrs. Lenhart. Then she looked at Mr. Pascotti. Then she picked up one of her knitting needles and looked at the pudgy joker across its sharp glittering point.

"Neither do we, Mr. Ferris," she said. "Neither do we."

LITTLE LAMB

The place where they met for
dinner was a Neapolitan res-
taurant on the edge of North Beach, not far from Don's apartment. The decor was very old-fashioned—red-and-white
checked tablecloths, Chianti bottles with candle drippings down
the necks and sides—but then Don was old-fashioned, too, at
least in some ways, so she wasn't surprised when he said it was
his favorite restaurant. Meg had never been there before. It
wasn't the kind of place Gene would ever have taken her, not in
a million years.

They sat at a little table in one corner, away from the windows that overlooked the street, and Don ordered a bottle of
wine, something called Valpolicella. He was nervous, probably
as nervous and tense as she was, but with him it was close to the
surface, not pushed down deep inside. Poor Don. He must suspect why she'd called him, why she'd coaxed him into meeting
her for dinner. How could he not suspect? He felt the same
about her as she felt about him, she was sure of that. She'd
noticed how he looked at her at the Currys' party that night
three years ago, felt the mutual attraction then and every time
they'd run into each other since. But he'd never done anything
about it—never called her or tried to see her alone somewhere.
And of course she'd never done anything about it, either. Until
tonight.

But I should have, she thought. I shouldn't have waited so long—all those bad, empty months and years with Gene. I should have arranged to see Don right away after that party at the Currys'. If I had . . .

But she hadn't. She was such a little lamb. That was what Gene said, anyway, what he always called her in private. His little lamb. He hadn't meant it affectionately, as her being cute and cuddly and soft. No, he'd meant she was placid, no mind of her own, lost without someone to guide her. Just a poor little lost lamb.

Not any more, though. Not tonight.

The waiter came with the wine and to take their orders. She'd asked Don to order for both of them, because he'd come here so often and knew what was especially good. She wanted the dinner, like everything else about this night, to be perfect. He must have wanted that, too, in his own way; he was very deliberate, asking the waiter several questions before he made up his mind. What he finally ordered was *zuppa di vongole*, green salad, breadsticks, and *fusilli alla Vesuviana*.

"What is *fusilli alla Vesuviana?*" she asked after the waiter went away.

"Pasta with tomato and cheese. Vesuvius style."

"Vesuvius? It won't erupt while we're eating, will it?"

He laughed, but it was a small laugh—forced, brittle. "You don't have to worry about that."

"I guess I'm not very good at making jokes . . ."

"No, no, it was a good joke."

There was an uncomfortable little silence. The only thing she could think to say was, "Don, aren't you glad you came?"

". . . Yes, I'm glad."

"You're not acting like it."

"It's just that . . . well . . ."

"Well what?"

"I don't think Gene would like it if he knew."

"He's not going to know. I told you, he's away."

"I know you did, but—"

"Until tomorrow," she said. "Sometime tomorrow."

Don seemed about to say something, changed his mind,

and took a too-quick drink from his glass and spilled a dribble of wine down over his chin. She had an impulse to reach over and wipe it away, touch him, but she didn't let herself do it. Not just yet.

She tasted her own wine. It was heavy, faintly sweet, not at all the kind of wine she usually liked. Tonight, though, it went with the ambiance here, with this special occasion. She drank a little more, watching Don drain his glass and pour another. She mustn't have too much herself before the food came. She had no tolerance for alcohol and she mustn't get tipsy, mustn't do anything to spoil things for either of them. When she got tipsy she would giggle or have an attack of the hiccups or knock over her glass—something silly and embarrassing like that. So she must be very careful. One glass of wine, no more.

It was just the opposite with Don. He drank two full glasses of Valpolicella and part of a third before he began to relax. Then she was able to draw him out a bit, get him to talk about his job—he was an editor with one of San Francisco's regional publishing firms—and about people they both knew. When she told him about Marian Cobb's latest trip to a fat farm, and he laughed a genuine laugh, she felt both relieved and reassured.

It's going to be all right, she told herself. It really is. Tonight is going to be just fine.

The *zuppa di vongole* came. She wasn't at all hungry, she had been sure she would only pick at her food, but she finished all of the soup; and all of the green salad that followed, and then most of the *fusilli alla Vesuviana*. It amazed her just how much of an appetite she had. And all the while they continued to talk, not about anything personal, just small talk, but there was an intimacy in it of the sort that she and Gene had never shared over a meal. Don felt it too. She could see him gradually give in to it, let the warmth of it enfold him as it was enfolding her.

Afterward they had espresso and a funny licorice-tasting liqueur—Zambucca?—that was served with a coffee bean floating in it. Over their second cup of espresso, she caught him looking at her, an unmistakably hungry look that he quickly covered up. It made her tingle, made her wet down below. She had never responded sexually when Gene looked at her that way. Oh, maybe in the beginning she had, a little. But not like this. She had never felt about Gene as she did about Don.

Why didn't I do this a long time ago? she asked herself again. Why, why, why didn't I?

The waiter came with the check. Don paid in cash, and when they were alone again she said, "What I'd like to do now is walk a bit. It's such a nice night."

"Good idea."

"Then what I want to do is go to your apartment."

She said it so casually, so boldly, it surprised her almost as much as it surprised Don. She hadn't meant to be so brazen; the words had just come out. He blinked in a way that was almost comical, like a startled owl. "Meg," he said, and then didn't go on.

"Wouldn't you like to?" she asked.

"I . . . don't think it would be a good idea."

"Why not?"

"You know why, for God's sake."

"Well, I think it's a wonderful idea," she said. "It's what I want and I think it's what you want too. Isn't it?"

He gave her a long searching look. Then he let his gaze slide away and said abruptly, almost painfully, "Yes, damn it. Yes."

"You mustn't be ashamed. I'm not."

"It isn't that I'm ashamed . . ."

She touched him then, touched his hand with the tips of her fingers. It made him jump as if with an electrical shock. "It's all right," she said. "Don—it's all right."

"It's not all right."

"But it is."

"You're a married woman . . ."

"I don't love Gene. I'm not sure I ever did."

"That isn't the point."

"It is the point. It *is*," she said. "Please, let's leave now. I'd like to walk."

She got to her feet and stood waiting for him to do the same. It wasn't a long wait, only a few seconds. They went outside together, along the crowded sidewalks of upper Grant. Somewhere she could hear music playing, guitar music—flamenco guitar? She smiled. It was such a nice night.

Beside her, Don said, "Meg, I don't understand this. Why? Tell me why."

"You know why," she said. "I've known all along how you felt about me. And I've felt the same about you, from the very first."

"Then why did you wait three years? That's what I don't understand. Why tonight, all of a sudden?"

"It was time," she said. "Past time. I couldn't wait any longer."

He was silent, walking.

"Don? You do want to be with me tonight, don't you? Alone together, the whole night?"

"You know I do. I won't deny it."

"Then that's all that matters, darling. Us together, tonight."

She heard him sigh softly. And then she heard him say, "God help us both."

Yes, she thought, God help us both.

She took his arm and moved close to him, as if they were already lovers. And for the first time, she thought about the bruises and wondered if the most recent ones still showed. Well, it didn't matter so much if they did. She would ask Don to turn the lights down low or shut them off altogether. That way, he would not notice tonight. Tomorrow . . . well, tomorrow was tomorrow. He would find out then, in any case, not so very long after he found out about Gene.

She thought about Gene, but only briefly. Only briefly did she picture him lying there in the bedroom they had shared, the bedroom where time and again he had beaten his poor little lamb, the bedroom where she had shot him to death at four o'clock this afternoon. *Yes, officer, I emptied the gun into him. He was coming at me, he was drunk and ready to beat me again, and I took the gun and I shot him and then I ran out and drove around and around—and then I called Don Murdock and arranged to have dinner with him and later spent the night with him for the first and last time. Do you think that's awful? Do you believe I'm some kind of monster?*

No, she mustn't think that way. All of that was tomorrow. First, there was tonight. And no matter what anyone believed, tonight was very important—very, very important. Like the last night before the end of the world.

She hugged Don's arm and smiled up at him, thinking about tonight.

ONCE A THIEF

(With Jeffrey M. Wallmann)

What I was doing, standing there in the shadow of a large oak at four o'clock on this clear moonlit morning, was considering the heist of a car. Not just any car, mind you, but a beautiful three-liter Lancelot Mark II, sitting in a secluded driveway less than a block away. The street—dark and deserted—was a tunnel of oaks, and the houses were nicely spaced apart. It was, as we say, a perfect setup.

But I was still only considering. Car thugging had been my trade for roughly half of my adult life; however, the other half has been spent in an assortment of state-maintained resorts run for the care and preservation of breeds such as myself. If I were to follow the mandates of my craft and once again be caught—well, the parting words of Warden Selkirk, when I was paroled from State Prison recently, were still heavy in my mind:

"Kenton, you're a loser, a perennial fixture here at the Camp. Much as I hate to say it, I'm afraid it won't be long before you're back with us again—for an even longer stay."

Nevertheless, I had been on the straight and narrow up until now. With the help of Feeney, my parole officer, I had gotten a worthwhile job as swing-shift dishwasher at the El Rancho Truck Stop and I had a room over the All-Nite Bowling Lanes; and saving bus fare the way I was, I would soon have a color television set. Maybe I shouldn't have scrimped on the fare, though, for walking to work brought me past the Lancelot every morning. And every morning I had been finding it harder and harder to continue walking and not driving.

You had to see that Lancelot to appreciate it. Sweet graceful lines, genuine leather throughout, crushed-velvet door panels, combination short wave and cassette mounted in the console, air conditioning, and power everything. The potential joy of wheeling it to Honest Jack's Auto Emporium, where it would receive a brand-new identity and eventually a brand-new home, made the palms of my hands itch.

Well, I was still trying to make up my mind—the Lancelot or another running of my personal gauntlet—when the kid appeared. He was on the sidewalk beyond the Mark II, moving with a kind of awkward stealth, looking furtively around him. When he reached the driveway he darted along it to where the Lancelot was parked. I could see him clearly in the moonlight—young, thin, scared, dressed in black—and I could see the bent wire he was clutching in one hand.

I recognized both the look of him and the wire. I had had both on my first heist those many years ago, the venture that had sent me down the broad path of crime. I saw the kid bend at the driver's door—and I knew I had to stop him. Before I could ponder the wisdom of this decision, I was hurrying silently away from the oak and down the sidewalk.

The kid was so intent on maneuvering the coat-hanger wire through the Lancelot's wing window that he didn't hear me at all. I eased up behind him and let my hand drop heavily onto his shoulder. "Son," I said in a low voice, "you're in trouble."

He turned, cringing. "Who—who are you?"

"Officer Stanislausky of the Special Citizen's Patrol," I said. "It's my job to watch this affluent neighborhood to make sure nobody heists iron belonging to the taxpayers."

"I—I wasn't going to steal this car."

"You were looking for a place to take a nap, maybe?"

"I just got a thing for Lancelots, that's all."

"That I can appreciate," I said. "But the fact remains, you're caught red-handed. I'm duty-bound to take you in."

"Give me a break, mister," the kid said. "I got a widowed mother to support, and if I'm arrested I'll lose my job."

"A widowed mother?"

"And a baby sister," he said.

"Well," I said, "that's a different story," even though I had used such a story myself on occasion. But he looked like a decent kid, just a little mixed up in his thinking.

"You mean, you'll let me go?" he said.

"Why not? I once supported a widowed mother, too."

"Thanks, mister—thanks!"

"You'll never try to heist another car?"

"Never!"

"Then you're now released on probation," I said, and let go of his shoulder. He gave me a weak grin, backed off two steps, then turned and ran down the driveway and out of sight along the oak-walled sidewalk.

I looked at the house to see if anyone had been aroused, but it was still dark and quiet. Then I looked at the Lancelot. The palms of my hands began to itch again, and I felt a weakness in the pit of my stomach. I began to shake. The Lancelot was so sleek, so beautiful—

And all at once I realized that I hadn't stopped the kid only for humanitarian reasons, that I had intervened partly because he was about to heist the Lancelot, *my* Lancelot. I knew then that I had to have it. I couldn't control myself any longer, the urge was too strong. Some men are born to write books and some to shape the destinies of the world; I was born to heist cars. There is no denying the inevitable.

The kid had left his bent coat hanger in the wing window. I touched it, almost nostalgically, and began to maneuver it. The old magic was still in my fingers. The door opened soundlessly under my hand and I slipped in behind the wheel. I ran my palms over the soft leather upholstery. Honest Jack was going to love this baby. Honest Jack had an eye for fine quality. He did not give new identities to anything but the best from both sides of the Atlantic.

I leaned down under the dash and began to cross the ignition wires. I didn't need a light—a craftsman works mainly by touch alone. As soon as I had her hot-wired, I would get out and roll the Lancelot into the street. Then—

The door was suddenly jerked open and the brilliant white light of a flash beam filled the Lancelot's interior. I sat up, blinking, and heard a sharp authoritative voice say, "Hold it right there. Put your hands where I can see them."

I put my hands where he could see them. The flashlight lowered slightly, and beyond the hazy glare was a big guy in a pair of pajamas. In his other hand he held an automatic. It was very steady. He said, "So you were trying to steal my car, eh?"

I sighed resignedly. Under the circumstances there was no point in trying to bluff it out; the proverbial egg was all over my face. "I couldn't control the urge," I said. "I have never been able to control the urge."

"In other words you're a professional car thief?"

"Reformed professional car thief—until just now."

"I thought so," the guy said. "I saw the way you got rid of that kid and the quick smooth way you opened the car."

In spite of the situation I felt a touch of pride. "How did you know something was going on out here?" I asked him.

"I was raiding the refrigerator," he answered, "and I happened to look through the kitchen window when the kid started up the drive. I got my gun and went out through the back door and by that time you were here talking to him. I knew you weren't what you claimed to be, so I just hid in the shrubbery to see what you were up to."

I sighed again. Would the local police and my parole board understand about birthrights and uncontrollable urges? Somehow I didn't think so; they had been unimpressed in the past. Well, maybe Warden Selkirk could arrange for me to have my old cell back. It had a nice view of the exercise yard.

"I tried to go straight," I told the guy philosophically. "I tried not to break my parole. But fate is a fickle woman, as the writers say. I guess I belong in the slammer, all right."

He lowered the flashlight, and the nose of the gun dipped as well. He was smiling—a sly and calculating smile. "Not necessarily," he said.

All that took place three months ago, and I can hardly believe what has happened to me since. I have moved into a posh residential apartment building called the Nabob Arms, and have acquired the color television set and a car of my own—not a Lancelot, but quality merchandise nonetheless. And Dolores, this very buxom blonde I met in the park a while back, has consented to become Mrs. Harold Kenton when her divorce is final.

Everything is coming up roses for the first time in my life, particularly and primarily because I am now able to pursue my calling on an average of six times a week—the heisting of iron, the finest of iron from both sides of the Atlantic. Bliss, sheer bliss. Oh, I don't get as much per as I did from Honest Jack, but I have to look at it from the volume and organizational aspects, not to mention the safety standpoint.

I know what you're thinking: the owner of the Lancelot happened to be the ringleader of a large-scale hot-car outfit, and he liked my style enough to take me into the fold.

But you're wrong. And that is the beauty part. What I'm doing, you see, is perfectly legitimate. The owner of the Lancelot is one of this community's most respected citizens, a shrewd business type who recognizes talent when he sees it. His name is Potter, Lawrence D. Potter, of Potter's Repossessions, Inc., and we work for only the best banks and new-car dealers when their paper turns sour, when their car loans are in default.

Like my parole officer, Feeney, says, "It's a modern Horatio Alger success story, if ever there was one."

UNDER THE SKIN

In the opulent lobby lounge of the St. Francis Hotel, where he and Tom Olivet had gone for a drink after the A.C.T. dramatic production was over, Walter Carpenter sipped his second Scotch-and-water and thought that he was a pretty lucky man. Good job, happy marriage, kids of whom he could be proud, and a best friend who had a similar temperament, similar attitudes, aspirations, likes and dislikes. Most people went through life claiming lots of casual friends and a few close ones, but seldom did a perfectly compatible relationship develop as it had between Tom and him. He knew brothers who were not nearly as close. Walter smiled. That's just what the two of us are like, he thought. Brothers.

Across the table Tom said, "Why the sudden smile?"

"Oh, just thinking that we're a hell of a team," Walter said.

"Sure," Tom said. "Carpenter and Olivet, the Gold Dust Twins."

Walter laughed. "No, I mean it. Did you ever stop to think how few friends get along as well as we do? I mean, we like to do the same things, go to the same places. The play tonight, for example. I couldn't get Cynthia to go, but as soon as I mentioned it to you, you were all set for it."

"Well, we've known each other for twenty years," Tom

said. "Two people spend as much time together as we have, they get to thinking alike and acting alike. I guess we're one head on just about everything, all right."

"A couple of carbon copies," Walter said. "Here's to friendship."

They raised their glasses and drank, and when Walter put his down on the table he noticed the hands on his wristwatch. "Hey," he said. "It's almost eleven-thirty. We'd better hustle if we're going to catch the train. Last one for Daly City leaves at midnight."

"Right," Tom said.

They split the check down the middle, then left the hotel and walked down Powell Street to the Bay Area Rapid Transit station at Market. Ordinarily one of them would have driven in that morning from the Monterey Heights area where they lived two blocks apart; but Tom's car was in the garage for minor repairs, and Walter's wife Cynthia had needed their car for errands. So they had ridden a BART train in, and after work they'd had dinner in a restaurant near Union Square before going on to the play.

Inside the Powell station Walter called Cynthia from a pay phone and told her they were taking the next train out; she said she would pick them up at Glen Park. Then he and Tom rode the escalator down to the train platform. Some twenty people stood or sat there waiting for trains, half a dozen of them drunks and other unsavory-looking types. Subway crime had not been much of a problem since BART, which connected several San Francisco points with a number of East Bay cities, opened two years earlier. Still, there were isolated incidents. Walter began to feel vaguely nervous; it was the first time he had gone anywhere this late by train.

The nervousness eased when a westbound pulled in almost immediately and none of the unsavory-looking types followed them into a nearly empty car. They sat together, Walter next to the window. Once the train had pulled out he could see their reflections in the window glass. Hell, he thought, the two of us even *look* alike sometimes. Carbon copies, for a fact. Brothers of the spirit.

A young man in workman's garb got off at the 24th and Mission stop, leaving them alone in the car. Walter's ears popped as the train picked up speed for the run to Glen Park. He said, "These new babies really move, don't they?"

"That's for sure," Tom said.

"You ever ride a fast-express passenger train?"

"No," Tom said. "You?"

"No. Say, you know what would be fun?"

"What?"

"Taking a train trip across Canada," Walter said. "They've still got crack passenger expresses up there—they run across the whole of Canada from Vancouver to Montreal."

"Yeah, I've heard about those," Tom said.

"Maybe we could take the families up there and ride one of them next summer," Walter said. "You know, fly to Vancouver and then fly home from Montreal."

"Sounds great to me."

"Think the wives would go for it?"

"I don't see why not."

For a couple of minutes the tunnel lights flashed by in a yellow blur; then the train began to slow and the globes steadied into a widening chain. When they slid out of the tunnel into the Glen Park station, Tom stood up and Walter followed him to the doors. They stepped out. No one was waiting to get on, and the doors hissed closed again almost immediately. The westbound rumbled ahead into the tunnel that led to Daly City.

The platform was empty except for a man in an overcoat and a baseball cap lounging against the tiled wall that sided the escalators; Walter and Tom had been the only passengers to get off. The nearest of the two electronic clock-and-message boards suspended above the platform read 12:02.

The sound of the train faded into silence as they walked toward the escalators, and their steps echoed hollowly. Midnight-empty this way, the fluorescent-lit station had an eerie quality. Walter felt the faint uneasiness return and impulsively quickened his pace.

They were ten yards from the escalators when the man in the overcoat moved away from the wall and came toward them.

He had the collar pulled up around his face and his chin tucked down into it; the bill of the baseball cap hid his forehead, so that his features were shadowy. His right hand was inside a coat pocket.

The hair prickled on Walter's neck. He glanced at Tom to keep from staring at the approaching man, but Tom did not seem to have noticed him at all.

Just before they reached the escalators the man in the overcoat stepped across in front of them, blocking their way, and planted his feet. They pulled up short. Tom said, "Hey," and Walter thought in sudden alarm: Oh, my God!

The man took his hand out of his pocket and showed them the long thin blade of a knife. "Wallets," he said flatly. "Hurry it up, don't make me use this."

Walter's breath seemed to clog in his lungs; he tasted the brassiness of fear. There was a moment of tense inactivity, the three of them as motionless as wax statues in a museum exhibit. Then, jerkily, his hand trembling, Walter reached into his jacket pocket and fumbled his wallet out.

But Tom just stood staring, first at the knife and then at the man's shadowed face. He did not seem to be afraid. His lips were pinched instead with anger. "A damned mugger," he said.

Walter said, "Tom, for God's sake!" and extended his wallet. The man grabbed it out of his hand, shoved it into the other slash pocket. He moved the knife slightly in front of Tom.

"Get it out," he said.

"No," Tom said, "I'll be damned if I will."

Walter knew then, instantly, what was going to happen next. Close as the two of them were, he was sensitive to Tom's moods. He opened his mouth to shout at him, tell him not to do it; he tried to make himself grab onto Tom and stop him physically. But the muscles in his body seemed paralyzed.

Then it was too late. Tom struck the man's wrist, knocked it and the knife to one side, and lunged forward.

Walter stood there, unable to move, and watched the mugger sidestep awkwardly, pulling the knife back. The coat collar fell away, the baseball cap flew off as Tom's fist grazed the side of the man's head—and Walter could see the mugger's face clearly: beard-stubbled, jutting chin, flattened nose, wild blaz-ing eyes.

The knife, glinting light from the overhead fluorescents, flashed between the mugger and Tom, and Tom stiffened and made a grunting, gasping noise. Walter looked on in horror as the man stepped back with the knife, blood on the blade now, blood on his hand. Tom turned and clutched at his stomach, eyes glazing, and then his knees buckled and he toppled over and lay still.

He killed him, Walter thought, he killed Tom—but he did not feel anything yet. Shock had given the whole thing a terri-ble dreamlike aspect. The mugger turned toward him, looked at him out of those burning eyes. Walter wanted to run, but there was nowhere to go with the tracks on both sides of the platform, the electrified rails down there, and the mugger blocking the escalators. And he could not make himself move now any more than he had been able to move when he realized Tom intended to fight.

The man in the overcoat took a step toward him, and in that moment, from inside the eastbound tunnel, there was the faint rumble of an approaching train. The suspended message board flashed CONCORD, and the mugger looked up there, looked back at Walter. The eyes burned into him an instant longer, holding him transfixed. Then the man turned sharply, scooped up his baseball cap, and ran up the escalator.

Seconds later he was gone, and the train was there instead, filling the station with a rush of sound that Walter could barely hear for the thunder of his heart.

The policeman was a short thick-set man with a black mustache, and when Walter finished speaking he looked up gravely from his notebook. "And that's everything that hap-pened, Mr. Carpenter?"

"Yes," Walter said, "that's everything."

He was sitting on one of the round tile-and-concrete benches in the center of the platform. He had been sitting there ever since it happened. When the eastbound train had braked to a halt, one of its disembarking passengers had been a BART security officer. One train too late, Walter remembered thinking dully at the time; he's one train too late. The security officer had asked a couple of terse questions, then had draped his coat over Tom and gone upstairs to call the police.

"What can you tell me about the man who did it?" the policeman asked. "Can you give me a description of him?"

Walter's eyes were wet; he took out his handkerchief and wiped them, shielding his face with the cloth, then closing his eyes behind it. When he did that he could see the face of the mugger: the stubbled cheeks, the jutting chin, the flat nose— and the eyes, above all those malignant eyes that had said as clearly as though the man had spoken the words aloud: *I've got your wallet, I know where you live. If you say anything to the cops I'll come after you and give you what I gave your friend.*

Walter shuddered, opened his eyes, lowered the handkerchief, and looked over to where the group of police and laboratory personnel were working around the body. Tom Olivet's body. Tom Olivet, lying there dead.

We were like brothers, Walter thought. We were just like brothers.

"I can't tell you anything about the mugger," he said to the policeman. "I didn't get a good look at him. I can't tell you anything at all."

CHANGES

The big flat-faced stranger came into the Elite Barber Shop just before closing that Wednesday afternoon.

Asa was stropping his old Spartacus straight razor, humming to himself and thinking how good a cold lemonade was going to taste. Over at the shoeshine stand Leroy Heavens sat on a three-legged stool, working on his own pair of brogans with a stained cloth; sweat lacquered his face and made it glisten like black onyx. The mercury in the courthouse thermometer had been up to 97 at high noon and Asa judged it wasn't much cooler than that right now: the summer flies were still heat-drugged, floating in circles on such breeze as the ceiling fan stirred up.

In the long mirror across the rear wall Asa watched the stranger shut the door and stand looking around. Leroy and the shoeshine stand got a passing glance; so did the three 1920s Otis barber chairs, the waiting-area furniture, the open door to Asa's living quarters in back, the counter full of clippers and combs and other tonsorial tools, and the display shelves of both modern and old-fashioned grooming supplies.

When the eyes flicked over him Asa said, "Sure is a hot one," by way of greeting. "That sun'll raise blisters, a person stands under it too long."

The big man didn't say anything. Just headed across to

where Asa was standing behind the number one chair. He wore a loose-fitting summer shirt and a pair of spiffy cream-colored slacks; dark green-tinted sunglasses hid his eyes. Asa took him to be somewhere in his middle fifties, reckoning from the lines in his face. Some face it was, too: looked as though somebody had beat on it with a mallet to flatten it that way, to get the nose and lips all spread out and shapeless.

The display shelves were to the left of the number-one chair; the stranger stopped there and peered down at the old-fashioned supplies. He picked up and inspected a silvertip-badger shaving brush, an ironstone mug, a block of crystal alum, a bottle of imported English lavender water. The left corner of his mouth bent upward in a sort of smile.

"Nice stuff you got here," he said, and Asa knew right off that he was from up North. New York, maybe; he had that kind of damn-Yankee accent you kept hearing on the TV. "Not too many places stock it nowadays."

"That's a fact," Asa agreed. "I'm just about the only barber in Hallam County that does."

"Sell much of it?"

"Nope, not much. Had that silvertip brush two years now; got a genuine tortoiseshell handle, too. Kind of a shame nobody wants it."

The stranger made a noise through his flattened nose. "Doesn't surprise me. All anybody wants these days is modern junk, modern ideas. People'd be a lot better off if they stuck to the old ways."

"Well," Asa said philosophically, "things change."

"Not for the better."

"Oh, I dunno. Sometimes I reckon they do." Asa laid the Spartacus razor down. "But sure not in the art of shaving. Now that silvertip there—a real fine piece of craftsmanship, hand made over in France. Make you a nice price on it if you're interested."

"Maybe," the big man said. He edged away from the shelves and went over by the open inner door. When he got there he paused and seemed to take inventory of the room beyond. "You live back there, old-timer?"

"I do."

"Alone?"

"Yep. You a census taker, maybe?"

The stranger barked once, like a hound on a possum hunt; then he came back to where Asa was and looked up at the clock above the mirror. "Almost five," he said. "Sign out front says that's when you close up."

"Most days the sign's right."

"How about today?"

"If you're asking will I still barber you, the answer's yes. Ain't my policy to turn a customer away if he's here before closing."

"Any after-hours appointments?"

Asa's brows pulled down. "I don't take after-hours appointments," he said. "Haircut what you're after, is it? Looks a mite long over the collar."

No answer. The big man turned his head and looked over at the front window, where the shade was three-quarters drawn against the glare of the afternoon sun. About all you could see below it was half of the empty sidewalk outside.

Asa ran a hand through his sparse white hair. Seemed pretty quiet in there, all of a sudden, except for the whisper of the push-broom Leroy had fetched and was sweeping up with in front of the shoeshine stand. There was hardly a sound out on Willow Street, either. Folks kept to home and indoors in this heat; hadn't been much foot or machine traffic all day, and no business to speak of.

"Don't recall seeing you around Wayville before," Asa said to the stranger. "Just passing through, are you?"

"You might say that."

"Come far?"

"Far enough. The state capital."

"Nice place, the capital."

"Sure. Lots of things happening there, right? Compared to a one-horse town like this, I mean."

"Depends on how you look at it."

"For instance," the big man said, "I heard there was some real excitement over there just last week. And I heard this barber named Asa Bedloe, from Wayville here, was mixed up in it."

Asa hesitated. Then, "Now where'd a Yankee like you hear that?"

The stranger's lips bent upward at the corner again. "The way I got it, Asa was in the capital visiting his nephew. While the nephew was at work, Asa wandered downtown to look through some secondhand bookstores because he likes to read. He took a short cut through an alley, heard two guys arguing inside an open doorway, and the next thing he knew, there was a shot and one guy came running out with a gun in his hand. Asa's already ducked out of sight, so the guy didn't see him. But Asa, he got a good look at the guy's face. He went straight to the cops and picked him out of a mug book—and what do you know, the guy's name is Rawles and he's a medium bigshot in the local rackets. So the cops are happy because they've got a tight eyewitness murder rap against Rawles, and Asa's happy because he's a ten-cent hero. The only one who isn't happy is Rawles."

Asa wet his lips. His eyes stayed fixed on the stranger's face.

"What I can't figure out," the big man went on, "is why old Asa went to the cops in the first place. I mean, why didn't he just keep his mouth shut and forget the whole thing?"

"Maybe he reckoned it was his duty," Asa said.

"Duty." The stranger shook his head. "That's another modern idea: instead of staying the hell out of things that don't concern them, everybody wants to do his duty, wants to get involved. Like I said before, people'd be better off if they stuck to the old ways."

"The old ways ain't always the right ways."

"Too bad you feel that way, old-timer," the stranger said. He glanced up at the clock again. "After five now. Time to close up."

"I ain't ready to close up just yet."

"Sure you are. Go on over and lock the front door."

"Now you listen here—"

The sly humor disappeared from the big man's face like

somebody had wiped it off with an eraser. His eyes said he was through playing games. And his actions said it even plainer: he reached down, hiked up the front of his loose-fitting shirt, and closed his big paw around the butt of a handgun stuck inside his belt.

"Lock the front door," he said again. "Then go over with the shoeshine boy—"

That was as far as he got.

Because by this time Leroy had come catfooting up behind him. And in the next second Leroy had one arm curled around his neck, his head jerked back, and the muzzle of a .44 Magnum pressed against his temple.

"Take the gun out and drop it," Leroy said. "Slow and careful, just use your thumb and forefinger."

The big man didn't have much choice. Asa watched him do what he'd been told. The look on his face was something to see—all popeyed and scrunched up with disbelief. He hadn't hardly paid any mind to Leroy since he walked in, and sure never once considered him to be listening and watching, much less to be a threat.

Leroy backed the two of them up a few paces. Then he said, "Asa, take charge of his gun. And then go ring up my office."

"Yes, sir, you bet."

The stranger said, "Office?"

"Why, sure. This fella's been pretending to work here for the past couple days, bodyguarding me ever since the capital police got wind Rawles had hired himself a professional gunman. Name's Leroy Heavens—*Sheriff* Leroy Heavens. First black sheriff in the history of Hallam County."

The big man just gawped at him.

Asa grinned as he bent to pick up the gun. "Looks like I was right and you were wrong, mister," he said. "Sometimes things change for the better, all right. Sometimes they surely do."

THE STORM TUNNEL

The two boys stood on the grassy creek bank, peering down through the darkness at the gaping mouth of the storm tunnel.

Raymond shivered. "It looks kind of spooky at night."

"Sure," Timmie said. "That's what makes it such a swell place to explore."

"You've really been inside before?"

"Lots of times."

"Alone?"

"Sure."

"Weren't you scared?"

"Not me," Timmie said.

"How far inside have you been?"

"Pretty far."

"What's it like?"

"Neat," Timmie said. "You can hear the water dripping down from the walls. And the river, too, farther inside."

Raymond shivered again. "You didn't . . . see anything, did you?"

"Like what?"

"You know."

Timmie laughed. "It's just an old storm tunnel."

"Rats and animals and . . . *things* live in old storm tunnels."

"Nothing lives in this one. You don't believe that junk?"

". . . I guess not."

"Come on, then." Timmie started down the bank.

Raymond didn't move. "My folks would skin me if they knew I was here."

"Well, they don't know, do they?"

"No. I snuck out my bedroom window like we said."

"Then it's okay."

"I don't know."

"You're not *scared*?"

"Who, me?"

"There's nothing to be afraid of," Timmie said.

"It's just spooky, that's all."

"Are you coming or not?"

Raymond took a long breath. "Yes," he said. "I'm coming."

The boys climbed down the steep, slippery bank, holding onto bushes and shrubs, digging their feet into the spongy earth. Soon they were standing on the sharp stones of the creek bed. In its center a thin stream of water flowed, disappearing into the tunnel.

It was very dark. There was no moon, and the trees and shrubs were shadows made quivery by the night breeze. The gurgle of water was the only sound.

Timmie said, "Follow me, Ray," and moved ahead along the stones. When he reached the tunnel opening he stopped again and took a flashlight from his pocket.

"Maybe I should have brought a flashlight too," Raymond said.

"One is all we need."

"I guess so."

They stepped into the storm tunnel.

The blackness was murky and damp. Timmie switched on his flashlight and played the beam along the concrete walls. They were dry and smooth at this point, but the floor was wet and littered with leaves, twigs, various bits of garbage. In the middle the stream flowed, slowly here, dying.

"I don't like this place," Raymond said.

"Oh, come on. You're not going to chicken out now?"

"No, but . . ."

"But what?"

"Nothing," Raymond said. "I'm ready."

"I'll lead the way."

They set off, Raymond hanging onto Timmie's jacket. The footing was treacherous, but Timmie moved with catlike sureness. The flickering light from his flash cast grotesque shadows on the walls. Outside the beam the blackness was absolute.

They had gone several hundred yards when Timmie halted.

"What's the matter?" Raymond asked, alarmed. The sound of his voice echoed hollowly off the thick concrete surrounding them.

"The tunnel curves around up ahead," Timmie said. "That's where it turns toward the river. The water gets deeper there, so you've got to watch your step. Stay close to the wall on your right."

". . . Okay."

Timmie led them around the gradual curve of the tunnel. Here, the dampness was pervasive. The walls were covered with a thin slime; water dripped from them, making tiny splashes on the floor like gently falling rain. The only other sounds were the shuffle of their sneakers and their raspy breathing.

When they had gone another hundred yards, the tunnel hooked sharply to the right. At that point they could hear a different sound in the blackness ahead.

"What's that?" Raymond asked, stopping.

"The river."

"Sounds like water boiling in a kettle."

"It does, kind of. Come on."

"We're not going up there, are we?"

"Sure."

"Is it safe?"

"How many times do I have to tell you? Just stay close to the wall on your right."

"Timmie . . . I think we ought to go back."

"What for?"

"I'm not going to pretend any more," Raymond said. "I'm scared, really scared."

"You're acting like a little kid."

"I don't care. I can't help it."

"Come *on*, Ray. We won't go far."

"You promise? Not far?"

"I promise," Timmie said.

He moved ahead into the sharp curve. After a few moments Raymond followed. The rushing whisper of the river grew louder. Raymond hugged the slimy wall on the right; Timmie, playing the flashlight beam ahead of them, walked a pace to his left.

Just before they reached the end of the curve, the narrow cone of light suddenly winked out.

"Timmie!" Raymond cried.

"Damn batteries must've died," Timmie said.

"Oh no! What'll we do?"

"Don't panic, Ray. Up ahead the tunnel straightens out again and there's a branch that leads to Orchard Street."

Raymond was trembling. "Let's just go back the way we came."

"It's shorter to Orchard Street," Timmie said. "We won't have so far to go in the dark."

"Can't you make the flashlight work?"

"It's no use. The batteries are dead."

"Timmie . . . I've never been this scared."

"There's nothing to be scared of."

"The river sounds awfully close."

"Just stay against the wall."

"How far is it?"

"Not more than fifty yards," Timmie said. "Let's go."

Raymond slid one foot forward, cautiously; brought the other one ahead to meet it. The deepening water saturated the thin canvas of his sneakers. The hissing rush of the river was close now; its dank odor filled the tunnel.

"Timmie?"

"I'm right here, Ray."

But Timmie's voice came from behind him. Raymond had raised his foot for another step, was already bringing it down. There was nothing to step on, no more floor.

In the blackness, Raymond's scream created a chaos of echoes. Then the scream ended abruptly in a heavy splash. Timmie stood motionless, listening, but now there was nothing to hear except the fading echoes and the voice of the river.

After a time Timmie raised the flashlight, touched the button on its side. A bright beam cut through the dark, illuminating the jagged-edged hole in the floor that extended from the middle of the tunnel to the wall on the right. He eased forward, shone the light down inside the hole. Not far below, he could see the black, swift-moving river. There was no sign of Raymond.

"You shouldn't have snitched," Timmie said softly. "I knew all along it was you, you and Peter Davis. I don't like snitches."

He turned, then, and followed the light back through the tunnel.

"I don't think this is such a good idea."

"Why not?"

"We shouldn't be out this late. Not after the way Ray Wilson disappeared so funny last week."

"You want to explore the storm tunnel, don't you?" Timmie asked.

"Well . . . I guess so."

Timmie started down the grassy creek bank. Then he paused, swung around to smile up at Peter.

"Come on," he said. "There's nothing to be afraid of."

DEFECT

Is glorious November morning,
here on decadent island of
Majorca if not in Mother Russia, and I am sitting on white-sand
beach at Palma Nova. On many such mornings I am coming
here from capital city, Palma, to mingle with unsavory tourists
from Scandinavia, England, and other bourgeois Western coun-
tries; to observe, to listen, to gather information which may be
useful. Is my duty as embassy officer.

I am observing from distance when Mikhail Pochenko
finds me. He does not look happy, but this is nothing unusual.
As good Russian and Party member, he seldom looks happy. He
sits down in chair next to mine, and before he speaks he glances
around to make certain *we* are not being observed.

"I have just communicated with Boris," he says. "There is
problem, comrade."

"Problem?" I say. We are speaking English today. On
other days away from embassy, we speak Spanish, German, and
French. To become fluent in many of disagreeable Western languages is another of our duties. "What is nature of problem?"

"Kempinski is planning to defect."

I narrow my eyes at Pochenko. "If this is jest," I say, "it is
in poor taste."

"I do not jest," Pochenko says. Which is truth. He does
not even smile often. "Kempinski intends to defect."

"When?"

"Today. While he is in Madrid."

"Can he be stopped?"

"Boris has dispatched agents, but it may already be too late."

"Kempinski," I say, and shake my head. "But why? Why would he do such a thing?"

"He has left word he desires to live in freedom."

"Freedom?"

"In United States of America," Pochenko says.

I am shocked. I stare out at sparkly calmness of Mediterranean Sea before I speak again. "To desire capitalist way of life, to defect . . . he must have defect of brain."

"Ah!" Pochenko says.

"Ah?"

"That was pun, comrade."

"It was?"

"*Da.* You said, 'To defect, he must have defect of brain.' In English language that is pun."

"It was slip of tongue, comrade."

"Puns in English language are unacceptable," Pochenko says. "Traitors such as Kempinski make puns in English language—men who have secret desires to live in United States of America."

"I have no such desire," I say. "Is unthinkable desire, depraved desire."

"Then be careful to make no more slips of tongue, comrade. I would not enjoy reporting you to Boris. *You* would not enjoy it."

"It will not happen again," I assure him. Pochenko is even greater patriot than I, Alexei Dorchev, and for this I cannot fault him or his suspicious nature. "Are we to return to embassy now?"

"No. There is nothing we can do. Boris will notify us when he receives further word about Kempinski."

We lapse into silence. Is not long before blonde girl in disgustingly tiny bikini bathing suit walks by and smiles at me. This is third time she has smiled at me this no-longer-glorious morning; is obvious she is attracted to dark Russian males with superb physiques, and wishes to make of me her sexual plaything. Soon I must go and acquaint myself with her. Is probable she is Scandinavian and will speak English—or French or one of other disagreeable languages in which I am becoming fluent. Perhaps she has useful information which I will cleverly obtain from her. But in any event I will permit her to make of me her sexual plaything so I may again observe repulsive love habits of Western women at close quarters. This, too, is one of duties I and Pochenko and Boris and other embassy officials must perform for good of Party.

But my heart will not be in it this time. Kempinski, the traitor, is too much heavy weight. His actions and motives are beyond comprehension of Alexei Dorchev, patriot.

Defect? Leave decadent island of Majorca, hotbed of capitalist corruption, when so much depends on workers in Soviet foreign service?

Kempinski *must* have defect of brain!

THE CLINCHER

They were forty-five minutes from the Oregon-California border when Cord noticed that the red needle on the fuel gauge hovered close to empty. He glanced over at Tyler. "Almost out of gas," he said.

Tyler grinned. "So am I. I could sure use some food."

In the backseat, Fallon and Brenner sat shackled close together with double cuffs. Fallon's eyes were cold and watchful—waiting.

"There you go," Tyler said suddenly, touching Cord's arm and pointing.

Cord squinted against the late afternoon sun. A couple of hundred yards to the right of the freeway was a small white building, across the front of which was a paved area and a single row of gasoline pumps. A sign lettered in faded red and mounted on a tall metal pole stood between the building and the highway. It read: ED'S SERVICE—OPEN 24 HOURS.

"Okay," Cord said. "Good as any."

A short distance ahead was an exit ramp. He turned there and doubled back along a blacktopped county road that paralleled the freeway, took the car in alongside the pumps. He shut off the engine and started to get out, but Tyler stopped him.

"This is Oregon, remember? No self-service here. It's a state law."

"Yeah, right," Cord said.

An old man with sparse white hair and a weather-eroded face came out of a cubbyhole office, around to the driver's window. "Help you?"

"Fill 'er up," Cord told him. "Unleaded."

"Yes, sir." Then the old man saw Fallon and Brenner. He moistened his lips, looking at them with bright blue eyes.

"Don't worry about them," Cord said. "They're not going anywhere."

"You fellas peace officers?"

Tyler smiled, nodding.

Cord said, "I'm a U.S. marshal and this is my guard. We're transporting these two down to San Francisco for federal court appearances."

"They from McNeil Island, up in Washington?"

"That's right."

Fallon said from the back seat, "Say, pop—"

"Shut up, Fallon," Tyler said sharply.

"Where's the rest rooms?" Fallon asked the old man.

"Never mind that now," Cord said. "Just keep quiet back there, if you know what's good for you."

Fallon seemed about to say something else, changed his mind, and sat silent.

The old man went to the rear of the car and busied himself with the gas cap and the unleaded hose. Then he came back with a squeegie, began to clean the windshield. In the front seat, Tyler yawned and Cord sat watching Fallon in the rearview mirror. The old man's eyes shifted over the four men as he worked on the glass, as if he were fascinated by what he saw.

There was a sharp click as the pump shut off automatically. The old man went to replace the hose and to screw the cap back on the tank. A few seconds later he was leaning down at the driver's window again.

"Check your oil?" he asked Cord.

"No, the oil's okay."

"That'll be twelve even, then. Credit card?"

Cord shook his head. "Cash." He got the wallet from his pocket, poked inside, gave the old man a ten and a five.

"Be right back with your change and receipt."

"Never mind, pop. Keep it. We're in a hurry."

"Not that much of a hurry," Tyler said. Then, to the old man, "You got anything to eat here?"

"Sandwich machine in the garage."

"Where's the garage?"

"Around on the other side. I'll show you."

"Better than nothing, I guess." Tyler looked at Cord. "What kind you want?"

"I don't care. Anything."

"I'll take ham on rye," Fallon said from the back.

Tyler said, "I thought we told you to shut up."

"Don't Brenner and I get anything to eat?"

"No."

"Come on, come on," Cord said. "Get the sandwiches, will you, Johnny? We've got a long way to go yet."

Tyler stepped out of the car and followed the old man around the side of the building. When they were out of sight Cord swiveled on the seat to stare back at Fallon. "Why don't you wise up?"

"I could ask you the same thing."

"Easy, Art," Brenner warned him.

"The hell with that," Fallon said. "This—"

"You keep pushing and pushing, don't you, Fallon?" Cord asked him. "You can't keep that smart mouth of yours closed."

Fallon's black eyes bored into Cord's; neither man blinked. Before long Brenner began to fidget. "Art . . ."

"Listen to your pal here," Cord said to Fallon. "He knows what's good for him."

Fallon remained silent, but his big hands clenched and unclenched inside the steel handcuffs.

Cord slid around to face front again. Pretty soon the old man came ambling back across the paved area, alone, carrying a square of rough, grease-stained cloth over one hand. He moved around to the driver's window again, bent down.

"What's keeping my guard?" Cord asked him. "Like I said before, we're in kind of a hurry."

"I guess you are," the old man said, and flicked the cloth away with his left hand.

Cord froze. In the old man's right hand was a .44 Magnum, pointed at Cord's temple.

"You make a move, mister, I reckon you're dead."

Fallon sucked in his breath; he and Brenner both sat forward. Cord remained frozen, staring at the Magnum.

The old man said to Fallon, "Where's the key to those cuffs?"

"On the ignition ring. Watch out he doesn't make a play for the gun."

"If he does he'll be minus a head." The old man reached down with his free hand, never taking his eyes from Cord, and pulled open the door. "Step out here. Slow. Hands up where I can see 'em."

Cord did as he was told. He stood holding his hands up by his ears, still watching the Magnum. The old man told him to turn around, pressed the muzzle against his spine, then removed the .38 revolver from the holster at Cord's belt. "Walk ahead a few steps," he said then. "And don't look around."

Cord took three forward steps and stopped. Behind him, the old man took the keys out of the ignition and passed them back to Fallon, who unlocked his and Brenner's handcuffs. Then the two of them got out and the old man let Fallon have the .38.

"The other one's around back," the old man said. "I slipped into the office while he was at the sandwich machine and got my gun and tapped him with it, then disarmed him. Here's his piece."

Brenner took the .38. "Go see about Tyler," Fallon told him, and Brenner nodded and went around the side of the building.

Fallon said to Cord, "You can turn around now." And when Cord had obeyed, "Lean your chest against the car, legs spread, hands behind you. You know the position."

Silently, Cord assumed it. Fallon gave the handcuffs to the

old man, who snapped them around Cord's wrists. Then Fallon slipped the wallet out of Cord's pocket, put it into his own.

Brenner came back, shoving a groggy Tyler ahead of him. There was a smear of blood on Tyler's head where the old man had clubbed him. His hands were also cuffed behind him now.

When Cord and Tyler were on the back seat of the car, Fallon gripped the old man's shoulder gratefully. "What can we say? You saved our lives."

"That's a fact," Brenner said. "All they talked about coming down from Washington was shooting us and leaving our bodies in the woods somewhere. They'd have done it sooner or later."

"What happened?" the old man asked.

"We got careless," Fallon admitted. "We stopped this morning for coffee and made the mistake of letting them have some. The next thing we knew, we had hot coffee in our faces and Cord there had my gun."

Brenner said, "How did you know, pop? They didn't give us the chance to say anything, to tip you off."

The old man had put the .44 Magnum into the pocket of his overalls; the heavy gun made them sag so much he looked lopsided. "Well," he said, "it was a number of things. By themselves, they didn't mean much, but when you put 'em all together they could only spell one thing. I was county sheriff here for twenty-five years, before I retired and opened up this station two summers ago. I seen a few federal marshals transporting prisoners to and from McNeil in my time. Housed federal prisoners in my jail more'n once, too, when an overnight stop was necessary. I know a few things about both breeds.

"First off, things just didn't seem right to me. The way they was acting, the way you was acting—there was something wrong about it. The way they looked, too, compared to you two. Whiter skin, kind of pasty, the way some Caucasians get when they've been in prison a while. And then neither of you lads was wearing those plastic identity bands around your wrists. I never seen a federal prisoner yet had his off outside, no matter what."

Fallon nodded. "They broke the ones they were wearing, so there was no way to get them on us."

"Another thing," the old man said, "they didn't want to let you go to the can or have anything to eat. No marshal treats his prisoners that way, not nowadays. They'd go screaming to their lawyers and anybody else who'd listen about abusive treatment, and the marshal'd find himself in hot water.

"Then there was the gasoline. The fella behind the wheel . . . Cord, is it?"

"Cord."

"Well, he paid me in cash," the old man said. "I never seen a marshal in recent years paid for gasoline 'cept with a credit card. Like the one I noticed peeking out of the wallet Cord had when he give me the two bills. Am I right?"

"Absolutely."

"And you get reimbursed for mileage, don't you?"

"We sure do."

"Well, that was the clincher," the old man said. "When I offered to give Cord a receipt he told me to keep it *and* a three-buck tip. No man on the federal payroll is gonna hand a gas jockey a three-dollar tip; and he sure as hell ain't gonna turn down a receipt that entitles him to get his money back from the government."

The old man passed a hand through his sparse white hair. "I'm getting on in years, but I ain't senile yet. I used to be a pretty fair lawman in my day, too, if I do say it myself. Reckon I haven't lost the knack."

Fallon glanced in at Cord and Tyler, now both sullen and quiet. "As far as Brenner and I are concerned, sir," he said, "you're the best there ever was."

THE FACSIMILE SHOP

(With Jeffrey M. Wallmann)

James Raleigh had just finished stenciling the words
THE FACSIMILE SHOP on the narrow front window when the
two men came in.

Raleigh, a plump jovial man with silvering hair, wiped his
hands on a chamois cloth and approached them, smiling. It was
almost three o'clock now and they were the first customers of
his first day. "Gentlemen," he said. "May I help you?"

Neither man spoke immediately. Their eyes were making a
slow inventory of the small shop, taking in the copy of Sesshu's
Winter Landscape on the wall beside the door, the gold-
painted, amber-inlaid replica of *Pectoral of Lioness from Kel-
ermes*, the fake gold and ivory Cretan snake goddess from the
sixteenth century B.C., the imitation Egyptian Seated Scribe of
red-hued limestone. The three statues, among others, adorned
separate and neatly arranged display stands.

The taller of the two men, dressed in a conservative gray
suit and a pearl-gray snap-brim hat, picked up the Seated Scribe
and rotated it in his hands. The eyes that studied it were a chilly
green. After a time he said conversationally, "Nice craftsmanship."

Raleigh nodded, still smiling. "Its prototype dates back to
2500 B.C."

"Prototype?"

"Yes. You see, everything in my shop is a facsimile of the original *objet d'art*. I specialize in genuine imitations—sculptures, paintings, and the like."

"In other words, junk, Harry," the second man said. He wore a glen plaid suit that was cut too tight across the shoulders and a green felt hat with a small red feather in the band. His nose had been broken at one time and improperly set.

The one named Harry gave him a look of mild reproach. "Now, Alex, that's no way to talk."

"I know," Alex said. He put his eyes on Raleigh. "What's your name, pal?"

Raleigh didn't particularly care for the man's tone, but he said, "James Raleigh. Really, gentlemen, if there is something I can—"

Harry held the Seated Scribe out toward his companion. "What do you think?"

Alex shrugged.

"How much is it, Mr. Raleigh?"

"Forty-nine ninety-five."

"Alex?"

"Too damned expensive."

"Just what I was thinking," Harry said. He turned toward the Scribe's display stand—and then seemed to spread his hands, allowing the sculpture to fall at his feet. It shattered with a dull hollow sound.

Raleigh stared down at the shards, feeling heat rise in his cheeks. The quiet in the shop now was charged with tension. At length he raised his head and looked at the two men; they returned his gaze steadily, expressionlessly.

"Why did you do that?"

"An accident," Harry said. "It slipped out of my hands."

"I don't think so."

"No?"

"No. You dropped it deliberately."

"Now why would I do a thing like that?"

"That's what I'm asking *you*."

Harry turned to the second man, Alex, and shrugged. Then he produced a wallet from inside his suit coat and took a small business card from it. He handed the card to Raleigh. On it were the words SENTINEL PROTECTIVE ASSOCIATION in black script. Below the words was an embossed drawing of a uniformed soldier with a rifle, standing at attention.

Harry said, "Accidents happen all the time to small-business men such as yourself, Mr. Raleigh. There's nothing that can be done to prevent them. But there *is* something you can do to prevent a lot of other costly business hazards—vandalism, burglary, shoplifting, wanton looting. This is kind of a bad neighborhood, you know—out of the way, poorly policed. The Sentinel Protective Association eliminates all such hazards here—except, of course, for simple accidents."

Raleigh's smile was faint and bitter. "And how much does the Sentinel Protective Agency charge for this service?"

"There is a membership fee of one hundred dollars," Harry said. "The weekly dues are twenty-five, payable on Fridays."

"Suppose I choose not to become a member?"

"Well, as I told you, this is a bad neighborhood."

"Very bad," Alex agreed. "Just last week old man Holtzmeier—he owns the delicatessen on the next block—old Holtzmeier had his store pretty near destroyed by vandals in the middle of the night."

"I suppose he wasn't one of Sentinel's clients."

"He was," Harry said sadly, "but he'd decided to discontinue our services only three days before the incident. An unfortunate decision on his part."

Raleigh moistened his lips. "They call this sort of thing 'juice,' don't they."

"Beg pardon?"

"These protective-association shakedown rackets like the one you're working here."

"I don't have any idea what you're talking about, Mr. Raleigh. The Sentinel Protective Association was formed on behalf of the small businessman in this neighborhood and operates solely with their best interests in mind."

"Sure it does," Raleigh said.

"Would you like us to put you on our membership list?"

Raleigh didn't answer at once. He glanced around the little

shop; it was a comfortable old place, one that suited him perfectly, and the rent was moderate. The thought of being forced out was not an appealing one.

After a time he turned back to the two men. "Yes," he said slowly. "I haven't any choice, have I?"

"A man always has a choice," Harry said. "In this case I'm sure you've made the right one."

"I suppose you'll want cash?"

"Naturally."

"A hundred dollars, you said?"

"For membership. Plus twenty-five for the first week's dues. One hundred and twenty-five dollars, total."

"I can have it for you by noon tomorrow . . ."

Harry shook his head. "We're sorry, Mr. Raleigh, but we couldn't possibly offer you any protection until we receive at least the membership fee."

Alex reached out to one of the display stands and began to rock a sculptured replica of the eleventh-century *Head of Divinity*. "And a lot of things can happen before noon tomorrow," he added meaningfully.

Raleigh sighed. "All right. One hundred dollars right now, the rest tomorrow."

"That's the spirit," Harry said affably.

"The money's in my safe. If you'll excuse me for a minute?"

"Of course, Mr. Raleigh. Take as much time as you need."

Raleigh disappeared through a door leading into the storage room at the rear. Two minutes later he emerged and stepped to the small check-out counter, where he fanned out ten twenty-dollar bills.

Both Harry and Alex looked at the money with surprise. "*Two* hundred dollars?" Harry said.

"I decided I might as well pay a full month's dues right now," Raleigh said resignedly. "That way, you won't have to bother coming back until the second Friday next month."

Harry smiled. "It's too bad all of our clients aren't as cooperative as you," he said.

Alex came forward, scooped up the bills, put them into his wallet. Then he produced a receipt book and a ballpoint pen and laboriously wrote out a receipt.

"Congratulations on becoming one of Sentinel's clients, Mr. Raleigh," Harry said. "You can rest assured that with us on the job, you won't have any trouble whatsoever."

Raleigh nodded wordlessly.

"Good-bye for now, then. It has been a pleasure doing business with you." And the two men left the shop.

As soon as they were out of sight, Raleigh hurried to the front door, locked it, and drew the shade. Then he went back into the storage room.

He sighed again, wistfully this time, as he set to work. This really was a very nice location. But then, he would have little difficulty finding another quiet, out-of-the way area, perhaps in another state, where he could set up his Facsimile Shop—and the Old Heidelberg printing press that he was now beginning to dismantle.

He smiled only once during the lengthy task, and that was when he thought of the inferior-quality throwaways he had run off for testing purposes that morning; and of what would happen when the Sentinel Protective Association tried passing those particular genuine imitation twenty-dollar bills.

WAITING, WAITING . . .

It was hot the day Kenner found me, the way it always was in San Pablo.

I was sitting in the cantina at the edge of town, beneath the old and tired fan, breathing the thick air with my mouth open. Drinking cheap Mexican *cerveza*, and through the windows watching the mid-afternoon sun bake a fresh network of cracks in the red adobe street.

Juan, the sad-eyed bartender, played dominoes at one end of the bar. At a table in the back a washed-out writer named Wurringer, the only other American in San Pablo, was sleeping off another drunk. That was all of us, and we had been there most of the day, as any day.

Nobody had said anything for more than an hour, but that would change when Wurringer came out of it. He was loud and profane, and when he was on a binge, as he was most of the time, he would ramble on at great length. He had been in San Pablo five years, three more than I had. He had come down from New York when it went sour for him, but he still got royalty checks now and then and was good for a few dollars. I spent time with him for that reason, and because sometimes I needed conversation to pass the long hot days and nights.

It was quiet in the cantina, with only the buzzing of flies and the sibilant hiss of the fan to mar the stillness. I had poured the last of my sixth or seventh bottle of beer into my glass, and was raising it to my lips, when I heard the screen door open and then bang closed. I looked—and he was standing there.

My heart skipped a single beat; my hand holding the glass stopped in midair. But that was all. In the beginning, two and a half years ago, I used to wonder what it would be like when he found me, as I knew he would one day. I would wake up in the night, my body leaking fluid, thinking of how I would feel and how I would react when this moment came.

Carefully, I set the glass down on the table. My hands were steady. Kenner stood by the door, not moving. He was just as I remembered him, though perhaps not as big, not as imposing; the waiting distorts a man's memory in some ways. The iron-gray hair was the same, and the lean body, and the bright, penetrating eyes.

Two and a half years, I thought. And now the waiting is over.

He crossed the room finally, sat down in the chair opposite me. His eyes bored into mine, sending little messages of hate, but I did not look away. We sat in silence that way. Juan, the bartender, left his dominoes and came toward us. But when he saw Kenner's eyes he stopped. Quickly he went back and sat down and did not look up again.

Kenner said, "Two and a half years, Larson." His voice was flat and emotionless—a hollow man's voice.

"Yes," I said. "A long time."

"I never expected to find you in a place like this. Not you."

"The money ran out in Mexico City," I said. "This was as far as I got."

Silence for a few seconds. Then he said, "Tell me about Marilyn."

"You know about her."

"I want you to tell me."

"She died," I said.

"How did she die?"

"By drowning."

"In the Bahamas, wasn't it?"

"You know it was."

"Tell me what happened."

"We hired a power boat for a cruise of the islands," I said. "We'd been out about an hour when the engine caught fire. We had to go overboard."

"Marilyn couldn't swim," Kenner said.

"No, she couldn't swim."

"But you could, Larson. You're a fine swimmer."

I didn't say anything.

"I talked to the people who pulled you out of the water," Kenner said. "They told me you might have saved her. They told me you panicked, and when you saw their boat you left her and swam toward them. She was screaming, they said. And you left her. By the time they got to where she'd been, she'd gone under."

I closed my eyes, and then opened them again slowly. I said, "Yes, I panicked and left her. That's why she drowned."

"I'm going to kill you, Larson," he said. "You know that, don't you?"

"I know."

"No man ever stole a thing from me before you. You were the first and the last. But that's not the reason. It's because you let her die that way. I would have taken her back, you know. Even after what she did with you, I would have taken her back. I loved her."

I said nothing. There was nothing to say.

"Aren't you going to beg?" Kenner asked. "Plead with me for your life?"

"No."

"I'd like it if you would. I'd enjoy seeing you crawl."

"I'm not going to beg," I said.

"I have a car outside," he said. "We're going to stand up now and go out to it. Will you try to run before we get there?"

"No. I won't run."

"I have a gun in my pocket. I'll shoot you in the knee if you try to run. They say the pain from a broken kneecap is the worst kind there is."

"I won't run," I said again.

"This isn't like you, Larson, this brave facade. A man who

lets a woman drown ought to act like the sniveling coward he is when he faces his own death."

I got to my feet. "All right," I said.

He smiled a bitter humorless smile. Then he stood, too, and we went to the door and out to the street. The sun spilled fire down from overhead. Kenner did not take his eyes off me as we walked to the car, a black, dust-streaked limousine. A man in a chauffeur's cap sat behind the wheel. He didn't look at us as we approached.

"Get in," Kenner said. "The backseat."

I got in, leaned back against the leather upholstery. Kenner sat in front, next to the driver, and then turned on the seat so he could look at me. The car started with a quiet rumble.

We drove for what seemed like a long time, out of San Pablo and along dusty, rutted cart tracks. The car was air conditioned but I sweated anyway, great oozes of perspiration that soaked my shirt and matted my hair to my forehead. Kenner's face and clothing were dry. Except for the hate shining in his eyes, his face was an expressionless mask.

Finally the car slowed, came to a stop. We were on a long, flat plain—barren, dead. Kenner said, "This is it, Larson."

I got out and stood beside the car. Small hot currents of air shimmered above the hood, above the distant wastes. I looked at the heat waves to keep from looking at Kenner when he came around to stand in front of me. The driver stayed behind the wheel.

"All right," I said. "Get it done with."

"Just like that? No last words from the condemned man?"

My hands had begun to tremble. "Get it done with, Kenner," I said again.

"There's no hurry. I've waited two and a half years. A few more minutes . . ."

"Damn you, get it over!"

The words ripped out of me before I could stop them. They seemed to echo across the heat-shrouded desert, reverberate, as if they had been flung instead against the side of a mountain.

Kenner stared at me for a long while, and now I could not

meet his eyes. When I did look at him again, he was smiling. It grew, that smile, until it split his face, until it became a kind of gargoyle grin. Then he said, "Get back in the car."

"No. Kenner, listen—"

"Get back in the car!"

He grabbed my shoulder, shoved me roughly into the rear. I sprawled across the seat and lay there, pressing my face to the cool leather. Then the car started to move again.

After a time I made myself sit up. Kenner was still looking at me; and I still could not meet his eyes. He knows, I thought. *He knows.*

We came back into San Pablo. The car stopped, and Kenner got out and pulled open the back door. When I was standing beside him he said, "For two and a half years I've lived with just one thought, Larson. Killing you. Seeing you dead. But that was before I came here, saw you again in this place. Now that I have, I'm not going to do it. I'm not going to put your blood on my hands."

"Kenner . . ."

"Because that's what you want, isn't it? That's the real reason you stopped running. You've been waiting here for me to find you, to do the thing you're not able to do yourself."

I tried to swallow into my parched throat, tried to find words. But there were no words, not anymore.

"It did something to you, didn't it? Letting Marilyn die that way. Do you think about her much? Have nightmares about her out there in the water, screaming—"

"Yes! Damn you, yes!"

"You're a bigger coward than I imagined, Larson. You don't have enough guts to put yourself out of misery, and you didn't have enough to come looking for me. So you just sat here for two years, waiting for me to come to you."

"Kenner, please, please . . ."

"I wanted to see you in hell," he said. "Well, now I have. You're already there, Larson. And you know it, don't you?"

I tried to claw at his arm, but he shook off my hand. Then he got back into the car, put the window down halfway.

"Goodbye, dead man," he said.

"No!"

I tried to reach him through the window, but it was too late. Much, much too late. The car pulled away, raising a cloud of dust. I fell to my knees in the street, watching after it, watching it grow smaller and smaller, the demon sun shining madly off the polished black metal of its top, until it was gone.

The waiting was over.

But now it would go on, and on, and on . . .

PEEKABOO

Roper came awake with the feeling that he wasn't alone in the house.

He sat up in bed, tense and wary, a crawling sensation on the back of his scalp. The night was dark, moonless; warm clotted black surrounded him. He rubbed sleep mucus from his eyes, blinking, until he could make out the vague grayish outlines of the open window in one wall, the curtains fluttering in the hot summer breeze.

Ears straining, he listened. There wasn't anything to hear. The house seemed almost graveyard still, void of even the faintest of night sounds.

What was it that had waked him up? A noise of some kind? An intuition of danger? It might only have been a bad dream, except that he couldn't remember dreaming. And it might only have been imagination, except that the feeling of not being alone was strong, urgent.

There's somebody in the house, he thought.

Or some *thing* in the house?

In spite of himself Roper remembered the story the nervous real-estate agent in Whitehall had told him about this place. It had been built in the early nineteen hundreds by a local family, and when the last of them died off a generation later it was sold to a man named Lavolle who had lived in it for forty years.

Lavolle had been a recluse whom the locals considered strange and probably evil; they hadn't had anything to do with him. But then he'd died five years ago, of natural causes, and evidence had been found by county officials that he'd been "some kind of devil worshiper" who had "practiced all sorts of dark rites." That was all the real-estate agent would say about it.

Word had gotten out about that and a lot of people seemed to believe the house was haunted or cursed or something. For that reason, and because it was isolated and in ramshackle condition, it had stayed empty until a couple of years ago. Then a man called Garber, who was an amateur parapsychologist, leased the place and lived here for ten days. At the end of that time somebody came out from Whitehall to deliver groceries and found Garber dead. Murdered. The real-estate agent wouldn't talk about how he'd been killed; nobody else would talk about it either.

Some people thought it was ghosts or demons that had murdered Garber. Others figured it was a lunatic—maybe the same one who'd killed half a dozen people in this part of New England over the past couple of years. Roper didn't believe in ghosts or demons or things that went bump in the night; that kind of supernatural stuff was for rural types like the ones in Whitehall. He believed in psychotic killers, all right, but he wasn't afraid of them; he wasn't afraid of anybody or anything. He'd made his living with a gun too long for that. And the way things were for him now, since the bank job in Boston had gone sour two weeks ago, an isolated back-country place like this was just what he needed for a few months.

So he'd leased the house under a fake name, claiming to be a writer, and he'd been here for eight days. Nothing had happened in that time: no ghosts, no demons, no strange lights or wailings or rattling chains—and no lunatics or burglars or visitors of any kind. Nothing at all.

Until now.

Well, if he *wasn't* alone in the house, it was because somebody human had come in. And he sure as hell knew how to deal with a human intruder. He pushed the blankets aside, swung his feet out of bed, and eased open the nightstand drawer. His fingers groped inside, found his .38 revolver and the flashlight he kept in there with it; he took them out. Then he stood, made his way carefully across to the bedroom door, opened it a crack, and listened again.

The same heavy silence.

Roper pulled the door wide, switched on the flash, and probed the hallway with its beam. No one there. He stepped out, moving on the balls of his bare feet. There were four other doors along the hallway: two more bedrooms, a bathroom, and an upstairs sitting room. He opened each of the doors in turn, swept the rooms with the flash, then put on the overhead lights.

Empty, all of them.

He came back to the stairs. Shadows clung to them, filled the wide foyer below. He threw the light down there from the landing. Bare mahogany walls, the lumpish shapes of furniture, more shadows crouching inside the arched entrances to the parlor and the library. But that was all: no sign of anybody, still no sounds anywhere in the warm dark.

He went down the stairs, swinging the light from side to side. At the bottom he stopped next to the newel post and used the beam to slice into the blackness in the center hall. Deserted. He arced it around into the parlor, followed it with his body turned sideways to within a pace of the archway. More furniture, the big fieldstone fireplace at the far wall, the parlor windows reflecting glints of light from the flash. He glanced back at the heavy darkness inside the library, didn't see or hear any movement over that way, and reached out with his gun hand to flick the switch on the wall inside the parlor.

Nothing happened when the electric bulbs in the old-fashioned chandelier came on; there wasn't anybody lurking in there.

Roper turned and crossed to the library arch and scanned the interior with the flash. Empty bookshelves, empty furniture. He put on the chandelier. Empty room.

He swung the cone of light past the staircase, into the center hall—and then brought it back to the stairs and held it there. The area beneath them had been walled on both sides, as it was in a lot of these old houses, to form a coat or storage closet; he'd found that out when he first moved in and opened the small door that was set into the staircase on this side. But it was just an empty space now, full of dust . . .

The back of his scalp tingled again. And a phrase from when he was a kid playing hide-and-seek games popped into his mind.

Peekaboo, I see you. Hiding under the stair.

His finger tightened around the butt of the .38. He padded forward cautiously, stopped in front of the door. And reached out with the hand holding the flash, turned the knob, jerked the door open, and aimed the light and the gun inside.

Nothing.

Roper let out a breath, backed away to where he could look down the hall again. The house was still graveyard quiet; he couldn't even hear the faint grumblings its old wooden joints usually made in the night. It was as if the whole place was wrapped in a breathless waiting hush. As if there was some kind of unnatural presence at work here. . . .

Screw that, he told himself angrily. No such things as ghosts and demons. There seemed to be presence here, all right—he could feel it just as strongly as before—but it was a human presence. Maybe a burglar, maybe a tramp, maybe even a goddamn lunatic. But *human.*

He snapped on the hall lights and went along there to the archway that led into the downstairs sitting room. First the flash and then the electric wall lamps told him it was deserted. The dining room off the parlor next. And the kitchen. And the rear porch.

Still nothing.

Where was he, damn it? Where was he hiding?

The cellar? Roper thought.

It didn't make sense that whoever it was would have gone down there. The cellar was a huge room, walled and floored in stone, that ran under most of the house; there wasn't anything in it except spiderwebs and stains on the floor that he didn't like to think about, not after the real estate agent's story about Lavolle and his dark rites. But it was the only place left that he hadn't searched.

In the kitchen again, Roper crossed to the cellar door. The knob turned soundlessly under his hand. With the door open a crack, he peered into the thick darkness below and listened. Still the same heavy silence.

He started to reach inside for the light switch. But then he remembered that there wasn't any bulb in the socket above the stairs; he'd explored the cellar by flashlight before, and he hadn't bothered to buy a bulb. He widened the opening and aimed the flash downward, fanning it slowly from left to right and up and down over the stone walls and floor. Shadowy shapes appeared and disappeared in the bobbing light: furnace, storage shelves, a wooden wine rack, the blackish gleaming stains at the far end, spiderwebs like tattered curtains hanging from the ceiling beams.

Roper hesitated. Nobody down there either, he thought. Nobody in the house after all? The feeling that he wasn't alone kept nagging at him—but it *could* be nothing more than imagination. All that business about devil worshiping and ghosts and demons and Garber being murdered and psychotic killers on the loose might have affected him more than he'd figured. Might have jumbled together in his subconscious all week and finally come out tonight, making him imagine menace where there wasn't any. Sure, maybe that was it.

But he had to make certain. He couldn't see all of the cellar from up here; he had to go down and give it a full search before he'd be satisfied that he really was alone. Otherwise he'd never be able to get back to sleep tonight.

Playing the light again, he descended the stairs in the same wary movements as before. The beam showed him nothing. Except for the faint whisper of his breathing, the creak of the risers when he put his weight on them, the stillness remained unbroken. The odors of dust and decaying wood and subterranean dampness dilated his nostrils; he began to breathe through his mouth.

When he came off the last of the steps he took a half-dozen strides into the middle of the cellar. The stones were cold and clammy against the soles of his bare feet. He turned to his right, then let the beam and his body transcribe a slow circle until he was facing the stairs.

Nothing to see, nothing to hear.

But with the light on the staircase, he realized that part of the wide, dusty area beneath them was invisible from where he stood—a mass of clotted shadow. The vertical boards between the risers kept the beam from reaching all the way under there.

The phrase from when he was a kid repeated itself in his mind: *Peekaboo, I see you. Hiding under the stair.*

With the gun and the flash extended at arm's length, he went diagonally to his right. The light cut away some of the thick gloom under the staircase, letting him see naked stone draped with more gray webs. He moved closer to the stairs, ducked under them, and put the beam full on the far joining of the walls.

Empty.

For the first time Roper began to relax. Imagination, no doubt about it now. No ghosts or demons, no burglars or lunatics hiding under the stair. A thin smile curved the corners of his mouth. Hell, the only one hiding under the stair was himself—

"Peekaboo," a voice behind him said.

WORDS DO NOT A BOOK MAKE

I went to the rear window, lifted the shade, and looked out. Then I pulled the shade down in a hurry and spun around to glare at Herbie.

"You fathead!" I yelled.

"What's the matter, boss?"

"The police station is across the street!"

"I know," Herbie said calmly.

"You know. Well, that's nice, isn't it?" I waved my hand at the telephones, the dope sheets, the rolls of flash paper, and the other stuff we had just unpacked. "Won't the cops be ever so happy when they bust in here? No long rides in the wagon. Just down the back stairs, across the street, and into a cell. Think of the time and expense we'll be saving the taxpayers. You fathead!"

"They aren't going to bust in here," Herbie said.

"No, huh?"

Herbie shook his head. "Don't you see? The setup is perfect. It couldn't be any better."

"All I see is a cold cell in that cop house over there."

"Didn't you ever read 'The Purloined Letter?'"

"The which letter?"

"Purloined," Herbie said. "'The Purloined Letter.' By Edgar Allan Poe."

"Yeah?" I said. "Never heard of him. What is he, some handicapper for one of the Eastern tracks?"

"He was a writer," Herbie said. "He died over a hundred years ago."

"What's some croaked writer got to do with this?"

"I'm trying to tell you, boss. He wrote this story called 'The Purloined Letter,' see, and everybody in it is trying to find a letter that was supposed to have been swiped, only nobody can find it. You know why?"

I shrugged. "Why?"

"Because it was under their noses all the time."

"I don't get it."

"Everybody's looking for the letter to be *hidden* some place," Herbie said. "So they never think to look in the only place left—the most obvious place, right in front of them."

"So?"

Herbie sighed. "We got the same type of thing right here. If the cops get wind a new bookie joint has opened up in town, they'll look for it everywhere *except* under their noses. Everywhere except right across the street."

I thought about it. "I don't know," I said. "It sounds crazy."

"Sure," Herbie said. "That's the beauty of it. It's so crazy it's perfect. It can't miss."

"What'd you tell the guy you rented this place from?"

"I said we were manufacturer's representatives for industrial valves. No warehouse stock; just a sales office. I even had some sign painters put a phony name on the windows, front and back."

"This landlord," I said. "Any chance of him coming up here when we ain't expecting him?"

"None, as long as we pay the rent on time. He's not that kind of guy."

"What's downstairs?"

"Insurance company. No bother on that end, either."

I did some more thinking. Herbie might be right, I decided. Why would the cops think of looking out their front door for the new book in town? No reason, none at all.

"Okay," I said, "we stay. But you better be right."

"Don't worry," Herbie said. "I am."

"All the contacts lined up?"

"I took care of everything before I called you, boss. I got eight guys—five bars, a cigar store, a billiards parlor, and a lunchroom. Phone number only, no address."

I nodded. "Put the word out, then. We're in business."

Herbie smiled. "'Of making many books there is no end,'" he said.

"Huh?"

"I read that somewhere once."

"Keep your mind off reading and on the book," I said.

For some reason Herbie thought that was funny.

At nine the next morning, the first contact phoned in his bets. The other seven followed at ten-minute intervals, just the way Herbie had set it up. From the size and number of the bets, I figured this town was going to be a gold mine.

We split up the work, Herbie taking the calls and putting the bets down on the flash paper, and me figuring odds and laying off some of the scratch with the big books in Vegas and L.A. The flash paper is thin stuff, like onionskin, and the reason we use it is that in case of a raid you just touch a match to it and the whole roll goes up in nothing flat. No evidence, no conviction.

So there we were, humming right along, getting ready for the first races at Santa Anita and Golden Gate Fields, when somebody knocked on the door.

Herbie and I looked at each other. Then I looked at my watch, as if the watch could tell me who was knocking on the damn door. It was ten forty-five, one hour and fifteen minutes after we'd opened for business.

"Who can that be?" Herbie said. "The landlord, maybe?"

"I thought you said he wouldn't bother us."

Two of the telephones began ringing at the same time.

I jumped. "Muffle those things!"

Herbie hauled up both receivers, said, "Ring back" into each one, and put them down again.

There was another knock on the door, louder this time.

"We better answer it," Herbie said. "If it's not the landlord, maybe it's the mailman."

"Yeah," I said.

"Anyway, it's nothing to worry about. I mean, cops wouldn't *knock*, would they?"

I relaxed. Sure, if it was the cops they would have come busting in already. They wouldn't stand out there knocking.

I got up and went over to the door and cracked it open. And the first thing I saw was a badge—a big shiny badge pinned to the front of a blue uniform shirt. My eyes moved upward to a neck, a huge red neck, and then on up to a huge, red head with a blue-and-gold cap perched on top of it.

"Hello," the head said.

I saw another blue uniform behind it. "Arrgh!" I said.

"I'm Chief of Police Wiggins," the head said, "and I—"

I slammed the door. "Cops!" I yelled. "The flash paper— Herbie, the flash paper!"

"*Cops?*" he yelled.

The door burst open. My backside was in the way, but not for long. It felt like a bull had hit that door, which in a manner of speaking was just what had happened. I flew into the room, collided with a chair, and fell down on my head.

A booming voice said, "What's going on in—" And then, "Well, I'll be damned!"

"Cops!" Herbie yelled.

"Watch it, Jed!" the booming voice boomed. "Flash paper!"

A blue uniform blurred past me as I struggled to my knees. I saw the uniform brush Herbie aside, saw a hand sweep across the desk. Saw all the paper flutter to the floor, intact.

"Bookies," the blue uniform said, amazed.

"Hoo-haw!" the booming voice said. "Hoo-haw-*haw*!"

"Right across the street," the blue uniform said, still amazed.

I reached up and touched my head. I could feel a lump sprouting there. Then I looked over at Herbie, who was now cowering in the grip of a long arm. "Herbie," I said, "I am going to kill you, Herbie."

"Right across the *street*," the blue uniform said again, shaking his head in wonder.

"Hoo, hoo, hoo!"

So, down the back stairs we went. Across the street we went. Into a cell we went.

Fortunately for Herbie, it wasn't the same cell.

I sat on the hard cot. The lump on my head seemed to be growing. But it was nothing, I told myself, to the lump that would soon grow on Herbie's head.

A little while later the blue uniform came back and took me to the chief's office. He took one look at me and broke off into a fresh series of hoo-hoos and hoo-haws. I sat in a chair and glared at the wall.

The chief wiped his eyes with a handkerchief. "Damnedest thing I ever heard of," he said. "Setting up a bookie joint within spitting distance of the police station."

I ground my teeth.

"It's one for the books, that's what it is," he said, and commenced hoo-hawing again.

I ground my teeth some more.

When his latest spasm ended the chief said, "What could have possessed you, son?"

Instead of answering I asked him, "Can I have a couple of minutes alone with Herbie?"

"What for?" Then he nodded his big red head and grinned and said, "Oh, I get it. His idea, was it?"

"Yeah. His idea."

"Damnedest thing I ever heard of," the chief said again. "It really is one for the—"

"All *right*," I said. "Look, how did you find out, anyway?"

"Well, to tell you the truth, we didn't."

"You . . . didn't?"

"We had no idea what you fellas were doing over there until we busted in."

"Then why were you there?"

"Business license. You got to have one to operate a business in this town."

I didn't get it. "I don't get it," I said.

"Saw some sign painters over there the other day," the chief said, "painting the name of a valve company on the windows."

"So?"

"New company setting up shop in town," the chief said. "Good for the growth of our fair city. But like I said, every business has got to have a license. So I did some checking, on account of it was a slow day, and found out this valve company never applied for one. Technically, they were breaking the law."

Herbie, I thought, I'm going to break your *head*.

"Wasn't a big deal, but still, the law's the law. So I figured to sort of welcome them officially and then bring up the matter of the license afterwards. Keep from ruffling feathers that way."

"You always go calling in person for something like that? Why didn't you use the phone?"

"Probably would have," the chief said. "Except for one thing."

I sighed. "What's that?"

"Well, son," he said with more hoo-haws lurking in his voice, "you were right across the street."

INCIDENT IN A NEIGHBORHOOD TAVERN

A "Nameless Detective" Story

When the holdup went down I was sitting at the near end of the Foghorn Tavern's scarred mahogany bar, talking to the owner, Matt Candiotti.

It was a little before seven of a mid-week evening, lull time in working-class neighborhood saloons like this one. Blue-collar locals would jam the place from four until about six-thirty, when the last of them headed home for dinner; the hard-core drinkers wouldn't begin filtering back in until about seven-thirty or eight. Right now I was the only customer.

But the draft beer in front of me wasn't the reason I was there. I'd come to ask Candiotti, as I had asked two dozen other merchants here in the Outer Mission, if he could offer any leads on the rash of burglaries that were plaguing small businesses in the neighborhood. The police hadn't come up with anything positive after six weeks, so a couple of the victims had gotten up a fund and hired me to see what I could find out. They'd picked me because I had been born and raised in the Outer Mission, which to them meant I understood the neighborhood better than any other private detective in San Francisco.

So far, though, I wasn't having any more luck than the SFPD. None of the merchants I'd spoken with today had given me any new ideas, and Candiotti was proving no exception. He stood slicing limes into wedges as we talked; they might have been onions the way his long, mournful face was screwed up, like a man trying to hold back tears. He reminded me of a tired old hound.

"Wish I could help," he said. "But hell, I don't hear nothing. Must be pros from Hunters Point or the Fillmore, hah?"

Hunters Point and the Fillmore were black sections of the city, which was a pretty good indicator of where his head was at. I said, "Some of the others figure it for local talent."

"Out of this neighborhood, you mean?"

I nodded, drank some of my draft.

"Nah, I doubt it," he said. "Guys that organized, they don't crap where they eat. Too smart, you know?"

"Maybe. Any break-ins or attempted break-ins here?"

"Not so far. I got bars on all the windows, double locks on the storeroom door off the alley. Besides, what's for them to steal except a few cases of whisky?"

"You don't keep cash on the premises overnight?"

"Fifty bucks in the till, that's all." He scraped the lime wedges off his board, into a plastic container. "One thing I did hear," he said. "I heard some of the loot turned up down in San José. You know about that?"

"Not much of a lead there. Secondhand dealer named Pitman had a few pieces of stereo equipment stolen from the factory-outlet store on Geneva. Said he bought it from a guy at the San José flea market, somebody he didn't know, never saw before."

"Yeah, sure," Candiotti said wryly. "What do the cops think?"

"That Pitman bought it off a fence."

"Makes sense. So maybe the boosters are from San José, hah?"

"Could be," I said, and that was when the kid walked in.

He brought bad air in with him; I sensed it right away and so did Candiotti. We both glanced at the door when it opened, the way you do, but we didn't look away again once we saw him. He was in his early twenties, dark-skinned, dressed in chinos and a cotton windbreaker. But it was his eyes that put the chill on my neck, the sudden clutch of tension down low in my belly. They were bright, jumpy, on the wild side. He had one hand in his jacket pocket and I knew it was clamped around a gun even before he took it out and showed it to us.

He came up to the bar a few feet on my left, the gun jabbing the air in front of him. He couldn't hold it steady; it kept jerking up and down, from side to side, as if it had a kind of spasmodic life of its own. I eased back a little on the stool, watching the gun and the kid's eyes flick between Candiotti and me. Candiotti didn't move at all, just stood staring with his hound's face screwed up tight.

"All right all right," the kid said. His voice was high-pitched, excited. You couldn't get much more stoned than he was and still function. Coke, crack, speed—maybe a combination of drugs. The gun that kept flicking this way and that was a goddamn Saturday Night Special. "Listen good, man, I don't want to kill anybody but I will if I got to, you believe it?"

Neither of us said anything. Neither of us moved.

The kid had a folded-up paper sack in one pocket; he dragged it out with his free hand, dropped it, broke quickly at the middle to pick it up without lowering his gaze. When he straightened again there was sweat on his face. He threw the sack on the bar.

"Put the money in there, Mister Cyclone Man," he said to Candiotti. "All the money in the register, no coins, you hear me, man?"

Candiotti nodded; reached out slowly for the sack and then turned toward the backbar with his shoulders hunched up against his neck. When he punched NO SALE on the register, the ringing thump of the cash drawer sliding open seemed overloud in the electric hush. For a few seconds the kid watched him scoop bills into the sack; then his eyes and the gun skittered my way again. I had looked into the muzzle of a handgun before and it was the same feeling each time: dull fear, helplessness, a kind of naked vulnerability.

"Your wallet on the bar, man, all your cash."

I did as I was told. But while I was getting my wallet out I managed to slide my right foot off the stool, onto the brass rail, and to get my right hand pressed tight against the edge of the bar. If I had to make any sudden moves I would need the leverage.

Candiotti finished loading the sack. There was a grayish cast to his face now—the wet gray color of fear. The kid said to him, "Pick up this dude's money, put it in the sack with the rest. Come on come on *come on!*"

Candiotti added my wallet to the contents of the paper sack, put the sack down carefully in front of the kid.

"Okay," the kid said, "okay, all right." He glanced over his shoulder at the street door, as if he'd heard something there; but it stayed closed. In his sweaty agitation the Saturday Night Special almost slipped free of his fingers. I watched him fumble a tighter grip on it, reach out and drag the sack in against his body. But he made no move to leave with it. Instead he said, "Now we go get the big pile, man."

Candiotti opened his mouth, closed it again. His eyes were almost as big and starey as the kid's.

"Come on Mister Cyclone Man, the safe, the safe in your office."

"No money in that safe," Candiotti said in a thin, scratchy voice. "Nothing valuable."

"Oh man I ain't playin' no games here, I want that money!"

He took two steps forward, jabbing with the gun up close to Candiotti's gray face. Candiotti backed off a step, took a tremulous breath. "All right," he said, "but I got to get the key to the office. It's in the register."

"Hurry up!"

Candiotti turned back to the register, rang it open, rummaged inside with his left hand. But with his right hand, shielded from the kid by his body, he eased up the top of a large wood cigar box nearby. The hand disappeared inside; came out again with metal in it, glinting in the backbar lights. I saw it, and I wanted to yell at him, but it wouldn't have done any good, would only have warned the kid—and Candiotti was already turning with it, bringing up that damn gun of his own in both hands. There was no time for me to do anything but shove away from the bar and sideways off the stool just as Candiotti opened fire.

The state he was in, the kid didn't realize what was happening until it was too late; he never even got a shot off. Candiotti's first slug knocked him halfway around, and one of the three others that followed took him in the face. He was dead before his body, driven backward, slammed into the cigarette machine near the door, slid down it to the floor.

When I came up out of my crouch, Candiotti was standing with his arms down at his sides, the gun out of sight below the bar. Staring at the bloody remains of the kid as if he couldn't believe what he was seeing, couldn't believe what he'd done.

Some of the tension in me eased as I went to the door, found the lock on its security gate and fastened it before anybody could come in off the street. The Saturday Night Special was still clutched in the kid's hand; I bent, pulled it free, broke the cylinder. Five live cartridges. I dropped the gun into my jacket pocket, thought about checking the kid's clothing for ID, didn't do it. It wasn't any of my business, now, who he'd been. And I did not want to touch him. There was a queasiness in my stomach, a fluttery weakness behind my knees—the same delayed reaction I always had to violence and death.

Candiotti hadn't moved. I walked over to him, pushed hard words at him in an undertone. "That was a damn fool thing to do. You could have got us both killed."

"I know," he said. "I know."

"Why'd you do it?"

"I thought . . . hell, you saw the way he was waving that piece . . ."

"Yeah," I said. "Call the police. Nine-eleven."

"Nine-eleven. Okay."

"Put that gun of yours down first. On the bar."

He did that. There was a phone on the backbar; he went away to it. While he was talking to the emergency operator I picked up his weapon, saw that it was a .32 Charter Arms revolver. I put it down again when he finished the call.

"They'll have somebody here in five minutes," he said.

I said, "You know that kid?"

"Christ, no."

"Ever see him before, here or anywhere else?"

"No."

"So how did he know about your safe?"

Candiotti blinked at me. "What?"

"The safe in your office. How'd he know about it?"

"How should I know. What difference does it make?"

"He seemed to think you keep big money in that safe."

"Well I don't. There's nothing in it."

"That's right, you told me you don't keep more than fifty bucks in the till overnight."

"Yeah."

"Then why have you got a safe, if it's empty?"

Candiotti's eyes narrowed. "I used to keep my cash receipts in it, all right? Before all these burglaries started. Then I figured I'd be smarter to take the money to the bank every night."

"Sure, that explains it. Still, a kid like that, looking for a big score to feed his habit, he wasn't just after what was in the till. No, it was as if he'd gotten wind of a heavy stash—a grand or more."

Nothing from Candiotti.

"Big risk you took, using that .32 of yours," I said. "How come you didn't make your play the first time you went to the register? How come you waited until the kid mentioned your safe?"

"Listen, what're you getting at, hah?"

"Another funny thing," I said, "is the way he called you Mister Cyclone Man. Now why would a hopped-up kid use a term like that to a bar owner he didn't know?"

"How the hell should I know?"

"Cyclone," I said. "What's a cyclone but a big destructive wind? Only one other thing I can think of."

"Yeah? What's that?"

"A fence. A cyclone fence."

Candiotti made a fidgety movement. Some of the wet gray pallor was beginning to spread across his cheeks again, like a fungus.

I said, "And a fence is somebody who receives and distributes stolen goods. A Mister Fence Man. But then you know that, don't you, Candiotti? We were talking about that kind of fence before the kid came in—how Pitman, down in San José, bought some hot stereo equipment off one. But that fence could just as easily be operating here in San Francisco. Right here in this neighborhood, in fact. Hell, suppose the stuff taken in all those burglaries never left the neighborhood. Suppose it was brought to a local place and stored until it could be trucked out to other cities—a tavern storeroom, for instance. Might even be some of it is *still* in that storeroom. And the money he got for the rest he'd keep locked up in his safe. Who'd figure it? Except maybe a poor junkie who picked up a whisper on the street somewhere—"

Candiotti made a sudden grab for the .32, backed up a step with it leveled at my chest. "You smart son of a bitch. I ought to kill you too."

"With the police due any second?"

"There's still enough time for me to get clear." He was talking to himself, not to me.

"I don't think so," I said.

"Goddamn you, you think I won't use this gun again?"

"I *know* you won't use it. I emptied out the last two cartridges while you were on the phone."

I held up the two shells I'd palmed, so he could see them. At the same time I got the kid's Saturday Night Special out of my jacket pocket and showed him that too. "You want to put your piece down now, Candiotti? You're not going anywhere, not for a long time."

He put it down—dropped it clattering onto the bar. And as he did, his sad hound's face screwed up again and wetness began to leak out of his eyes. He was leaning against the bar, crying like a woman, submerged in his own outpouring of self-pity, when the cops showed up a little while later.

THE TERRARIUM
PRINCIPLE

Andrea Parker was on the back porch, working on her latest project—the planting of seeds in a bottle terrarium—when she heard Jerry's car in the driveway. She took off her gloves, brushed flecks of potting soil off her gardening shirt, and went into the kitchen to meet him as he opened the garage door.

There was a preoccupied scowl on Jerry's face. He looked rumpled, the way Columbo used to look on television. Which was unusual; her husband may have been a police lieutenant attached to the Homicide Division, but he definitely was not the Peter Falk type.

He brushed his lips over hers—not much of a kiss, Andrea thought—and said, "I could use a drink." He went straight to the refrigerator and began tugging out one of the ice trays.

"Rough day?" she asked him.

"You can say that again. Except that the operative word is frustrating. One of the most frustrating days I've ever spent."

"Why?"

"Because a man named Harding committed murder in a locked room this morning and I can't prove it. *That's* why."

"Want to talk about it?"

He made a face. But he said, "I might as well. It's going to be on my mind all evening anyway. You can help me brood."

Andrea took the ice tray away from him, shooed him into

the living room, and made drinks for both of them. When she brought them in, Jerry was sitting on the couch with his legs crossed, elbow resting on one knee and chin cupped in his palm. He really did look like Columbo tonight. All he needed, she thought, was a trench coat and a cigar.

She handed him his drink and sat down beside him. "So why can't you prove this man Harding committed murder? You did say it happened in a locked room, didn't you?"

"Well, more or less locked. And I can't prove it because we can't find the gun. Without it we just don't have a case."

"What exactly happened?"

"It's a pretty simple story, except for the missing gun. The classic kind of simple, I mean. Harding's uncle, Philip Granger, has—or had—a house out in Roehampton Estates; wealthy guy, made a lot of money in oil stocks over the years. Harding, on the other hand, is your typical black-sheep nephew—drinks too much, can't hold down a job, has a penchant for fast women and slow horses.

"This morning Harding went out to his uncle's house to see him. The housekeeper let him in. According to her, Harding seemed upset about something, angry. Granger's lawyer, Martin Sampson, happened to be there at the time, preparing some papers for Granger to sign, and he confirms the house-keeper's impression that Harding was upset.

"So Harding went into his uncle's study and either he or Granger locked the door. Fifteen minutes later both Sampson and the housekeeper heard a gunshot. They were sure it came from the study; they both ran straight for that door. But the door was locked, as I said. They pounded and shouted, and inside Harding yelled back that somebody had shot his uncle. Only he didn't open the door right away. It took him eight and one-half minutes by Sampson's watch to get around to it."

"Eight and a half minutes?" Andrea said. "What did he say he was doing all that time?"

"Looking out the window, first of all, for some sign of a phantom killer. Harding's claim is that window was open and Granger was shot through the window from outside; he says Sampson and the housekeeper must have been mistaken about where the shot came from. The rest of the time he was supposedly ministering to his uncle and didn't stop to open the door until the old man had died."

"But you think he spent that time hiding the gun somewhere in the room?"

"I *know* that's what he was doing," Jerry said. "His story is implausible and he'd had arguments with his uncle before, always over money and sometimes to the point of violence. He's guilty as sin—I'm sure of it!"

"Couldn't he have just thrown the gun out the window?"

"No. We searched the grounds; we'd have found the gun if it had been out there."

"Well, maybe he climbed out the window, took it away somewhere, and hid it."

"No chance," Jerry said. "Remember the rain we had last night? There's a flower bed outside the study window and the ground there was muddy from the rain; nobody could have walked through it without leaving footprints. And it's too wide to jump over from the windowsill. No, the gun is in that room. He managed to hide it somewhere during those eight and one-half minutes. His uncle's stereo unit was playing, fairly loud, and if he made any noise the music covered it—Sampson and the housekeeper didn't hear anything unusual."

"Didn't one of them go outdoors to look in through the study window?"

"Sampson did, yes. But Harding had drawn the drapes. In case the phantom killer came back, he said."

"What's the study like?" Andrea asked.

"Big room with masculine decor: hunting prints, a stag's head, a wall full of books, overstuffed leather furniture, a large fireplace—"

"I guess you looked up the fireplace chimney," Andrea said.

He gave her a wry smile. "First thing. Nothing but soot."

"What else was in the room?"

"A desk that we went over from top to bottom. And model airplanes, a clipper ship in a bottle, a miniature train layout—all kinds of model stuff scattered around."

"Oh?"

"Evidently Granger built models in his spare time, as a hobby. There was also a small workbench along one wall."

"I see."

"The only other thing in there was the stereo unit—radio, record player, tape deck. I thought Harding might have hidden the gun inside one of the speakers, but no soap."

Andrea was sitting very still, pondering. So still that Jerry frowned at her and then said, "What's the matter?"

"I just had an idea. Tell me, was there any strong glue on the workbench?"

"Glue?"

"Yes. The kind where you only need a few drops to make a bond and it dries instantly."

"I guess there was, sure. Why?"

"How about a glass cutter?"

"I suppose so. Andrea, what are you getting at?"

"I think I know what Harding was doing for those eight and a half minutes," she said. "And I think I know just where he hid the gun."

Jerry sat up straight. "Are you serious?"

"Of course I'm serious. Come on, I want to show you something." She led him out through the kitchen, onto the rear porch. "See that terrarium?"

"What about it?"

"Well, it's a big glass jar with a small opening at one end, right? Like a bottle. There's nothing in it now except soil seeds, but pretty soon there'll be flowers and plants growing inside and people who don't know anything about terrariums will look at it and say, 'Now how in the world did you get those plants through that little opening?' It doesn't occur to them that you *didn't* put plants in there; you put seeds and they grew into plants."

"I don't see what that has to do with Harding—"

"But there's also a way to build a bottle terrarium using full-grown plants," she went on, "that almost never occurs to anybody. All you have to do is slice off the bottom of the container with a glass cutter; then, when you've finished making your garden arrangement inside, you just glue the bottom back on. That's what some professional florists do. You can also heat the glass afterward, to smooth out the line so nobody can tell it's been cut, but that isn't really necessary. Hardly anyone looks that close."

A light was beginning to dawn in Jerry's eyes. "Like we didn't look close enough at a certain item in Granger's study."

"The ship in a bottle," Andrea said, nodding. "I'll bet you that's where Harding put the gun—inside the ship that's inside the bottle."

"No bet," Jerry said. "If you're right, I'll buy you the fanciest steak dinner in town."

He hurried inside, no longer looking like Columbo, and telephoned police headquarters. When he was through talking he told Andrea that they would have word within an hour. And they did—exactly fifty-six minutes had passed when the telephone rang. Jerry took it, listened, then grinned.

"You were right," he said when he'd hung up. "The bottom of the bottle had been cut and glued back, the ship inside had been hollowed out, and the missing gun was inside the ship. We overlooked it because we automatically assumed nobody could put a gun through a bottle neck that small. It never occurred to us that Harding didn't *have* to put it through the neck to get it inside."

Andrea smiled. "The terrarium principle," she said.

"I guess that's a pretty good name for it. Come on, get your coat; we'll go have that steak dinner right now."

"With champagne, maybe?"

"Sweetheart," he said, "with a whole magnum."

ON GUARD!

(With Michael Kurland)

At ten-thirty Saturday morning I parked my van in front of 2419 Melrose Place, on the fashionable north side of St. Albans. The house was a two-story Colonial set behind high, neatly trimmed hedges and a rolling sweep of lawn. All very posh.

Mr. James Gregg was obviously well off, and could no doubt afford to buy just about any type of sophisticated theft-proofing apparatus. But then, some people are stingy and others are cautious. In any event, I would soon find out why Gregg had answered my ad in the *St. Albans Press*.

I got out of the van and went around to the rear. When I opened the rear doors, Sam Boy barked softly and leaned his head out to nuzzle my hand. He was a ninety-pound German shepherd and a product of the specialized training course I devised a number of years ago—one of the finest, most intelligent animals I've ever worked with.

After he had jumped down, I closed the doors again and then walked up to the front door of the Colonial. Sam Boy followed obediently at my side, and sat when I stopped on the porch.

I rang the bell, waited half a minute. Finally the door was opened by a middle-aged, red-haired guy wearing an alpaca golf sweater. He was no servant, which meant that Gregg probably didn't employ servants; the house wasn't really that large, anyway.

"Yes?" he said. Then he noticed Sam Boy sitting behind me. "Oh, you must be the man from *On Guard!*"

"Paul Ferguson," I answered, nodding. "Mr. Gregg?"

"Yes. Come in, please. That's quite a . . . an *imposing* animal you have there."

"He is that," I said. Different people have different reactions to ninety pounds of German shepherd, but Gregg struck me as the kind of man who wouldn't be intimidated by man or beast.

My ad in the *Press* said, "*Expertly trained guard dogs are the best home security—satisfaction guaranteed. Write On Guard!, Box 238, this paper.*" But I've found that most people have no idea of what an expertly trained guard dog is, or what to expect from one. Some think it's merely a large dog that barks a lot if someone passes too close to the house, while others expect the animal to patrol the house and grounds constantly, identify burglarious intent in the mind of the trespasser, and hold him in one place until the return of the owners. Still other people expect a friendly companion who can babysit the kids; and yet another group looks for a ravening monster who must be kept chained and can be handled safely by none but his master.

Gregg led Sam Boy and me down a richly carpeted hall into the living room. He invited me to sit on the couch, and then brought in cups and a silver pot of coffee. His wife was out shopping, he explained, but whatever he decided would be fine with her.

Then he asked, "Just what are this animal's capabilities?"

"Were you thinking of using him inside or outside?"

"Inside. I want to safeguard my collection, among other things." He patted the side of a glass-fronted cabinet.

"China?" I asked.

"It's called majolica," he said. "Actually, it's a type of earthenware."

"Very pretty."

"And very expensive. Every time I go out I'm afraid that when I come home I'll find that I've been cleaned out."

"Surely with this valuable collection and your other property, you've installed a burglar alarm."

"Yes, but I don't trust it," Gregg said. "Burglars are clever, as I'm sure you know. Besides, my neighbors are some distance away on both sides. If the alarm went off, they might not even hear it."

"Well, the ringing alone would probably scare off any housebreaker."

"So I've been told. But I prefer not to take any chances. I might reasonably expect a dog to keep burglars out of the house, mightn't I?"

"Absolutely," I said. "No one but yourself or members of your family would be allowed admittance unless accompanied by one of you."

"What will he do if a burglar shows up?"

"Stop him," I said. "By brute force, if necessary. Before one could get past Sam Boy, he'd have to kill him; and killing an animal like Sam Boy in a darkened house, while the dog is making one heck of a racket *and* trying to tear his arm off, is a job no sane burglar will undertake."

Gregg thought this over.

"You'd have to take proper care of him, of course," I said. "Both to keep him in top shape and to win his lasting affection. But a dog that loves you is an animal that would do anything for you. You need only to communicate to him what you want done; German shepherds are surprisingly intelligent. I'm not exaggerating, sir. You can't beat a good, well-trained guard dog."

"I don't know," Gregg said, but I could tell that he was already about half-sold.

"I'll tell you what, Mr. Gregg," I said. "The animal is expensive, and I want to be sure you're satisfied and Sam Boy is happy with you before final placement; I'll give you a two-week trial period at no charge. At the end of that time, you either write me a check for five hundred dollars or I take him back."

"Five hundred is a lot of money."

"The dog, untrained, is worth over two hundred, Mr. Gregg. But you'll have two weeks to decide. Why don't I just let Sam Boy sell himself?"

I called Sam Boy over and formally introduced him to Gregg. Customers always like that sort of thing, and Gregg was no exception. Just watching the way he ruffled the dog's fur and responded to the way Sam Boy nuzzled his hand told me we had him sold on the trial-period idea. And he confirmed it a moment later.

For the next half-hour Gregg and I went over the details of feeding, watering, grooming, and otherwise caring for the dog, and I taught him the half-dozen basic commands he would need to work Sam Boy. "I think that's everything," I told him finally. "You won't have any problems, I'm sure, but I'll check back with you periodically just in case."

"Very good, Ferguson."

I declined another cup of coffee, and Gregg took me back into the foyer. That was where the box for the burglar alarm he'd mentioned was, on the wall to one side of the front door. It was a common type that could be turned on or off by a simple lever switch on the box, or from the outside by a key. But as Gregg had said, this kind of system isn't really foolproof; guard dogs, on the other hand, *are* when properly handled.

I said good-bye to Gregg and Sam Boy, and drove back into downtown St. Albans.

At seven-forty that night I called Gregg from a telephone booth in the Golden Mandarin Chinese restaurant. "How are you getting along with Sam Boy, Mr. Gregg?" I asked him.

"Beautifully," he answered. "What a marvelous animal."

"Isn't he? I was wondering, sir, if I could drop out to see you again one of these evenings? I've just picked up an excellent new book on dog handling and I thought you might enjoy reading it."

"That's good of you, Ferguson," he said. "Come by any night but tonight. My wife and I have a late dinner engagement with friends."

After we said good-byes, I went back to my table and

sipped a final cup of tea and broke open my fortune cookie. *Early preparations make for early rewards,* the fortune said.

I drove around St. Albans for a while, killing time; then, at ten-thirty, I went to Melrose Place. When I saw that Gregg's house was dark I pulled the van into his driveway and parked in the shadows of one of the hedges. I went over and rang the bell a couple of times. Not a sound inside but the padding of a dog's paws coming to the door.

"Hi, Sam Boy," I whispered, and then I blew two short blasts on my silent dog whistle. Inside, as he had been so patiently trained to do—and as he had done so many times before, in a score of towns like St. Albans in eight different states—Sam Boy stood up on his hind legs, with his forepaws on the wall near the door, and used his teeth to flip the lever switch on the burglar alarm box to Off.

When I heard him come back to the door and bark once, I knew that he'd done his job. I hurried around the side of the house to the nearest window, used my glass cutter, and then reached in and opened the window and slid up the sash. Sam Boy was sitting on the floor inside; I leaned in and patted his head.

Yes, sir, I thought, you really can't beat a good, well-trained guard dog. Satisfaction guaranteed. Then I climbed over the sill and began teaching a valuable lesson in home security to another of *On Guard's* burglar-conscious customers . . .

MEMENTO MORI

There are murder weapons and there are murder weapons, but the thing used to bludgeon Philip Asher to death was the grisliest I'd seen in more than two decades on the police force.

It was a skull—a human skull.

Ed Crane and I stood staring down at what was left of it, lying splintered and gore-streaked to one side of the dead man. It had apparently cracked like an eggshell on the first or second blow, but that had been enough to shatter Asher's skull as well. Judging from the concavity of the wound, he had been struck with considerable force.

I pulled my gaze away and let it move over the room, a large masculine study. Well-used, leather-bound books covered two walls, and a third was adorned with what appeared to be primitive Mexican or Central American art and craftwork: pottery, statuary, wood carvings, weaponry. There were two teakwood desks arranged so that they faced each other—one large and ostentatious, the other small and functional—and several pieces of teak-and-leather furniture. It should have been a comfortable room, but for me it wasn't; there seemed to be a kind of cold, impersonal quality to it, despite the books and art.

Crane said, "If I wasn't seeing it for myself, I don't think I'd believe it."

"Yeah."

He rubbed at the bald spot on the crown of his head. "Well, I've had enough in here if you have."

"More than enough," I agreed.

We crossed to the double entrance doors and went into the hallway beyond. At its far end was a large living room containing more teakwood furniture and primitive art. One of the two patrolmen who had preceded us on the scene stood stoically beside a long sofa; the other officer was waiting outside for the arrival of the lab crew and the coroner. Sitting stiff-backed in middle of the sofa was Douglas Falconer—hands flat on his knees, eyes blinking myopically behind thick-lensed glasses. He was about forty, with a thin, chinless face and sparse sand-colored hair, dressed in slacks and a navy-blue shirt. He looked timid and harmless, but when he'd called headquarters a half-hour earlier, he had confessed to the murder of Philip Asher. The dried stains on his right shirt sleeve and on the back of his right hand confirmed his guilt well enough.

All we knew about Falconer and Asher was that the deceased owned this house, an expensive Spanish-style villa in one of the city's finer residential areas; that Falconer had been his secretary; that no one else had been present at the time of the slaying; and that the crime had been committed, in Falconer's words, "during a moment of blind fury." We had no idea as to motive, and we hadn't been prepared at all for the nature of the murder weapon.

Falconer kept on blinking as Crane and I approached and stopped on either side of him, but his eyes did not seem to be seeing anything in the room. I thought maybe he'd gone into delayed shock, but when I said his name, his head jerked up and the eyes focused on me.

I said, "You want to tell us about it, Falconer?" We'd already apprised him of his rights, and he had waived his privilege of presence of counsel during questioning.

"I murdered Asher," he said. "I already told you that. At first I thought of trying to cover it up, make it look as though a burglar had done it. But I'm not a very good liar, even though I've had a lot of practice. Besides, I . . . I don't much care what happens to me from now on."

"Why did you kill him?" Crane asked.

Falconer shook his head—not so much a refusal to answer as a reluctance or inability to put voice to the reason. We would get it out of him sooner or later, so there was no point in trying to force it.

I said, "Why the skull, Mr. Falconer? Where did you get a thing like that?"

He closed his eyes, popped them open again. "Asher kept it on the shelf behind his desk. He was sitting at the desk when I . . . when I did it."

"He kept a human skull in full view in his study?" Crane's tone was incredulous. "What the hell for?"

"He had a macabre sense of humor. He claimed to enjoy the reactions of visitors when they saw it. It was his *memento mori*, he said."

"His what?"

"Reminder of death," Falconer said.

"That sounds pretty morbid to me."

"Philip Asher was a fearless, cold-blooded man. Death never bothered him in the least. In one sense, it was his life; he devoted his life to the dead."

Crane and I exchanged glances. "You'd better explain that," I said.

"He was an anthropologist, quite a renowned one," Falconer said. "He published several books on the Mayan and Aztec races, and was in great demand as a lecturer and as a consultant to various university anthropological departments specializing in pre-Columbian studies."

"You were his full-time secretary, is that right?"

"Yes. I helped him with research, accompanied him on his expeditions to the Yucatán and other parts of Mexico and Central America, correlated his notes, typed his book manuscripts and business correspondence."

"How long did you work for him?"

"Eight years."

"Do you live here?"

"Yes. I have a room in the south wing."

"Does anyone else live in this house?"

"No. Asher never remarried after his wife left him several years ago. He had no close relatives."

Crane said, "Did you premeditate his death?"

"I didn't plan to kill him today, if that's what you mean."

"The two of you had an argument, then?"

"No, there wasn't any argument."

"Then what triggered this murderous rage of yours?" I asked.

He started to shake his head again, and then slumped backward bonelessly. His eyes seemed to be looking again at something not in the room.

At length he said, "It was a . . . revelation."

"Revelation?"

A heavy sigh. "I received a letter yesterday from another anthropologist I'd met through Asher," he said, "asking me to become his personal secretary at a substantial increase in salary. I considered the offer, and this morning decided that I couldn't afford to turn it down. But when I talked to Asher about it, he refused to accept my resignation. He said he couldn't be certain of my continued silence if I were no longer in his employ or in his house. He ordered me to remain. He said he would take steps against me if I didn't . . ."

"Wait a minute," I said. "Your continued silence about what?"

"Something that happened six years ago."

"*What* something?"

He didn't speak again for several seconds. Then he swallowed and said, "The death of his wife and her lover at Asher's summer lodge on Lake Pontrain."

We stared at him. Crane said, "You told us a couple of minutes ago that his wife had left him, not that she was dead."

"Did I? Yes, I suppose I did. I've told the same lie, in exactly the same way, so many times that it's an automatic response. Mildred and her lover died at Lake Pontrain; that is the truth."

"All right—how did they die?"

"By asphyxiation," he said. "It happened on a Saturday in September, six years ago. Early that morning Asher decided on the spur of the moment to spend a few days at the lodge; the book he was writing at the time was going badly and he thought a change of scenery might help. He drove up alone at eight; I had an errand to do and then followed in my own car about an hour later. When I reached the lodge I found Asher inside with the bodies. They were in bed—Mildred, who was supposed to have been visiting a friend in Los Angeles, and the man. I'd never seen him before; I found out later he was an itinerant musician." Pause. "They were both naked," he said.

"What did Asher say when you walked in?"

"That he'd found them just as they were. The lodge had been full of gas when he arrived, he said, and he'd aired it out. A tragic accident caused by a faulty gas heater in the bedroom."

"Did you believe that?" I asked.

"Yes. I was stunned. I'd always thought Mildred above such a thing as infidelity. She was beautiful, yes—but always so quiet, so dignified . . ."

"Was Asher also stunned?"

"He seemed to be," Falconer said. "But he was quite calm. When I suggested we contact the authorities he wouldn't hear of it. Think of the scandal, he said—the possible damage to his reputation and his career. I asked what else we could do. I wasn't prepared for his answer."

"Which was?"

"He suggested in that cold, calculating way of his that we dispose of the bodies, bury them somewhere at the lake. Then we could concoct a story to explain Mildred's disappearance, say that she had moved out and gone back to Boston, where she was born. He insisted no one would question this explanation, because he and Mildred had few close friends and because of his reputation. As it happened, he was right."

"So you went along with this cover-up?"

"What choice did I have? I'm not a forceful man, and at the time I respected Asher and his judgment. And as I told you, I was stunned. Yes, I went along with it. I helped Asher transfer the bodies to a promontory a mile away, where we buried them beneath piles of rocks."

Crane said, "So for six years you kept this secret—until today, until something happened this morning."

"Yes."

"These 'steps' Asher told you he'd take if you tried to leave his employ—were they threats of bodily harm?"

Falconer nodded. "He said he would kill me."

"Pretty drastic just to insure your silence about two accidental deaths six years ago."

"Yes. I said the same thing to him."

"And?"

"He told me the truth," Falconer said.

"That his wife and her lover *didn't* die by accident? That he'd murdered them?"

"That's right. He found them in bed together, very much alive; his massive ego had been wounded, the sin was unforgivable and had to be punished—that was how Philip Asher was. He knocked them both out with his fists. I suppose I would have seen evidence of that if I'd looked closely at the bodies, but in my distraught state I noticed nothing. Then he suffocated them with a pillow. I arrived before he could remove the bodies by himself, and so he made up the story about the faulty gas heater. If I hadn't believed it, if I hadn't helped him, he would have killed me too, then and there."

"Did he tell you that too?"

"Yes."

"So when you found out you'd been working for a murderer the past six years, that you'd helped cover up a cold-blooded double homicide, you lost control and picked up the skull and bashed his head in with it."

"No," Falconer said. "No, not exactly. I was sickened by his confession and by my part in the whole ugly affair; I loathed him and I wanted to strike back at him. But I'm not a violent man. It was his *second* revelation that made me do what I did."

"What was it, this second revelation?"

"Something else he'd done, a year after the murders. I don't know why he told me about it, except that he was quite mad. A mad ghoul." Falconer laughed mirthlessly. "Mad ghoul. It sounds funny, doesn't it? Like an old Bela Lugosi film. But that's just what Asher was, always poking around among the dead."

"Mr. Falconer—"

He let out a shuddering breath. "Asher's *memento mori* didn't come from Mexico, as I always believed; it came from that promontory at Lake Pontrain. I killed him, using the one fitting weapon for his destruction, when he told me I'd been working in that study of his all these years, *all these years,* with the skull of the only woman I ever loved grinning at me over his shoulder . . ."

A LITTLE LARCENY

Dalton Truax smiled at Margo and me across his desk. He was short and round, with a receeding hairline and soft smooth jowls; he reminded me of a large, pink, mostly hairless panda bear. "You brought the money, I trust?"

I lifted the briefcase from beside my chair and set it in front of him. "Seventy-five thousand dollars."

"Very good, Bob," he said. "Shall we sign the contracts?"

I nodded, but Margo said, "I still don't see why we have to pay cash. Why couldn't we just give you a bank draft?"

"I explained that, Mrs. London," Truax said patiently. "But let me go over it again, in simpler terms. Dealings in land speculation these days are, by necessity, complicated and difficult. Sometimes the strict letter of the law must be, ah, shall we say slightly revised, in order to assure a satisfactory outcome for all concerned."

"In other words," Margo said, "you have to pay people off under the table."

Truax chose to ignore that. "Now in this case," he said, "the undeveloped property that Consolidated Development Corporation will soon purchase is valuable only as second-growth timberland. It is owned by a small independent logging company that is willing to part with it for five thousand dollars an acre."

"Because they don't know the state is planning to build a freeway through the area," I said.

"Correct. It so happens that a close friend of mine is an official with the State Highway Commission. He came to me recently with a proposition: He would divulge certain classified information—in fact, the secret freeway project—in exchange for a one-fifth share in the Consolidated Development Corporation, which I would set up. This share was to be purchased for him in cash by the other four stockholders, each contributing twenty thousand dollars of their total purchase price of seventy-five thousand, so as to prevent any link between himself and the corporation. To put it another way, corporation documents show a total of four stockholders, when in reality there are five; the official's stock will be held in trust. Do you see now?"

"Not really," Margo said. "Oh, I understand why twenty thousand has to be paid in cash, but why the other fifty-five thousand?"

"I'll try to simplify that, too. The logging company wants to avoid a large capital-gains tax, so they've agreed to sell Consolidated the land at a much lower official price than its actual market value. We in turn will give them the difference in cash." He smiled disarmingly. "As you say, Mrs. London, 'under the table.' Therefore, the logging company pays less tax and Consolidated outlays less for the property."

Margo was silent for a time. Then she said, "I see." Finally.

"Fine. Any more questions, then?"

"I don't have any," I said. "Margo?"

"No, I suppose not."

Truax beamed at us again. "Then shall we sign the papers and complete the transaction?"

We signed them. Truax countersigned, gave us our copy of the agreement, put the others away in a portfolio. He made no move toward the briefcase.

Margo asked him, "Aren't you going to count the money?"

"No, that's not necessary. I trust you and Bob implicitly, Mrs. London."

"You don't know us very well," she said. "We don't know

you very well, for that matter. Robert only met you a month ago."

"Indeed. But trust is vital in this sort of business dealing, when the eventual rewards are so great. Don't you agree?"

"Mm. You're sure we won't have to wait more than two years?"

"Not absolutely positive, no. It might take as many as three before you begin to reap the profits. No longer than three, though; I think I can guarantee that."

The light of greed glittered in Margo's eyes again. "Several million dollars for each of the stockholders, you said?"

"Exactly. Five million, minimum. Perhaps as much as ten."

We shook hands all around, and Margo and I left Truax's offices and rode the elevator down to the lobby. As we left the building, Margo said, "I'm still not convinced we've done the right thing, Robert."

"Why not?"

"Seventy-five thousand dollars is all the money I . . . we have in the world. After all, Aunt Lucinda intended it for our golden years—a retirement home like the one she had in Suncrest Acres."

"There isn't any reason we can't still buy a retirement home in Suncrest Acres," I said. "In fact, we can probably afford to buy Suncrest Acres itself with ten million dollars. Think about that."

She thought about it, and the greed came back into her eyes. "Ten million dollars," she said. And nothing more.

The following afternoon I was sitting in the parlor of our small house near one of the city's shopping centers. I sometimes have occasion to work on Saturday afternoons—I am an accountant at Hardiman and Waycroft—but this was not one of them.

I put down the travel magazine I had been reading and said to Margo, who was crocheting, "I've been thinking, dear. It might be a good idea for us to take a drive upstate tomorrow."

She looked up. "What for?"

"Well, to look at the property we bought," I said. "I think I'd like to see our investment first-hand."

"It's just timberland. You saw that in those aerial and ground photos Mr. Truax showed us."

"I'd still like a close-up look. I think I'll call Truax, see if he'll join us. He told me he works a full day on Saturdays."

I went to the phone and dialed Truax's number. And a recorded voice answered, saying, "We're sorry, the number you've reached is no longer in service." Frowning, I tried the number again, with the same results.

"What's the matter, Robert?"

"His phone has been disconnected."

"Disconnected? I don't understand."

"Neither do I."

I called the company that handles the renting and leasing of offices in the Wainwright Building; I happened to know which one it was because Hardiman and Waycroft is their accounting firm. I got through to a man I knew slightly named Corday, identified myself, and then told him that I had been trying to reach a Mr. Dalton Truax who occupied an office in the Wainwright Building.

"Not any longer," Corday said.

"What?"

"Mr. Truax vacated this morning. I spoke with him personally, as a matter of fact. He was apologetic that he would have to vacate after only one month, but business pressures and lack of funds made it necessary."

"Only one month? But . . . but he told me he'd been there for *years*!"

"No, only one month. Is something wrong, Mr. London?"

"No, I . . . no."

I hung up quickly and turned to face Margo. She was livid. "I should have known something like this would happen," she said. "I should have known he was a crook!"

"Maybe he isn't," I said in stunned tones. "Maybe it's some sort of misunderstanding . . ."

"No it isn't. He stole my seventy-five thousand dollars! And it's your fault, Robert, all your fault!"

"But . . ."

"No buts! Get your hat and coat—we're going to the police!"

I had been just about to suggest the same thing.

The bunco-squad detective was named Helwig. He listened to our story with a mixture of sympathy and mild reproach in his eyes, and then he did some checking through police channels.

"There's no such person as Dalton Truax," he told us then. "Which means that there's no Consolidated Development Corporation, no undeveloped parcel of land upstate, no crooked official in the State Highway Department, and no secret freeway project. I'm afraid you're the victims of an elaborate con game."

Neither Margo nor I had anything to say. I could feel her eyes boring into me, but I refused to look at her.

"You're not the first and you won't be the last," Helwig said, "if that's any consolation. Land speculation, particularly the shady variety, is one of the con man's stocks in trade. Everybody wants to get rich quick, and it's said there's a little larceny in us all. The con artist counts on that; it's what makes any swindle work."

I said miserably, "But how did he know about my wife's inheritance? How could he have known we had seventy-five thousand dollars in cash?"

"You'd be amazed at the number of ways he might have found out. And at the lengths a con man will go to set up a mark, especially when the score is a big one."

"Have you any idea who he is?" Margo asked. "Or where to find him?"

"No, Mrs. London, I'm sorry. His description and his M.O.—his method of operation—are unfamiliar to us."

"Are you saying you may never recover my money?"

"We'll do what we can," Helwig said. "I'll be frank with you, though: the prospects aren't good. Seventy-five thousand dollars is a large price to pay for a lesson in honesty and common sense, I know, but . . . well, you may end up having to pay it."

Margo and I rode home in a frigid silence. When we arrived I said I was going for a walk, that I needed to be alone for a while, and left the house. For a block I shuffled along with head down and shoulders slumped, in case she was looking out the window. Once I turned the corner, however, I straightened my back and began to walk quite jauntily.

P.T. Barnum was right, I was thinking. There *is* a sucker born every minute!

It had all gone beautifully. Margo hadn't suspected a thing, and still didn't. Truax—or rather, Arthur Byrnes—had played his part to perfection, winning her confidence with his disarming and sincere manner. Of course, as a part-time actor in another city's local theater, a man I had met through a casual acquaintance, Byrnes was used to playing affably trustworthy roles. And I *was* paying him five thousand dollars to ensure a flawless performance.

I smiled. A retirement home in Suncrest Acres indeed! Such was not for Robert London. Not with the wide world filled with exotic ports of call, and not with seventy thousand tax-free dollars.

After a suitable period of time, during which I would be making circumspect arrangements, I would one day disappear. Certainly I expected Margo to realize the truth after I was gone, but would she be able to convince Helwig? A mild-mannered husband plotting an elaborate swindle of his wife with an unknown party, and capping it off with a report to the police? Well, I rather thought Helwig would be inclined to view that theory as the vindictive fabrication of a woman deserted in middle age. But even if she did manage to convince him, what could the police do? A man can't be extradited for stealing from his wife, not without proof, and not from Brazil in any case.

They say Rio is a beautiful city, full of alluring and tractable women. It wouldn't be long before I found out for myself if that were true.

I was whistling when I reached the shopping center. On the mall I entered a public telephone booth and rang the number of Arthur Byrnes's rooming house. I would keep the seventy thousand in a safe deposit box in a cross-town bank, I thought, until the time came to—

A woman's voice answered and I asked to speak to Mr. Byrnes.

"Mr. Byrnes?" the woman said. "Oh, I'm sorry, sir. Mr. Byrnes turned in his key last evening. You see, he came into a sizable inheritance quite suddenly and left for South America first thing this morning."

MRS. RAKUBIAN

Three days after she murdered him with a hatchet and put his body down the dry well, Mrs. Rakubian's husband showed up alive and kicking on the front porch.

It was a hot day and Mrs. Rakubian had been in the kitchen mixing some lemonade. She mixed it tart, real tart, because Charlie always liked it sweet and made her put too much sugar in it. That was one of the reasons she'd killed him—one of three or four hundred. It wasn't the one that made her pick up the hatchet, though. That one was him blowing his nose on the front of his bib overalls. When he done that again, even after she warned him, she went and got the hatchet and give him half a dozen licks and that was that. Except for fetching the wheelbarrow and carting him off to the dry well, but that was one chore she hadn't minded at all.

Things had been mighty peaceful ever since. So peaceful that she'd taken to humming a little ditty to herself while she worked. She was humming it when she carried the tart lemonade out to the front porch. But she stopped humming it when she saw Charlie sitting there in the shade of the cottonwood tree, wiping his sweaty face with his handkerchief.

"Morning, Maude," he said. "Made some fresh lemonade, I see."

Mrs. Rakubian stared at him goggle-eyed for a few seconds. There wasn't a mark on him, not a mark!

"Something wrong, Maude?"

Mrs. Rakubian didn't answer. She put the lemonade down on the porch table, went into the house, took the varmint gun off the rack, walked back out to the porch, and let Charlie have it with both barrels. Then she fetched the wheelbarrow and trundled what was left of him to the dry well.

"You stay dead this time, Charlie Rakubian," she said after she'd dumped him again. "Thirty years of you haunting me alive was bad enough. Don't you dare keep coming back to haunt me dead too. This time you stay put."

But Charlie didn't stay put. He was back again the next morning, all smiley and chipper, like butter wouldn't melt in his mouth and the hatchet and varmint gun hadn't durned near taken his head off twice.

Mrs. Rakubian was ready for him, though. She'd decided not to take any chances and it was a good thing she had. She didn't let him say a word this time. As soon as she saw him, she took Papa's old Frontier Colt out from under her apron and shot him right between the eyes.

"Now I'm not going to tell you again, Charlie," she said when she got him to the well. "Don't come bothering me no more. You're dead three times now and you'd better start acting like it."

She had a day and a half of peace before the sheriff's car drove in through the farm gate and stopped right in front of where she was sitting under the cottonwood tree drinking tart lemonade. The driver's door opened and Charlie got out.

Mrs. Rakubian was used to his tricks by now. She stared at him in disgust.

"Maude," Charlie said, "I got some questions to ask you. Seems Ed Beemis, the mailman, and Lloyd Poole from the gas company have disappeared and they was both last seen out this way—"

She didn't let him finish. She yanked Papa's Colt out from under her apron and let fly at him. One bullet knocked him down but the others ones missed, which allowed him to crawl to safety behind the sheriff's car. Then durned if he didn't pull a gun of his own and start blasting away at *her.*

Mrs. Rakubian flung herself into the house just in the nick of time. She locked the door behind her, reloaded Papa's Colt, and took the varmint gun down and made sure it was loaded too. Then she waited.

For a time there wasn't much noise out in the yard. Then there was—a regular commotion. Cars, voices . . . why, you'd of thought it was the Fourth of July picnic out there. Pretty soon Charlie started yelling at her over some contraption that made his voice real loud, only she didn't pay much attention to what he was saying. Instead she yelled right back at him.

"You Charlie, you go back into the well where you belong! Go on, git, and leave me be!"

Charlie didn't git and leave her be—not that she'd expected he would, after all the times he'd come back from the dead to devil her. So she was ready for him again with Papa's Colt and the varmint gun when he busted down the door and come in after her.

She *thought* she was ready, anyhow. In fact she wasn't, not with just six bullets and two loads of buckshot. Mrs. Rakubian took one look at what come piling through the door, screamed once, and swooned on the spot.

It was Charlie, all right.

But the sneaky old booger had brought a dozen other dead Charlies along with him.

TOY

It was Jackey who found the toy, on a Saturday afternoon in mid-July.

Mrs. Webster was in the kitchen when he came home with it. "Look at this, Mom," he said. "Isn't this neat?"

She looked. It was an odd gray box, about the size of a cigar box; Jackey lifted its lid. Inside were a score or more of random-shaped pieces made out of the same funny-looking material as the box. It seemed to be some sort of slick, shiny plastic, only it didn't really look like plastic. Or feel like plastic when she ran her finger over the lid.

"What is it, Jackey?"

"I dunno. Some kind of model kit, I think."

"Where did you get it?"

"Found it, in the vacant lot by the Little League field. I was hunting lost balls. It was just lying there under a bunch of leaves and junk."

"Well, someone must have lost it," Mrs. Webster said. "I suppose we'll have to put an ad in the Lost and Found."

"Maybe nobody'll claim it," Jackey said. "I'm going to put it together, see what it is."

"I don't think you should . . ."

"Oh, come on, Mom. I won't use glue or anything. I just want to see what it is."

"Well . . . all right. But don't break anything."

"I don't think you *can* break this stuff," Jackey said. "I dropped the box on the way home, right on the sidewalk. It landed on its edge and didn't even get a scratch."

He went upstairs with the toy. Mrs. Webster had no doubt that he would be able to fit the pieces of the model together; for a boy of twelve, he had a remarkable engineering aptitude.

And he *did* fit the pieces together. It took him two hours. Mrs. Webster was out on the back porch, putting new liner on the pantry shelves, when she heard the first banging noise—low and muffled, from up in Jackey's room. A minute later there was another one, and a minute after that, a third. Then Jackey yelled for her to come up. The fourth bang, exactly a minute after the third, sent her straight to his room.

The box and the assembled toy were sitting on Jackey's "workbench," the catchall table his father had built for him. What the toy most resembled, she thought, was a cannon; at least, there was a round barrel-like extremity with a hole in it, set at an upward angle to the model's squarish base. She was sure it was a cannon moments later, when it made the banging noise again and a round, gray, pea-sized projectile burst out of it and arced two thirds of the way across the room.

"Neat, huh?" Jackey said. "I never saw one like this before."

"Cannons," Mrs. Webster said, and shook her head. "I don't like that sort of toy. I don't like you playing with it."

"I'm not. It sort of works by itself."

"By itself?"

"I don't even know where those cannonballs come from. I mean, *I* didn't put 'em in there."

"What *did* you do, then?"

"I didn't do anything except stick the pieces together the way I thought they ought to go. When I snapped the barrel on, something made a funny noise down inside the base. Next thing, it started shooting off those little balls."

It shot off another one just then, and the projectile—slightly larger than the last one, Mrs. Webster thought—went a foot farther this time. An uneasiness formed in her. She didn't like the look of the model cannon or whatever it was. Toys like that . . . they shouldn't be put on the market.

"You dismantle that thing right now," she said. "You hear me, Jackey? And be careful—it might be dangerous."

She went downstairs. But the banging noise came again, and again after exactly one minute. Each seemed a little louder than the last. The second one brought her back to the foot of the stairs.

"Jackey? I thought I told you to dismantle that thing."

Bang! And there was a thud, a crash from inside Jackey's room.

"What was that? What are you doing up there?"

Silence.

"Jackey?"

"Mom, you better come in here. Quick!"

She hurried up the stairs. There was another bang just as she reached the door to Jackey's room, followed by the sound of glass breaking. She caught the knob, jerked the door open.

She saw Jackey first, cowering back alongside the bed, his eyes wide and scared. Then she saw the far wall, opposite the workbench—the dents in the plasterboard, the jagged hole in the window, the projectiles on the floor ranging from pea-sized to apricot-sized. And then she saw the toy. Chills crawled over her; she caught her breath with an audible gasp.

The model had grown. Before, less than five minutes ago, it had been no larger than a small model tank; now it was three times that size. It had subtly changed color, too, seemed to be glowing faintly now as if something deep inside it had caught fire.

"Jackey, for God's sake!"

"Mom, I couldn't get near it, I couldn't touch it. It's *hot*, Mom!"

She didn't know what to do. She started toward Jackey, changed her mind confusedly and went to the workbench instead. She reached out to the toy, then jerked her hand back. Hot—it gave off heat like a blast furnace.

Oh my God, she thought, it's radioactive—

Bang!

A projectile almost as large as a baseball erupted from the toy's muzzle, smashed out the rest of the window and took part of the frame with it. Jackey yelled, "Mom!" but she still didn't know what to do. She stared at the thing in horror.

It had grown again. Every time it went off it seemed to grow a little bigger.

That's not a toy, that's some kind of weapon . . .

Bang!

A projectile just as large as a baseball this time. More of the window frame disappeared, leaving a gaping hole in the wall. From outside, Mrs. Webster could hear the Potters, their neighbors to the north, shouting in alarm. For some reason, hearing the Potters enabled her to act. She ran to where Jackey was crouched, caught hold of his arm, pulled him toward the door.

On the workbench, the gray thing was the size of a portable TV set. She thought she could see it pulsing as she and Jackey stumbled out.

Bang!

Bang!

On the street in front, she stood hugging Jackey against her. He was trying not to cry. "I didn't mean to do anything, Mom," he said. "I didn't *mean* it. I only wanted to see how it worked."

Bang!

Flames shot up from the rear of the house, from the back yard: the big oak tree there wore a mantle of fire. People were running along the street, crowding around her and Jackey, hurling frightened questions at them.

"I don't know," she said. "I don't *know!*"

And she was thinking: Where did it come from? How did it get here? Who would make a monstrous thing like that?

Bang!

Bang!

BANG!

The projectile that blew up the Potters' house was the size of a cantaloupe. The one a few minutes later that destroyed the gymnasium two blocks away was the size of a basketball. And the one a little while after that that leveled the industrial complex across town was the size of a boulder.

The thing kept growing, kept on firing bigger and bigger projectiles. By six o'clock that night it had burst the walls of the Webster house, and most of the town and much of what lay within fifty miles north-by-northwest had been reduced to flaming wreckage. The National Guard was mobilizing, but there was nothing they could do except aid with mass evacuation proceedings; no one could get within two hundred yards of the weapon because of the radiation.

At six-thirty, half a dozen Phantom jets from the Air Force base nearby bombarded it with laser missiles. The missiles failed to destroy it; in fact, it seemed to feed on the heat and released energy, so that its growth rate increased even more rapidly.

In Washington, there was great consternation and panic. The President, his advisers, and the Joint Chiefs of Staff held an emergency meeting to decide whether or not to use an atomic bomb. But by the time they made up their minds it was too late. Much too late.

The thing was then the size of two city blocks, and still growing, and the range of its gigantic muzzle extended beyond the boundaries of the United States—north-by-northwest, toward the Bering Sea and the vast wastes of Russia beyond . . .

HOUSE CALL

(With Jeffrey M. Wallmann)

It was a few minutes past three o'clock when Christine Taylor parked her compact on San Lorenzo Way, in front of the Morris home and directly behind a dusty Ford station wagon with a personalized license plate that read O HENRY. Both cars seemed out of place in the forested elegance of St. Francis Wood, one of San Francisco's wealthier neighborhoods.

She took the packages of Beauty Express cosmetics from the seat beside her, closed the car door with her foot, and started up the broad flagstone path that led to the Morris veranda. The house was set apart from its neighbors by stands of eucalyptus and landscaped gardens and lawns; dwarf cypress and shrubbery grew along the veranda and the side walls. The overall effect was of a small country estate rather than a house on an urban street.

When Chris neared the veranda, peering around the tiered boxes so she could see where she was going, she caught a glimpse of the small discreet sign that said TRADESMEN USE SIDE ENTRANCE. Although she was not a tradesperson in the strictest sense of the term, and had been admitted through the front door three days before, when her first visit here had produced a sale to old Mrs. Roberta Morris, she felt it would be proper to make the delivery at the side entrance. Besides, Mrs. Morris suffered from an inflammation of the joints called *brachial radiculitis,* coupled with muscle spasms of the trapezius—the old lady had explained this to Chris in great detail—and consequently spent most of her time upstairs in her bedroom. Her live-in maid handled most household matters.

Turning onto the path to her left, Chris made her way around to the north side. A thick screen of oleander bushes partially obscured the side entrance from the path, so that you couldn't see the door until you were within a few feet of it. The boxes of cosmetics further hampered her vision; Mrs. Morris had bought over fifty dollars' worth of lotions, powders, and makeup.

A half-dozen paces from the entrance, she felt the boxes start to slip in her grasp. She was so busy trying to keep them balanced that she didn't hear the door open or see the man who came around the oleanders on a sudden collision course.

When they ran into each other, the impact sent her sprawling onto the lawn and the packages flying. She landed on her hip, without damage to anything except her dignity, but a startled "Ouf!" came out of her. She pushed onto one knee and stared up at the man standing on the path.

He was tall, middle-aged, distinguished-looking, dressed in a chalk-striped suit and carrying a black doctor's satchel. He looked almost as amazed as she felt. He also looked harried and preoccupied; running his free hand through his salt-and-pepper hair he asked in a peremptory manner, "Who are you?"

"Aren't you going to help me up, Doctor?"

"Oh—yes, of course. Sorry." He extended his hand. Chris took it and let him pull her to her feet. He looked at her, at the packages strewn over the lawn out toward the front of the house. His distracted manner reminded her of her father, who was a resident physician at St. Theresa's Memorial Hospital here in the city.

"Is Mrs. Morris ill?" she asked him.

"Yes, but it's nothing serious." He glanced again at the packages, but when Chris bent to restack them he made no move to help her. "Are you making a delivery?"

"I was about to, yes. Beauty Express Cosmetics. May I ask

what's wrong with Mrs. Morris, Doctor? Is it the *brachial radiculitis* again?"

He raised an eyebrow. "How do you know about that?"

"She told me about it the last time I was here."

"I see. Well, you're right—that's the problem."

"I hope it doesn't put her back in her wheelchair," Chris said. "She says she hates it when her trapezius muscles get so bad she can't walk."

"It probably won't come to that. I gave her something to relieve the pain." He looked at his watch. "If you'll excuse me—" And he started away along the path.

Chris finished stacking the boxes, lifted them in her arms, and hurried after him. When she caught up she said, "I might as well leave too. If Mrs. Morris is ill, I don't want to disturb her."

The tall man nodded distractedly.

"Are your offices near here, Doctor?" she asked him.

"Yes, they are."

"Then you've done some work at St. Theresa's."

"That's right, I have."

"My father is on the staff there, so you probably know him. Vincent Taylor."

"Why, yes, I do know Vincent. An excellent man."

"I think so too," Chris said. "I'll mention that we met. Doctor—?"

"Hoskins." They had reached the sidewalk and he started toward the dusty station wagon. "Sorry again about bumping into you, Miss Taylor," he said over his shoulder. "Have a good day."

"You too, Dr. Hoskins."

Chris moved over to her compact and stood watching him get inside the station wagon and drive away. As soon as he had disappeared around the first curve, she tossed her packages into the backseat and ran back up the driveway. When she reached the side entrance she opened the door, not bothering to knock first, and went inside.

It took her less than thirty seconds to find Mrs. Morris and her maid. They were in the sitting room, bound to a pair of wing-back chairs and gagged with handkerchiefs.

Swiftly she untied them. She paused long enough to determine that neither of the frightened women had been harmed, then she hurried to one of the downstairs extension phones to call the police.

"There's been a robbery at Number 79 San Lorenzo Way in St. Francis Wood," she told the officer who answered. "The man responsible claims to be a doctor, but he isn't. He just drove off in a Ford station wagon with a personalized license plate that says O HENRY. If you hurry you probably can catch him before he gets too far away."

"They did hurry," Chris said to her father that evening, "and they caught him about twenty minutes later, over in Golden Gate Park. The station wagon didn't belong to him; he stole it this morning from a parking lot downtown. His real name is Hammond, not Hoskins, and he's a professional burglar who specializes in robbing wealthy homes. The police found five hundred dollars in cash and all of Mrs. Morris's jewelry in the doctor's satchel."

"But how did you know he was a thief and not a doctor?" her father asked.

"He made me suspicious right from the first. So I maneuvered him into saying two things that convinced me he was neither a doctor nor an invited guest of Mrs. Morris."

"What two things?"

"I said I hoped Mrs. Morris' brachial radiculitis wasn't serious enough to confine her to a wheelchair again, because she hated it when her trapezius muscles got so bad she couldn't walk. He said it probably wouldn't come to that. But there isn't a doctor alive who doesn't know that brachial radiculitis is an inflammation of the *shoulder* joints, not the leg joints—or that the trapezius muscles are in the upper back—and that it wouldn't confine anybody to a wheelchair."

"What was the second thing?"

"You were, Dad. I got him to say he'd done some work at

St. Theresa's, and then I said my father, Vincent Taylor, was on the staff there and he must know you. He said he did."

"Ah," Philip Taylor said.

"And if I needed any more proof, there was that license plate on the station wagon. O HENRY. It's doubtful a doctor making a house call would drive a car with a personalized license plate and no caduceus."

Her father nodded. "Now tell me why you were suspicious enough at first to go on and bait your verbal traps."

"Two reasons," Chris said. "When he knocked me down he didn't ask if I'd hurt myself; he didn't even offer to help me up. A real doctor wouldn't have been that careless. But it's the other thing that really made me suspicious." She reached out and took his hand. "Dad, if you'd been attending a woman like Mrs. Morris, would you have left the house by the tradesmen's entrance when the front door is much closer to the street where you'd left your car? No. And no other physician would either. The front door is always the proper entrance for a visiting doctor."

Philip Taylor shook his head admiringly. "You're quite a detective, you know that?"

"Not really, Dad. It was all a simple matter of house calls."

"House calls?"

"Sure," Chris said, smiling. "The burglar picked this day to make his, ran into me as I was making mine, and made the mistake of pretending to be a doctor on a medical one. You don't have to be Sherlock Holmes to figure out that that's one house call too many."

DEATHWATCH

They just came and told me I'm dying.

I've got first and second degree burns over sixty percent of my body, and the doctors—two of them—said it's hopeless, there's nothing they can do. I don't care. It's better this way. Except for the pain. They gave me morphine but it doesn't help. It doesn't keep me from thinking either.

Before the doctors, there were two county cops. And Kjel. The cops told me Pete and Nicky are dead, both of them killed in the explosion. They said Kjel and me were thrown clear, and that he'd come out of it with just minor burns on his face and upper body. They said he hung onto me until another boat showed up and her crew pulled us out of the water. I don't understand that. After what I did, why would he try to save my life?

Kjel told them how it was. The cops didn't say much to me about it, just wanted to know if what Kjel said was the truth. I said it was. But it doesn't make any difference, why or how. I tried to tell them that, and something about the light and the dark, but I couldn't make the words come out. They wouldn't have understood anyway.

After the cops left, Kjel asked to see me. One of the doctors said he had something he wanted to say. But I wouldn't let him come in. I don't want to hear what he has to say. It doesn't matter, and I don't want to see him.

Lila is in the waiting room outside. The same doctor told me that, too. I wouldn't let her come in either. What good would it do to see her, talk to her? There's nothing she can say, nothing I can say—the same as with Kjel. She's been sitting out there sixteen hours, ever since they brought me here from the marina. All that time, sitting out there, waiting.

They have a word for it, what she's doing.

Deathwatch.

The pain . . . oh God, I've never hurt like this. Never. Is this how it feels to burn in hell? An eternity of fire and pain . . . and light? If that's what's in store for me, it won't be so bad if there's light. But what if it's dark down there? Christ, I'm so scared. What if the afterlife is dark, too?

I want to pray but I don't know how. I never went to church much, I never got to know God. The doctors asked if I wanted to see a minister. I said no. What could a minister do for me? Would a minister understand about the light and the dark? I don't think so. Not the way I understand.

The lights in this room are bright, real bright. I asked the doctors to turn the lights up as high as they would go and one of them said he would and he did. But outside, it's night—it's dark. I can see it, the dark, pressing against the window, if I look over that way. I don't look. Dying scares me even more when I look at the night—

I just looked. I couldn't stop myself. The dark, always the dark, trying to swallow the light. But not the black dark that comes with no moon, no stars. Gray dark, softened by fog. High fog tonight, high and heavy, blowing cold. It'll drop by morning, though. There won't be much visibility. But that won't stop the boats from going out. Never has, never will. Wouldn't have stopped us from going out—me and Kjel and Pete and Nicky. It's the season and the big Kings are running. Christ, it's been a good salmon run this year. One of the best in the last ten. If it keeps up like this, Kjel said this morning, we'll have the mortgage on *The Kingfisher* paid off by the end of the year.

But he said that early this morning, while we were still fishing.

He said that before the dark came and swallowed the light.

It seems like so long ago, what happened this morning. And yet it also seems like it must have been just a minute or two . . .

We were six miles out, finished for the day and on our way in—made limit early, hit a big school of Kings. Whoo-ee! They were practically jumping into the boat. I was in the wheelhouse, working on the automatic depth finder because it'd been acting up a little, wishing we could afford a better one. Wishing, too, that we could afford a Loran navigation system like some of the other skippers had on their boats. Kjel and Pete and Nicky were working the outriggers, hauling in the lines by hand. We didn't have one of those hydraulic winches, either, the kind with an automatic trigger that pulls in a fish as soon as it hits the line. The kind that does all the work for you. We had to do it ourselves.

The big Jimmy diesel was rumbling and throbbing, loud, at three-quarters throttle. I shouldn't have been able to hear them talking out on deck. But I heard. Maybe it was the wind, a trick of the wind. I don't know. It doesn't matter. I heard.

I heard Nicky laugh, and Pete say something that had Lila's name in it, and Kjel said, "Shut up, you damn fool, he'll hear you!"

And Nicky said, "He can't hear inside. Besides, what if he does? He knows already, don't he?"

And Kjel said, "He doesn't know. I hope to Christ he never does."

And Pete said, "Hell, he's got to have an idea. The whole village knows what a slut he's married to . . ."

I had a box wrench in my hand. I put it down and walked out there and I said, "What're you talking about? What're you saying about Lila?"

None of them said anything. They all just looked at me. It was a gray morning, no sun. A dark morning, not much light. Getting darker, too. I could see clouds on the horizon, dark hazy things, swallowing the light—swallowing it fast.

I said, "Pete, you called my wife a slut. I heard you."

Kjel said, "Danny, take it easy, he didn't mean nothing—"

I said, "He meant something. He meant it." I reached out and caught Pete by the shirt and threw him up against the port outrigger. He tried to tear my hands loose; I wouldn't let go. "How come, Pete? What do you know about Lila?"

Kjel said, "For Christ's sake, Danny—"

"What do you know, goddamn you!"

Pete was mad. He didn't like me roughing him up like that. And he didn't give a damn if I knew—I guess that was it. He'd only been working for us a few months. He was a stranger in Camaroon Bay. He didn't know me and I didn't know him and he didn't give a damn.

"I know because I was with her," he said. "You poor sap, she's been screwing everybody in the village behind your back. Everybody! Me, Nicky, even Kjel here—"

Kjel hit him. He reached in past me and hit Pete and knocked him loose of my hands, almost knocked him overboard. Pete went down. Nicky backed away. Kjel backed away too, looking at me. His face was all twisted up. And dark—dark like the things on the horizon.

"It's true, then," I said. "It's true."

"Danny, listen to me—"

"No," I said.

"It only happened once with her and me. Only once. I tried not to, Danny, Jesus I tried not to but she . . . Danny, listen to me . . ."

"No," I said.

I turned around, I put my back to him and the other two and the dark things on the horizon and I went into the wheelhouse and shut the door and locked it. I didn't feel anything. I didn't think anything either. There was some gasoline in one of the cupboards, for the auxiliary engine. I got the can out and poured the gas on the deckboards and splashed it on the bulkheads.

Outside Kjel was pounding on the door, calling my name.

I lit a match and threw it down.

Nothing happened right away. So I unlocked the door and

opened it, and Kjel started in, and I heard him say, "Oh my God!" and he caught hold of me and yanked me through the door.

That was when she blew.

There was a flash of blinding light, I remember that. And I remember being in the water, I remember seeing flames, I remember the pain. I don't remember anything else until I woke up here in the hospital.

The county cops asked me if I was sorry I did it. I said I was. And I am, but not for the reason they thought. I couldn't tell them the real reason. They wouldn't have understood, because first they'd have had to understand about the light and the dark.

I close my eyes now and I can see my old man's face on the night *he* died. He was a drunk and the liquor killed him, but nobody ever knew why. Except me. He called me into his room that night, I was eleven years old, and he told me why.

"It's the dark, Danny," he said. "I let it swallow all the light." I thought he was babbling. But he wasn't. "Everything is light or dark," he said. "That's what you got to understand. People, places, everything, the whole world—light or dark. You got to reach for the light, Danny. Sunshine and smiles, everything that's light. If you don't you'll let the dark take over, like I did, and the dark will destroy you. Promise me you won't let that happen to you, boy. Promise me you won't."

I promised. And I tried—Christ, Pa, I *tried*. Thirty years I reached for the light. But I couldn't hold onto enough of it, just like you couldn't. The dark kept creeping in, creeping in.

Once I told Lila about the dark and the light. She just laughed. "Is that why you always want to make love with the light on, sleep with the light on?" she said. "You're crazy sometimes, Danny, you know that?" she said.

I should have known then. But I didn't. I thought *she* was light. I reached for her six years ago, and I held her and for a while she lit up my life . . . I thought she was light. But she wasn't, she isn't. Underneath she's the dark. She's always been the dark, swallowing the light piece by piece—with Nicky, with

Pete, with all the others. Kjel, too, my best friend. Turning him dark too.

I did it all wrong, Pa. All of it, right to the end. And that's the real reason I'm sorry about what I did this morning.

I shouldn't have blown them up, blown me up. I should have blown *her* up, lit up the dark with fire and light.

Too late now. I did it all wrong.

And she's still out there, waiting.

The dark out there, waiting.

Deathwatch.

The pain isn't so bad now, the fire on me doesn't burn so hot. The morphine working? No, it isn't the morphine.

Something cool touches my face. I'm not alone in the room any more.

The bastard with the scythe is here.

But I won't look at him. I won't look at the dark of his clothes and the dark under his hood. I'll look at the light instead . . . up there on the ceiling, the big flourescent tubes shining down, light shining down, look at the light, reach for the light, the light . . .

And the door opens, I hear it open, and from a long way off I hear Lila's voice say, "I couldn't stay away, Danny, I had to see you, I had to come—"

The dark!

OUTRAGEOUS

Dunsett had two things Burke coveted and one habit Burke hated, so Burke decided to murder him.

He walked over to Dunsett's neighboring dairy ranch, which was one of the things he coveted, and stole a glance through the kitchen window at Dunsett's wife, which was the other thing he coveted, and then he went into the milking barn. Dunsett was there, using a hose on the floor near an overturned bucket. The barn and all the dairy equipment gleamed spotlessly; Dunsett was a fastidious man, and a fanatical one when it came to his cattle. He claimed he had a kind of mystical communion with them—that he would do anything for them and in return they would do anything for him. Which was a lot of nonsense, of course, although Burke had to admit that Dunsett's dairy ranch *was* the most productive in the state.

He went up to where Dunsett stood working with the hose. "Hello, Dunsett," he said. "What are you doing?"

"Well, I'll tell you," Dunsett said. "I was using a lye soap solution to wash the floor and I knocked over the bucket accidentally. So I'm cleaning it up now." He grinned. "After all, there's no use milking over spilt lye."

That was the habit Burke hated—outrageous punning. It cemented his decision. He walked over and picked up a metal bar that was part of the vacuum milking machine and hit Dunsett over the head with it.

Dunsett make a cowlike bleating sound and toppled over on the floor. Outside, somewhere in the north pasture, several cattle began to make noise—a new low for them, as if they had heard Dunsett and were responding to his cry. But then, after a few seconds, they stopped and it was quiet again, inside and out.

Burke determined to make the murder look like an accident. First, he dragged the body over near one of the cattle stalls and arranged it so that it seemed as though Dunsett had slipped and fallen against a stanchion. Then he wiped off the bar with his handkerchief and returned it to the vacuum machine. When he stepped back to examine it he was satisfied that it appeared clean and homogenous, like every milk bar he had ever seen.

He turned and started across to the doors. Just before he got there, he heard voices outside. He looked around frantically, but there was no other immediate exit from the barn. Which meant that he had to find a place to hide, and the only place he saw nearby was a stack of large stainless-steel milk pails painted in Dunsett's favorite color of crimson.

Burke ran there and dropped down on all fours behind the stack, just as the barn doors opened. There was a narrow crawlspace between some of the containers; he eased his way along it to the front, where he could see a narrow aperture between two of them. He knelt there and peered past the red pails at Dunsett.

The voices belonged to Mrs. Dunsett and one of the ranchhands. They found the body right away, and there was a lot of excitement and confusion for the next couple of minutes. Burke held his breath and sat perfectly still as he watched them. He knew he was lost if he was found.

Mrs. Dunsett left finally to notify the authorities, but the ranchhand stayed there to watch over the body. After a time he began to pace back and forth in heavy-footed strides. Burke remained motionless and watched and waited, listening to the sound of the one hand clopping.

Before long the sheriff arrived from the nearby village, along with the local mortician, who was also the county coroner; the mortician drove his hearse right inside the barn. They examined the body while Dunsett's wife and the ranchhand looked on. Then the sheriff glanced around the barn, and for a moment Burke was afraid he would want to search it.

But the mortician said, "Looks like an accident to me. Fell and hit his head on that stanchion. Probably slipped on the wet floor."

The sheriff agreed. And he stopped looking around.

Burke breathed an inaudible sigh of relief as they loaded Dunsett's remains into the hearse and prepared to depart. He was home free. All he had to do was leave his hiding place, slip outside, and close the barn door after the hearse was gone.

Which he did, five minutes later. There was no sign of anyone in the vicinity; apparently they had all gone into the village. Smiling, Burke moved away from the barn and headed for the north pasture, a shortcut to his own property. He thought he had committed the perfect crime.

But he was wrong.

When he got out in the middle of the pasture, Dunsett's outraged cattle converged on him, knocked him flat on his face, piled on top of him, and crushed him to death.

First moral: Murderers often get it in the end.
Second moral: Never underestimate the herd mentality.
Third moral: Milk and beef can put a lot of weight on you.
Fourth moral: When walking in a pasture, always be on the alert for cow flops.

MUGGERS' MOON

I was walking along one of the cinder paths in the southern end of the park when the blond guy in the Navy pea jacket tried to mug me.

I caught a glimpse of him in the pale moonlight as he came out of the shrubbery that bordered the path on one side, but before I could react he threw an arm around my neck and put a knee in the small of my back. Pain lanced across my throat and suddenly there was no more air in my lungs. Bright white lights flashed in back of my eyes. I felt myself being bent backwards. In another second he would have had me.

I had just enough time to piston my left elbow backward. He took it under the wishbone, and air exploded against the back of my neck. I gave him another one, felt his arm loosen around my throat; then I had *him*. I twisted off his knee, wrenching my head down—and I was free. I hit him with a right and a left, very fast, and he went down and stayed there. He wasn't going anywhere for a while.

I stood over him, trying to pull breath into my aching lungs, rubbing my throat where he'd held me. My ears were ringing. The damned bum!

I was still standing over him, gasping for breath, when a big uniformed patrolman came running up out of nowhere. He had his service revolver ready in his right hand, a flashlight with a bright beam slicing the darkness in his left. He put the light on me. "What's going on here?"

The light was blinding; I raised my hand against it. "Where'd you come from?" I asked him.

"Never mind that." He swung the flash down to the mugger lying on the ground, then brought it up to me again. "What happened here?"

"I was coming along the path when he jumped me out of those shrubs?"

"Tried to mug you?"

"Yeah."

"How'd you get him?"

"Some elementary judo."

"Nice work."

"I'm trained for it, same as you," I said, and I let him see the badge and identification in the leather case in my coat pocket. "I'm Andrews, with the Twenty-ninth Detective Squad—over on the other side of the park."

"A dick," the patrolman said. He put his revolver away and lowered the flash. "Well, well. What are you doing here this time of night?"

"I'm on special assignment, working with your precinct on this mugger case," I told him. "There's four of us spread through the area."

"Nobody ever lets us poor foot jockeys in on anything."

"You think we got nothing better to do than tell you guys about every stakeout we go on?"

"Okay, okay."

"How'd you get here so fast, anyway?"

"I was rousting a vag sleeping on one of the benches near the fountain," the patrolman said. "Heard all the noise on the path here. Lucky thing, you know? I mean, he could have put you out before you had the chance to use your judo. If he had I would've been right on top of him."

"Sure," I said. I was still having difficulty breathing.

"How's your throat?"

"He damned near crushed my windpipe."

"Just like those two women."

"Yeah."

The patrolman went to one knee beside the mugger and looked him over. Young, well set up, with huge hands that had thick blond hair growing on their backs. Wearing black denims and black leather boots along with the pea jacket.

"Big and plenty strong, looks like," the patrolman said. "You figure this is the guy, Andrews? The one the papers are calling the Park Stalker?"

"Figures that way," I said. "His technique is right. We'll find out for certain when we get him to the Twenty-ninth."

The patrolman nodded. He turned the mugger over and ran a quick frisk and didn't find any weapons. He took a thin cowhide wallet out of the back pocket of the denims and shined his flash on it. "Name's David Lee," he said. "You make him?"

I shook my head.

"Lives over on Madison, a few blocks from here," the patrolman said. "Can you beat that? Right in our own backyard."

"Yeah," I said.

He got to his feet and took off his cap and looked up at the thin lunar slice in the dark sky—a muggers' moon. "Man, I sure hope he's the one."

"That makes two of us."

"Whole city is in a panic over this rash of muggings, especially with those two women dead and the one guy critical in the hospital. Been eleven assaults up to now, hasn't there?"

"That's right," I said. "Eleven."

"There's a lot of parks in this city," the patrolman said, "and he's never hit the same one twice in a row. Smart bastard. We'll play hell catching him if it isn't this baby here."

"He's the one," I said. "He's got to be."

"I hope you're right, Andrews."

"Listen, you watch him while I go over to the Twenty-ninth. Captain's going to want to set up for plenty of publicity on this pinch before we bring him in."

"Well, I don't know . . ."

"You'd like to get your name in the papers, wouldn't you?"

The patrolman's face brightened. "Mean you'll let me share in a little of the glory?"

"Why not? Might mean a promotion for both of us."

"Hell, Andrews, that's decent of you."

I shrugged. "Just don't let him get away, that's all."

The patrolman had already unhooked handcuffs from his belt. "You don't have to worry none about that," he said.

I left him and went back to the fountain. From there I cut across the grass and came out of the park on Dunhill Street. Then I headed west, downtown—away from the Twenty-ninth Precinct.

That had been too damn close, I thought. If I'd been Mr. Average Citizen, the patrolman would have taken me in to sign a complaint. Then suppose somebody got suspicious? They'd have run a routine fingerprint check, and I'd have been a dead goose, brother. I've got an assault record in two cities down South.

It's a lucky thing I had that police badge and ID, all right.

But it's an even luckier thing that Number Twelve, the guy I'd mugged ten minutes before that stupid blond amateur jumped me, had been a real detective on stakeout duty in the park.

HERO

A Tale of the Old West

The mob boiled upstreet from Saloon Row toward the jailhouse. Some of the men in front carried lanterns and torches made out of rag-wrapped sticks soaked in coal oil; Micah could see the flickering light against the black night sky, the wild quivering shadows. But he couldn't see the men themselves, the hooded and masked leaders, from back here where he was at the rear of the pack. He couldn't see Ike Dall neither. Ike Dall was the one who had the hang rope already shaped out into a noose.

Men surged around Micah, yelling, waving arms and clubs and sixguns. He just couldn't keep up on account of his damn game leg. He kept getting jostled, once almost knocked down. Back there at Hardesty's Gambling Hall he'd been right in the thick of it. He'd been the center of attention, by grab. Now they'd forgot all about him and here he was clumping along on his bad leg, not able to see much, getting bumped and pushed with every dragging step. He could feel the excitement, smell the sweat and the heat and the hunger, but he wasn't a part of it no more.

It wasn't right. Hell damn boy, it just wasn't right. Weren't for him, none of this would be happening. Biggest damn thing ever in Cricklewood, Montana, and all on account of him. He was a hero, wasn't he? Back there at Hardesty's, they'd all said so. Back there at Hardesty's, he'd talked and they'd listened to every word—Ike Dall and Lee Wynkoop and Mack Clausen, all of them, everybody who was somebody in and around Cricklewood. Stood him right up there next to the bar, bought him drinks, looked at him with respect, and listened to every word he said.

"Micah seen it, didn't you, Micah? What that drifter done?"

"Sure I did. Told Marshal Thrall and I'm tellin' you. Weren't for me, he'd of got clean away."

"You're a hero, Micah. By God you are."

"Well, now. Well, I guess I am."

"Tell it again. Tell us how it was."

"Sure. Sure I will. I seen it all."

"What'd you see?"

"I seen that drifter, that Larrabee, hold up the Wells, Fargo stage. I seen him shoot Tom Porter twice, shoot Tom Porter dead as anybody ever was."

"How'd you come to be out by the Helena road?"

"Mr. Coombs sent me out from the livery, to tell Harv Perkins the singletree on his wagon was fixed a day early. I took the shortcut along the river, like I allus do when I'm headin' down the valley. Forded by Fisherman's Bend and went on through that stand of cottonwoods on the other side. That was where I was, in them trees, when I seen it happen."

"Larrabee had the stage stopped right there, did he?"

"Sure. Right there. Had his sixgun out and he was tellin' Tom to throw down the treasure box."

"And Tom throwed it down?"

"Sure he did. He throwed it right down."

"Never made to use his shotgun or his side gun?"

"No sir. Never made no play at all."

"So Larrabee shot him in cold blood."

"Cold blood—sure! Shot Tom twice. Right off the coach box the first time, then when Tom was lyin' there on the ground, rollin' around with that first bullet in him, Larrabee walked up to him cool as you please and put his sixgun agin Tom's head and done it to him proper. Blowed Tom's head half off. Blowed it half off and that's a fact."

"You all heard that. You heard what Micah seen that son of a bitch do to Tom Porter—a decent citizen, a man we all liked and was proud to call friend. I say we don't wait for the circuit judge. What if he lets Larrabee off light? I say we give that murderin' bastard what he deserves here and now, tonight. Now what do you say?"

"Hang him!"

"Stretch his dirty neck!"

"Hang him high!"

Oh, it had been fine back there at Hardesty's. Everybody looking at him the way they done, with respect. Calling him a hero. He'd been somebody then, not just poor crippled-up Micah Hays who done handy work and run errands and shoveled manure down at the Coombs Livery Barn. Oh, it had been fine! But now—now they'd forgot him again, left him behind, left him out of what was going to happen on *his* account. They were all moving upstreet to the jailhouse with their lanterns and their torches and their hunger, leaving him practically alone where he couldn't do or see a damn thing . . .

Micah stopped trying to run on his game leg and limped along slow, watching the mob, wanting to be a part of it but wanting more to see everything that happened after the mob got to the jailhouse. Then he thought: Why, I *can* see it all! Sure I can! I know just where I got to go.

He hobbled ahead to the alley alongside Burley's Feed and Grain, went down it to the staircase built up the side wall. The stairs led to a railed gallery overlooking the street, and to the offices of the town lawyer, Mr. Spivey, that had been built on top of the feed-store roof. Micah stumped up the stairs and went past the dark offices and on down to the far end of the gallery.

Hell damn boy! He sure *could* see from up here, clear as anybody could want. The mob was close to the jailhouse now; in the dancy light from the lanterns and torches, he could make out the hooded shape of Ike Dall with his hang-rope noose held high, the shapes of Lee Wynkoop and Mack Clausen and the others who were leading the pack. He could see that big old shade cottonwood off to one side of the jail, too, with its one gnarly limb that stretched out over the street. That was where they was going to hang the drifter. Ike Dall had said so, back there at Hardesty's. *"We don't have to take him far, by Christ. We'll string him up right there next to the jail."*

The front door of the jailhouse opened and out come Marshal Thrall and his deputy, Ben Dietrich. Micah leaned out over the railing, squinting, feeling the excitement scurry up and down inside his chest like a mouse on a wall. Marshal Thrall had a shotgun in his hands and Ben Dietrich held a rifle. The marshal commenced to yelling, but whatever it was got lost in the noise from the mob. Mob didn't slow down none, neither, when old Thrall started waving that Greener of his. Marshal wasn't going to shoot nobody, Ike Dall had said. *"Why, we're all Thrall's friends and neighbors. Ben Dietrich's, too. They ain't goin' to shoot up their friends and neighbors, are they? Just to stop the lynching of a murderin' son of a bitch like Larrabee?"*

No sir, they sure wasn't. That mob didn't slow down none at all. It surged right ahead, right on around Marshal Thrall and Ben Dietrich like floodwaters around a sandbar, and swallowed them both up and carried them right on into the jailhouse.

A hell of a racket come from inside. Pretty soon the pack parted down the middle and Micah could see four or five men carrying that drifter up in the air, hands tied behind him, the same way you'd carry a side of butchered beef. Hell damn boy! Everybody was whooping it up, waving torches and lanterns and swirling light around in the dark like a bunch of kids with pinwheel sparklers. It put Micah in mind of an Independence Day celebration. By grab, that was just what it was like. Fireworks on the Fourth of July.

Well, they carried that murdering Larrabee on over to the shade cottonwood. He was screaming things, that drifter was— screaming the whole way. Micah couldn't hear most of it above the crowd noise, but he caught a few of the words. And one whole sentence: "I tell you, I didn't do it!"

"Why, sure you did," Micah said out loud. "Sure you did. I seen you do it, didn't I?"

Ike Dall throwed his rope over the cottonwood's gnarly limb, caught the other end and give it to somebody, and then he put that noose around Larrabee's neck and drew it tight.

Somebody else brung a saddle horse around, held him steady whilst they hoisted the drifter onto his back. That Larrabee was screaming like a woman now.

Micah leaned hard against the gallery railing. His mouth was dry, real dry; he couldn't even work up no spit to wet it. He'd never seen a lynching before. There'd been plenty in Montana Territory—more'n a dozen over in Beaverhead and Madison counties a few years back, when the vigilantes done for Henry Plummer and his gang of desperadoes—but never one in Cricklewood nor any of the other towns Micah had lived in.

The drifter screamed and screamed. Then Micah saw everybody back off some, away from the horse Larrabee was on, and Ike Dall raised his arm and brought it down smack on the cayuse's rump. Horse jumped ahead, frog-stepping. And Larrabee quit screaming and commenced to dancing in the air all loosey-goosey, like a puppet on the end of a string. Before long, though, the dancing slowed down and then it quit altogether. That's done him, Micah thought. And everybody in the mob knew it, too, because they all backed off some more and stood there in a half-circle, staring up at the drifter hanging still and straight in the smoky light.

Micah stared too. He leaned against the railing and stared and stared, and kept on staring long after the mob started to break up.

Hell damn boy, he thought over and over. Hell damn, boy, if that sure wasn't something to see!

It took the best part of a week for the town to get back to normal. There was plenty more excitement during that week—county law coming in, representatives from the territorial governor's office in Helena, newspaper people, all kinds of curious strangers. For Micah it was kind of like the lynching went on and on, a week-long celebration like none other he'd ever been part of. Folks kept asking him questions, interviewing him for newspapers, buying him drinks, shaking his hand and clapping his back and calling him a hero the way the men had done that night at Hardesty's. Oh, it was fine. It was almost as fine as when he'd been the center of attention before the lynch mob got started.

But then it all come to an end. The law and the newspaper people and the strangers went away; Cricklewood settled down to what it had been before the big event, and Micah settled back into his humdrum job at the Coombs Livery Barn and his nights on the straw bunk in one corner of the loft. He did his handy work, ran errands, shoveled manure—and the townsfolk and ranchers and cowhands stopped buying him drinks, stopped shaking his hand and clapping his back and calling him hero, stopped paying much attention to him at all. It was the same as before, like he was nobody, like he didn't hardly even exist. Mack Clausen snubbed him on the street no more than two weeks after the lynching. The one time he tried to get Ike Dall to talk with him about that night, how it had felt putting the noose around Larrabee's neck, Ike wouldn't have none of it. Why, Ike claimed he hadn't even been there that night, hadn't been part of the mob—said that lie right to Micah's face!

Four weeks passed. Five. Micah did his handy work and ran errands and shoveled manure and now nobody even *mentioned* that night no more, not to him and not to each other. Like it never happened. Like they was ashamed of it or something.

Micah was feeling low the hot Saturday morning he come down the loft ladder and started toward the harness room like he always done first thing. But this wasn't like other mornings because a man was curled up sleeping in one of the stalls near the back doors. Big man, whiskers on his face, dust on his trail clothes. Micah had never seen him before.

Mr. Coombs was up at the other end of the barn, forking hay for the two roan saddle horses he kept for rent. Micah went on up there and said, "Morning, Mr. Coombs."

"Well, Micah. Down late again, eh?"

". . . I reckon so."

"Getting to be a habit lately," Mr. Coombs said. "I don't like it, Micah. See that you start coming down on time from now on, hear?"

"Yes sir. Mr. Coombs, who's that sleepin' in the back stall?"

"Just some drifter. He didn't say his name."

"Drifter?"

"Came in half-drunk last night, paid me four bits to let him sleep in here. Not the first time I've rented out a stall to a human animal and it won't be the last."

Mr. Coombs turned and started forking some more hay. Micah went away toward the harness room, then stopped after ten paces and stood quiet for a space. And then, moving slow, he hobbled over to where the fire ax hung and pulled it down and limped back behind Mr. Coombs and swung the axe up and shut his eyes and swung the ax down. When he opened his eyes again Mr. Coombs was lying there with the back of his head cleaved open and blood and brains spilled out like pulp out of a split melon.

Hell damn boy, Micah thought.

Then he dropped the ax and run to the front doors and threw them open and run out onto Main Street yelling at the top of his voice, "Murder! It's murder! Some damn drifter killed Mr. Coombs! Split his head wide open with a fire ax. I seen him do it, I seen it, I seen the whole thing!"

THE MAN
WHO COLLECTED
"THE SHADOW"

Mr. Theodore Conway was a nostalgiac, a collector of memorabilia, a dweller in the uncomplicated days of his adolescence when radio, movie serials, and pulp magazines were the ruling forms of entertainment and super-heroes were the idols of American youth.

At forty-three, he resided alone in a modest apartment on Manhattan's Lower East Side, where he commuted daily by subway to his position of file clerk in the archives of Baylor, Baylor, Leeds and Wadsworth, a respected probate law firm. He was short and balding and very plump and very nondescript; he did not indulge in any of the vices, major or minor; he had no friends to speak of, and neither a wife nor, euphemistically or otherwise, a girlfriend. (In point of fact, Mr. Conway was that rarest of individuals, an adult male virgin.) He did not own a television set, did not attend the theater or movies. His one and only hobby, his single source of pleasure, his sole purpose in life, was the accumulation of nostalgia in general—and nostalgia pertaining to that most inimitable of all super-heroes, The Shadow, in particular.

Ah, The Shadow! Mr. Conway idolized Lamont Cranston, loved Margo Lane as he could never love any living woman. Nothing set his blood to racing quite so quickly as The Shadow on the scent of an evildoer, utilizing the Power that, as

Cranston, he had learned in the Orient—the Power to cloud men's minds so that they could not see him. Nothing gave Mr. Conway more pleasure than listening to the haunting voice of Orson Welles, capturing The Shadow as no other had over the air; or reading Maxwell Grant's daring accounts in *The Shadow Magazine*; or paging through one of the starkly drawn Shadow comic books. Nothing filled him with as much delicious anticipation as the words spoken by his hero at the beginning of each radio adventure: *Who knows what evil lurks in the hearts of men? The Shadow knows* . . . and the eerie, bloodcurdling laugh that followed it. Nothing filled him with as much security as, when each case was closed, this ace among aces saying words of warning to criminals everywhere: *The weed of crime bears bitter fruit. Crime does not pay. The Shadow knows!*

Mr. Conway had begun collecting nostalgia in 1944, starting with a wide range of pulp magazines. (He now had well over ten thousand issues of *Wu Fang, G-8 and his Battle Aces, Black Mask, Weird Tales, Doc Savage,* and two hundred others.) Then he had gone on to comic books and comic strips, to premiums of every kind and description—decoders and secret-compartment belts and message flashlights and spy rings and secret pens that wrote in invisible ink. In the 1950s he had begun to accumulate tapes of such radio shows as *Jack Armstrong, the All-American Boy* and *Buck Rogers in the 25th Century.* But while he amassed all of these eagerly, he pursued the mystique of The Shadow with a fervor that bordered on the fanatical.

He haunted secondhand bookshops and junk shops, pored over advertisements in newspapers and magazines and collectors' sheets, wrote letters, made telephone calls, spent every penny of his salary that did not go for bare essentials. And at long last he succeeded where no other nostalgiac had even come close to succeeding. He accomplished a remarkable, an almost superhuman feat.

He collected the complete Shadow.

There was absolutely nothing produced about his hero— not a written word, not a spoken sentence, not a drawing or gadget—that Mr. Conway did not own.

The final item, the one that had eluded him for so many years, came into his possession on a Saturday evening in late June. He had gone into a tenement area of Manhattan, near the East River, to purchase from a private individual a rare cartoon strip of *Terry and the Pirates*. With the strip carefully tucked into his coat pocket, he was on his way back to the subway when he chanced upon a small neighborhood bookshop in the basement of a crumbling brownstone. It was still open, and unfamiliar to him, and so he entered and began to browse. And on one of the cluttered tables at the rear—there it was.

The October 1931 issue of *The Shadow Magazine*.

Mr. Conway emitted a small, ecstatic cry. Caught up the magazine in trembling hands, stared at it with disbelieving eyes, opened it tenderly, read the contents page and the date, ran sweat-slick fingers over the rough, grainy pulp paper. Near-mint condition. Spine undamaged. Colors unfaded. And the price—

Fifty cents.

Fifty cents!

Tears of joy rolled unabashedly down Mr. Conway's cheeks as he carried this treasure to the elderly proprietor. The bookseller gave him a strange look, shrugged, and accepted two quarters from Mr. Conway without a word. Two quarters, fifty cents. And Mr. Conway had been prepared to pay *hundreds* . . .

As he went out into the gathering darkness—it was almost nine by this time—he could scarcely believe that he had finally done it, that he now possessed the total word, picture, and voice exploits of the most awesome master crime fighter of them all. His brain reeled. The Shadow was *his* now; Lamont Cranston and Margo Lane (beautiful Margo!)—his, all his, his alone.

Instead of proceeding to the subway, Mr. Conway impulsively entered a small diner not far from the bookshop and ordered a cup of coffee. Then, once again, he opened the magazine. He had previously read a reprint of the novel by Maxwell Grant—*The Shadow Laughs!*—but that was not the same as reading the original, no indeed. He plunged into the story again, savoring each line, each page, the mounting suspense, the seemingly inescapable traps laid to eliminate The Shadow by archvillains Isaac Coffran and Birdie Crull, the smashing of their insidious counterfeiting plot: justice triumphant. *The weed of crime bears bitter fruit, crime does not pay* . . .

So engrossed was Mr. Conway that he lost all track of time. When at last he closed the magazine he was startled to note that except for the counterman, the diner was deserted. It had been nearly full when he entered. He looked at his wristwatch, and his mouth dropped open in amazement. Good heavens! It was past midnight!

Mr. Conway scrambled out of the booth and hurriedly left the diner. Outside, apprehension seized him. The streets were dark and deserted—ominous, forbidding.

He looked up and down without seeing any sign of life. It was four blocks to the nearest subway entrance—a short walk in daylight but now it was almost the dead of night. Mr. Conway shivered in the cool night breeze. He had never liked the night, its sounds and smells, its hidden dangers. There were stories in the papers every morning of muggers and thieves on the prowl . . .

He took a deep breath, summoning courage. Four blocks. Well, that really wasn't very far, only a matter of minutes if he walked swiftly. And swift was his pace as he started along the darkened sidewalk.

No cars passed; no one appeared on foot. The hollow echo of his footfalls were the only sounds. And yet Mr. Conway's heart was pounding wildly by the time he had gone two blocks.

He was halfway through the third block when he heard the muffled explosions.

He stopped, the hairs on his neck prickling, a tremor of fear coursing through him. There was an alley on his left; the reports had come from that direction. Gunshots? He was certain that was what they'd been—and even more certain that they meant danger, sudden death. *Run!* he thought. And yet, though he was poised for flight, he did not run. He peered into the alley, saw a thin light at its far end.

Run, run! But instead he entered the alley, moving slowly, feeling his way along. *What am I doing? I shouldn't be here!* But still he continued forward, approaching the narrow funnel of light. It came from inside a partly open door to the building on his right. Mr. Conway put out a hand and eased the door open wider, peered into what looked to be a warehouse. The thudding of his heart seemed as loud as a drum roll as he stepped over the threshold.

The sourse of the light was a glassed-in cubicle toward the middle of the warehouse. Shadowy shapes—crates of some kind—loomed toward the ceiling on either side. He advanced in hesitant, wary steps, seeing no sign of movement in the gloom around him. At last he reached the cubicle, stood in the light. A watchman's office. He stepped up close to look through the glass.

A cry rose in his throat when he saw the man lying motionless on the floor inside; he managed to stifle it. Blood stained the front of the man's khaki uniform jacket. He had been shot twice.

Dead, murdered! Get out of here, call the police!

Mr. Conway turned—and froze.

A hulking figure stood not three feet away, looking straight at him.

Mr. Conway's knees buckled; he had to put a hand against the glass to keep from collapsing. The murderer! His mind once again compelled him to run, *run*, but his legs would not obey. He could only stare back in horror at the hulking figure—at the pinched white face beneath a low-brimmed cloth cap, at rodentlike eyes and a cruel mouth, at the yawning muzzle of a revolver in one fist.

"No!" Mr. Conway cried then. "No, please, don't shoot!"

The man dropped into a furtive crouch, extending the pistol in front of him.

"Don't shoot!" Mr. Conway said again, putting up his hands.

Surprise, bewilderment, and a sudden trapped fear made a twisted mask of the man's face. "Who's that? Who's there?"

Mr. Conway opened his mouth, then closed it again. He could scarcely believe his ears. The man was standing not three feet away, looking right at him!

"I don't understand," Mr. Conway said before he could stop the words.

The murderer fired. The sudden report caused Mr. Conway to jump convulsively aside; the bullet came nowhere near him. He saw the gunman looking desperately from side to side, everywhere but at him—and in that instant he did understand, he knew.

"You can't *see* me," he said.

The gun discharged a second bullet, but Mr. Conway had already moved again. Far to one side of him a spiderwebbed hole appeared in the glass wall of the cubicle. "Damn you!" the murderer screamed. "Where are you? *Where are you?*"

Mr. Conway remained standing there, clearly outlined in the light, for a moment longer; then he stepped to where a board lay on the floor nearby, picked it up. Without hesitation, he advanced on the terrified man and then struck him on the side of the head; watched dispassionately as the other dropped unconscious to the floor.

Mr. Conway kicked the revolver away and stood over him. The police would have to be summoned, of course, but there was plenty of time for that now. A slow, grim smile stretched the corners of his mouth. Could it be that the remarkable collecting feat he had performed, his devotion and his passion, had stirred some supernatural force into granting him the Power that he now possessed? Well, no matter. His was not to question why; so endowed, his was but to heed the plaintive cries of a world ridden with lawlessness.

A deep, chilling laugh suddenly swept through the warehouse. "The weed of crime bears bitter fruit!" a haunting, Wellesian voice shouted. "Crime does not pay!"

And The Shadow wrapped the cloak of night around himself and went out into the mean streets of the great metropolis . . .

FOR LOVE

The taxi let Giroux off in a residential area six blocks from Hopper Industrial Park. The night wind was chill; he turned up the collar on his overcoat as he walked rapidly toward the park. The gun in his right coat pocket was cold against his palm.

It was just past nine when he reached the deserted industrial complex. There was no sign of the night security patrol. Keeping to shadows, he made his way to the squat structure that housed the Moore Plumbing Supply Company. A single light burned in the office, behind blind-covered front windows. As was his custom on Thursday evenings, Moore was working late and alone on the company books.

Giroux moved around to the rear of the building. Only one car waited in the parking area—Moore's, of course, one he knew well. Not only did he see it every day, parked in the drive of the Moore house diagonally across the street from his own home, but he had written the insurance policy on it.

He walked to the base of the cyclone fence that ringed the supply-yard enclosure, blended into the blackness there. Now, as he waited, he did not feel the chill of the wind. His thoughts insulated him—thoughts of Judith. She was vivid in his mind, as always: long dark hair, gentle brown eyes, high cheekbones, and slim sensuous body. How often did he dream of her? How often did he long to hold her in the warm silent hours of all the nights to come?

"Soon now, Judith," he whispered in the cold silent hour of this night. "Soon . . ."

He did not have to wait long. Habitually precise, Moore left the building at ten o'clock. Giroux tensed, his fingers moving over the surfaces of the gun, as he watched Moore walk to his car and begin to unlock it. Then, quickly, he stepped out and approached the other man.

Moore heard him and glanced around in a jerky way, startled. Giroux stopped two paces away. "Hello, Frank," he said.

Recognition smoothed the nervous frown on Moore's face. "Why—hello, Martin. You gave me a jolt, coming out of the darkness like that. What are you *doing* here at this hour?"

"Waiting for you."

"What on earth for?"

"Because I'm going to kill you," Giroux said.

Moore stared at him incredulously. "Kill me?"

"That's right."

"Hey, listen, that's not funny. Are you drunk?"

Giroux took out the gun. "Not at all. I'm quite serious."

"Martin, for God's sake, put that thing away." There was a mixture of fear and anger in Moore's voice now. "What's the matter with you? Why would you even think of killing *me*?"

"For love," Giroux said.

"For . . . what?"

"Love. You're in the way, Frank; you stand between Judith and me. Does it all become clear now?"

"You and Judith? No, I don't believe it. My wife loves me, she's devoted to me . . ."

Giroux smiled faintly. "Have you ever wondered about the perfect murder, Frank? Whether there is such a thing? I have, often. And I believe there is, if it's properly planned and executed."

"Judith would never be party to such a thing!"

"Whether she would is irrelevant, isn't it?"

"This is insane," Moore said. "*You're* insane, Giroux!"

"Not at all. I'm merely in love. Of course, I do have my

practical side as well. There's the hundred-thousand-dollar double-indemnity policy my company has on your life, which will take care of Judith's and my needs quite nicely once we're married. After a decent interval of mourning, naturally. We can't have the slightest suspicion cast on her good name or mine."

"You can't do this," Moore said. "I won't *let* you do it." And he made a sudden jump forward, clawing at the gun.

But his fear and his anger made him clumsy, and Giroux was able to sidestep with ease and then club him with the barrel. Moore fell moaning to the pavement. Giroux hit him again, even more sharply. Then he finished opening the car door, dragged the unconscious man onto the floor in back, and slid in under the wheel.

As he drove out of Hopper Industrial Park, he was watchful for the night security patrol; still saw no sign of it. Observing the exact speed limit, he followed the route Moore always took home—a route that included a one-mile stretch through Old Mill Canyon. The canyon road was little used since the construction of a bypassing freeway, but Moore considered it a shortcut.

At the top of the canyon road was a sharp curve with a bluff wall on the left and a wide shoulder edged by a guardrail on the right. Beyond the rail was a sheer two-hundred-foot drop into the canyon below. No cars were behind Giroux as he drove up to the crest. From there he could see for perhaps a quarter of a mile past the curve, and that part of the road also seemed empty.

Giroux stopped the car a hundred feet from the shoulder. He took and held a long breath, then pressed down hard on the accelerator and twisted the wheel until the car was headed straight for the guardrail. While it was still on the road he braked sharply; the tires burned against the asphalt, providing the skid marks that would make Moore's death seem a tragic accident.

He managed to fight the car to a stop ten feet from the guardrail. Rubbing sweat from his forehead, he reversed to the roadway, set the emergency brake, and got out to look both ways along the road. Still no headlights in either direction. He dragged Moore out of the rear, propped him behind the wheel, and wedged his foot against the accelerator pedal. The engine roared. Giroux grasped the release lever for the emergency brake, braced himself, jerked the brake off, and flung his body out of the way.

The car hurtled forward. An edge of the open driver's door slapped against his hip, knocking him down, but he wasn't hurt. He rolled over in time to see the car crash through the guardrail, seem to hang in space for a moment amid a shower of splinters, and plunge downward. The thunderous rending of metal filled the night as the machine bounced and rolled into the canyon.

Giroux gained his feet, went to the edge. There was no fire, but he could make out the mangled wreckage far below. He said softly, "I'm sorry, Frank. It's not that I hated you, or even disliked you. It's just that you were in the way."

Then, keeping to the side of the road, he began the long three-mile trek home.

At six the following evening, Giroux stepped up onto the front porch of the Moore house. He rang the bell, waited with damp palms and constricted chest for Judith to answer.

There were steps inside, the door opened—and at the sight of her his love swelled inside him until it was almost like physical pain.

"Hello, Judith," he said gravely. "I just heard about Frank, and of course I came right over."

Her grief-swollen mouth trembled. "Thank you, Martin. It was such a terrible accident, so . . . so *sudden*. I guess you know how devoted Frank and I were to each other; I feel lost and terribly alone without him."

"You're not alone," Giroux told her, and silently added the words *my love*. "It's true that we've never been anything but casual neighbors, Judith, but I want you to know that there isn't anything I wouldn't do for you. Not *anything* I wouldn't do . . ."

UNCHAINED

The woods were dark and wet and cold after the recent rain. The old man could feel the chill and dampness against his face, against the whole of his left hand—but nowhere else. Except for that left hand, resting on the arm of his wheelchair, he was completely paralyzed from the neck down.

He did not know these woods, though he had lived at the edge of them for eighteen years. His spinster daughters, Madeline and Caroline, never took him there. But he had sat many times on the enclosed back porch of their house, looking out at the unbroken line of green and brown, thinking of what lay within, and wishing he could go there. Alone. That was the important thing: alone.

The opportunity had finally come.

Today, as on every Thursday afternoon, Madeline had left at two o'clock to do the week's shopping and Caroline had gone off to her Literary Society meeting; but on this Thursday, the remainder of the ritual had been broken. Mrs. Gregor, who always arrived promptly at two-thirty to care for him until his daughters returned at five, had not come.

He didn't know why she failed to show up, and he didn't care; he was merely thankful that she hadn't, and that he had been able to talk Caroline into leaving on faith that Mrs. Gregor *would* come. It had been eighteen years since the accident, when the drunken salesman had run Martha and him down as they were crossing a rain-slick street, killing her instantly and permanently damaging his spine. Eighteen years, and at long last he was *alone*. No one in the next room, listening; no one in the house popping in to see if he needed anything, to bother him with unwanted chatter. Alone!

Getting out of the house had not been easy. All the doors were open leading to the rear porch, beyond which a ramp had been installed in place of the back stairs; but the screen door that gave access to the ramp was closed with an eye hook—a barrier, a wall, a simple screen door that he could not open.

Still, he had managed it. The wheelchair was motorized, with a control panel on the left arm. By using his thumb on the forward and reverse buttons and hooking his ring finger around the steering mechanism, he could take himself from room to room, propel himself along sidewalks when Madeline and Caroline took him out for one of his periodic airings. (They hadn't wanted to let him have the motorized chair—though they were well-meaning, they thought of him as a helpless child—but he had pleaded and demanded and refused to eat until finally they had given in.)

At a distance of ten feet, he had pressed down on the forward button and sent the chair rushing into the screen door. Seven times he had done that, before the eye hook finally popped loose and the door fluttered open. Then he was down the ramp and moving slowly across the rear yard toward the woods.

Now he was deep among the tall trees—he wasn't sure exactly how far he had come or how long it had taken him—and the only sounds were the occasional cry of a bird, the hum of the wheelchair's motor, the liquid whisper of the tires tracking through wet leaf mold. Ahead was a brushy deadfall, which a man with legs could have penetrated but the wheelchair could not. He turned laterally along it, found the remnants of an old path at its end, and maneuvered his way into a large, grassy glade.

It was peaceful there, serene. The old man smiled faintly, remembering another glade in another wood decades earlier:

Martha sitting beside him, and the touch of her lips, and the softness of her hair. Then the smile faded, blotted out by another memory—the still-vivid image of the night on the rain-slick street. He blanked his mind again. He had become quite adept at blanking his mind the past eighteen years.

The old man rolled across the glade. Through the trees on the far side he could see the dull gray reflection of water. He changed direction, moving diagonally to where the ground sloped upward and the undergrowth was thinner. There he found himself at the edge of a steep, twenty-foot embankment, looking down into a small vale that contained an even smaller pond. Three wild ducks floated placidly in the pond's center, like a child's toys in an oversized wading pool. Patterns of leaves and water lilies rimmed its edges.

He sat watching the ducks. One of them lifted up, spreading wings that slapped and rippled the surface, and soared away into the overcast sky. *Free*, he thought. *No chains on him. Free.*

He lowered his chin to his chest, sighing softly. When he raised his head again a few seconds later, he noticed movement far down to his left, in the trees close to the pond. A young man and a young woman came into view, hands clasped, moving along the shore in his direction.

Lovers, the old man thought—and then realized with sudden alarm that the girl was struggling, trying to free herself of the young man's grip. The youth kept moving forward, half-dragging her now. In the forest hush the old man could hear her voice, shrill and frightened: "Please, please, let me go. I won't tell anyone about you, I swear I won't!"

The youth swung around, caught her shoulder with his free hand, and shook her roughly. "Shut up! You hear me? Keep your mouth shut!"

"Don't hurt me, please don't hurt me—"

He slapped her openhanded, with enough force that the sound of it reverberated like a pistol shot. "I'll hurt you plenty if you don't keep that mouth of yours *shut.*"

Watching, the old man felt an almost forgotten rage well up inside him. His right hand gripped the wheelchair's arm. *If I had legs!* he thought impotently. *If I could walk and use my body!* He craned his head forward and shouted, "You, down there! Leave that girl alone!"

Both their heads jerked around and they stared upward, locating him. The girl cried, "Help, help!" not realizing he was in a wheelchair. The old man strained futilely in the contraption, like someone straining against unbreakable bonds.

In a frenzy the youth released the girl and then hit her with a closed fist. She fell and lay still. He fumbled under the jacket he wore, and the metal of a handgun flashed in his right hand. Brandishing the weapon, he ran to the embankment.

The old man did not touch the chair's control panel. He sat with his lips pulled in against his teeth, eyes bright and hard as they followed the youth's struggles up the rocky, root-tangled slope. As he came closer, the old man saw that he was in his early twenties, tall and bony, with a wild tangle of reddish hair—and knew then that the youth was Rusty Jaynes, one of two young thugs who had gone on a brutal crime spree in the area. The other fugitive had been captured by state police two days before. The old man knew all this because one of the few hollow pleasures he had left was television.

Jaynes, panting, reached the top of the embankment and stood five feet from the old man, pointing a snub-nosed revolver at him. He wiped his mouth on the sleeve of his jacket before he said, "A cripple, a damned old cripple in a wheelchair. You got some moxie, grandpa, yelling at me that way."

"Let the girl go, Jaynes," the old man said.

"So you know who I am. Well, that's just too bad for you."

"Let the girl go," the old man said again. "Take me as your hostage—that's what you've got her for, isn't it?"

Jaynes laughed shrilly. "Man, you're something else. I'm gonna push you in that chair? A hostage in a *wheelchair?*"

"Then shoot me now and have done with it."

"If that's the way you want it, grandpa—"

The old man pressed down hard on the wheelchair's forward control button. The chair rolled ahead so abruptly that Jaynes was startled into momentary inaction. At the last second he tried to dodge, squeezing the revolver's trigger at the same time. An echoing roar hammered in the old man's ears; the bullet sang past his head. And then the chair's raised metal footrest struck the youth on one shin and pitched him off balance, sent him toppling backward down the embankment.

Jaynes made a screeching sound that cut off when his body jarred into the earth; the revolver popped loose and arced to one side. The old man managed to brake inches from the edge of the slope, in time to see Jaynes roll and slide down over the rough ground. The youth was trying desperately to check his momentum when his head cracked against an upthrust rock; then he went limp. Moments later his body came to a sprawled rest near the bottom. There was blood on the side of his head, blood at one corner of his mouth. He did not move.

The old man reversed a few feet back from the edge. He sat stoically in the heavy silence, looking toward the girl. There was no way he could get down to her, nothing he could do except to wait. Long minutes passed, five or more, before she began to stir, and it was another two before she sat up and rubbed her jaw. She seemed dazed, disoriented.

Some of the tenseness went out of the old man. He shouted, "Girl! Up here, girl!"

He had to call out a second time before her head twisted around and she looked his way. Then she seemed to remember where she was, what had happened to her; she got jerkily to her feet, poised for flight.

"It's all right," the old man told her. "He can't hurt you now. Look below me, on the slope—you can see him lying there."

The girl located Jaynes, stared at his sprawled body for a few seconds before her gaze shifted upward again to the old man. Fear gave way to confusion, and finally to understanding and relief.

"Get the police. I'll wait here. Hurry, now. Run!"

She hesitated, as if she wanted to say something to him. Then she turned and ran swiftly along the edge of the pond, back into the trees where she and Jaynes had first appeared.

Sitting there after she was gone, waiting, the old man wondered what the police would say when they arrived, if any of them would recognize his name. Probably not; eighteen years was a long time. The news people would make the connection, though: Ben Frazer, the crippled old man who had miraculously saved a young woman's life and brought about the capture of a dangerous felon, was the same Ben Frazer who had for thirty years been a lieutenant of detectives in the state capital—the officer they had called "Bulldog" because of his refusal to let go once he had his teeth into a case.

Funny, but he hadn't thought of that bulldog business in a long time. All his life, until that night eighteen years ago, he had been tenacious; then the bulldog in him had simply let go, given up. For almost two decades he had lived with a single purpose: to find a way to get out from under the watchful eyes of his two daughters, and then find a way to end what remained of his life. That was why he had come into these woods today; that was what he had been thinking of, sitting here watching the ducks. If it hadn't been for the appearance of Jaynes and the girl, he would have pressed down on the Forward button and sent himself over the edge. It would have been Bulldog Ben Frazer, not Rusty Jaynes, lying broken and bloody down there now.

He thought of the girl, the look on her face just before she'd fled. And for the first time since Martha's death and his own paralysis, he felt as he once had. Useful to others and to himself. Tenacious. Unchained.

A small smile curved the corners of his mouth. There would be no more thoughts of suicide, no more self-pity. He could wait now, in peace, because in a way he was already free. . . .

TIGER, TIGER

(With John Lutz)

Kerry Maitland, who had been standing at the Fine Watches and Jewelry counter for the past five minutes, thought that this was one of the few times she was glad to be ignored. And glad to seem like just another browser taking up space. Because she wasn't browsing. Nor was she there to buy anything.

The heavy-set woman on her left kept studying a velvet-lined tray full of 24-carat gold rings, all of them with expensive jeweled settings. The salesperson behind the counter kept studying the woman and trying not to look impatient. And Kerry, feigning interest in a modest cameo locket, kept covertly studying the pigeon's-blood ruby ring in the nearest corner of the tray. The ruby had been cut *cabochon*—in convex form and not faceted—and in its deep purplish-red depths you could see a six-rayed star. It was a very valuable stone.

There was a good deal of milling about in the area, and a good deal of noise, too, as other customers began to besiege the salesperson with demands for attention. Finally, in self-defense, she let some sort of her impatience show through and asked the heavy-set woman to please make up her mind. A little snappishly, the woman said she was trying to do just that.

At which point an irritable-looking man suggested in a loud voice that the woman quit being so selfish and let other people take their turn. The woman glared at him and told him to mind his own business. He glared back and told her to go fall down the escalator. She made an indignant squeaking sound, then appealed to the salesperson, who was already making a half-hearted effort to restore order.

While all this was going on Kerry plucked the ruby ring out of the tray, palmed it, turned from the counter, and dropped the ring into her coat pocket as she started away.

Without looking back, she hurried through the crowd toward the escalators. She was not quite halfway there when the tall man materialized beside her and laid a heavy hand on her arm. "Hold it right there, lady," he said in an undertone.

Kerry stiffened. "Who are you? What do you want?"

"The name's Cassidy," the tall man said. He was bland-featured, except for a pair of canny brown eyes, and dressed in a conservative suit and tie. "Store security officer. You better come with me."

"Come with you where? You have no right—"

"Look lady, just come along. It'll be easier for both of us if you don't make a scene."

He steered her to the escalators, still holding tightly onto her arm. Kerry didn't try to resist; there would have been no point in it. They rode to the fourth floor, and from there took an elevator to the fifth where the credit department and managerial offices were located. At the end of a long hallway Cassidy knocked on a door marked Cassidy knocked on a door marked *Lawrence Tinker, Assistant Manager*, opened it, and ushered her inside.

The only occupant was a chubby bald-headed man in his forties, with pointy ears like Mr. Spock. He peered at Kerry from behind a cluttered desk, frowned slightly, and said, "Well, what have we here?"

"Shoplifter," Cassidy told him. "I spotted her an hour ago, down in Perfumes; she swiped a bottle of the eighty-dollar-an-ounce French stuff."

Tinker raised an eyebrow. "Is that so?"

"Yep. I wondered if maybe she had other plans, too, so I decided to follow her a while and see. She hit Men's Sundries next, for a pair of silver cufflinks. Then she went up to Fine

Watches and Jewelry and nailed a fancy ruby ring. I figured it was time to move in then, before she managed to slip away."

"Where are these items now?"

"In her right coat pocket."

Biting her lip, Kerry said, "This isn't what you think. I'm not a criminal . . ."

"Please put the ring and the other things on my desk," Tinker said. "Then let me have your purse."

Kerry did as ordered. Tinker picked up the ring first and peered at it as if trying to estimate its value. After which he opened her purse, rummaged through the keys, tissues, compact, and other items inside, and finally withdrew her wallet. He thumbed through that, too, and spent some time studying her driver's license.

"You're married, I see," he said. "And you live on Waverly Drive; that's in Forest Hills, isn't it?"

"Yes."

"A nice address." His eyes seemed to take inventory of her coiffed red hair, her alpaca coat, her smartly styled wool suit, her Gucci shoes and bag. "You're obviously not poor, Mrs. Maitland; yet here you are, guilty of shoplifting."

Kerry averted her eyes. "I didn't want to take those things," she said in a small voice. "It's just that I . . . I couldn't help it. It was a compulsion."

"Have you had compulsions like that before?"

"I . . . yes. Not very often, but . . ." She broke off and shivered.

Tinker was silent for a time. Then he asked Cassidy, "What do you think, George?"

"Well," Cassidy said, "could be she's one of these rich types that does it for kicks; we've had them in here before. But she doesn't fit the pattern. She's either telling the truth—a klepto—or she's a pretty clever pro. Either way, it looks like we got a tiger on our hands."

"Tiger?" Kerry asked.

"That's what George and I call practiced, compulsive shoplifters," Tinker said. "They blend in with their background so you hardly notice them watching and waiting. Then they pounce."

Kerry had never thought of herself as a tiger. But she understood the analogy. For a few moments she had felt as if she were stalking each of her preys.

"What are you going to do with me?" she asked anxiously. "Are you going to have me arrested?"

Tinker said, "I'm afraid so, Mrs. Maitland."

"But you *can't*. What would my family say? Oh, please, can't you just let me go? I promise I'll never come here again . . ."

Tinker sighed. "You seem to be a decent person; maybe you couldn't help what you did. But store policy is to turn all shoplifters over to the police. No exceptions."

"Please," Kerry said again. "Isn't there *some* way. . . ?"

"You know, Mr. Tinker," Cassidy said, "I kind of feel sorry for the lady. Maybe she's not a genuine tiger at that. Couldn't we give her a break?"

Another frown wrinkled Tinker's puffy face. "I tend to agree with you, George. But we'd be taking a big risk. If our superiors found out, we could lose our jobs."

"I'd never tell anyone," Kerry said fervently. "Never."

"Well . . ." Tinker leaned forward and lowered his voice to a near-whisper. "Maybe we *could* make an arrangement, at that."

"Arrangement?"

"Yes. Where you could leave here free and clear, with no report made to the police. And where Mr. Cassidy and myself would be, ah, rewarded for the risk we'd be taking."

"You mean . . . money?"

"Yes, dear lady. Money."

Cassidy said, "We'd even let you keep the items you stole. It'd be kind of like a trade."

"Oh," Kerry said. "Oh, I see. And since I did keep the stolen merchandise, I could never reveal the truth to anyone. Yes, I'd be willing to make that sort of arrangement." She cleared her throat. "How much would you want?"

"How about two thousand dollars apiece?" Cassidy suggested. "That's one month's salary for each of us, more or less; and it could take us a month to find new jobs if we got fired."

"Does that sound fair to you, Mrs. Maitland?"

"Yes, all right. But I couldn't get that much money until Monday morning . . ."

"Tell you what," Tinker said. "You trust us, we'll trust you. We won't even think about contacting the police until Monday noon; all you have to do is come in before then with the cash."

Kerry nodded. "Before noon on Monday," she said. "Two thousand dollars for each of you, in cash."

"Very good."

"May I leave now? I . . . I'm not feeling very well."

"Of course," Tinker said. "I'll just keep your driver's license, though, if you don't mind. As a sort of insurance." He took it out of its card pocket and then handed wallet, purse, and stolen items back to Kerry. "Until Monday, then, Mrs. Maitland."

"Yes. Until Monday." Hastily she put the merchandise into her purse.

Cassidy opened the door for her; she went into the hallway and around to the elevators. The first one that came was empty. She stepped inside, pushed the button for the main floor, and waited for the doors to close.

Then she relaxed, smiled, reached into her purse, took out her compact—which wasn't a compact at all—and opened it.

And switched off the miniature tape recorder concealed inside.

The tape had been recording ever since she entered the store, because she hadn't known at which point in her shoplifting spree Cassidy would appear. But it was a long-playing tape; the entire conversation in Tinker's office would be on it.

She couldn't wait to play that tape for her husband Jim. She couldn't wait to see the look on his face when she told him how she'd been shopping here six Saturdays ago and seen Cassidy apprehend and take away one of two well-dressed women; how that same woman had reappeared a half-hour later and Kerry had overheard her tell the friend that she'd "bought her way out of trouble"; how Kerry's suspicions of an extortion scheme had brought her back on several occasions to watch Cassidy surreptitiously—and watch the same thing happen again last week, with another shoplifter; and how she'd set out today to put an end to larceny by using a little larceny of her own.

Oh yes, she would enjoy telling Jim. It might just convince Police Captain James Maitland that he'd been wrong about his new young wife; that she shouldn't simply sit home like a lump in posh Forest Hills, living off her inheritance while he pursued a career. Maybe she could even become a policewoman. . . .

She smiled again as the elevator reached the main floor. No one accosted her on her way out of the store.

In the privacy of her richly furnished living room, Kerry laid the stolen ring, cufflinks, and perfume on the marble-topped coffee table and examined them. She would give them to Jim when he got home from the afternoon shift.

As she stared at the gleaming merchandise, she recalled the rather delicious thrill of stealing it. And a thought struck her. She didn't *have* to give Jim the—for some reason she relished the word—loot. She could simply pay Tinker and Cassidy their money, retrieve her driver's license and destroy the tape. If she could never reveal their extortion scheme, neither could Tinker or Cassidy reveal her crime.

The gold mantel clock ticked loudly, in rhythm with Kerry's pulse and her rapid, shallow breathing. She had always craved beautiful things—for what they were, not for their cash value. And to take them from time to time, simply take them in carefully and cunningly planned raids. . . . The idea was exhilarating. Sort of like Salome contemplating the head of John the Baptist—chilling, thrilling, and revolting, all at the same time.

She couldn't do it, of course. Not really.

Or could she?

Kerry remembered Cassidy's allusion to a tiger, a thief who blended in with his background so you hardly noticed him watching and waiting until he pounced. Then she remembered a story she had read as a girl, a story about a young man forced to choose between opening one of two identical doors; behind one was salvation in the form of a benign woman, while behind the other was danger in the form of a deadly tiger. The title of the story was "The Lady or the Tiger?"

"Which am I?" Kerry wondered aloud, staring into the blood-red depths of the ruby.

HERE LIES
ANOTHER BLACKMAILER

My Uncle Walter studied me across the massive oak desk in his library, looking at once irascible, anxious, and a little fearful. "I have some questions to ask you, Harold," he said at length, "and I want truthful answers, do you understand?"

"I am not in the habit of lying," I lied stiffly.

"No? To my mind your behavior has always left much to be desired, and has been downright suspect at times. But that is not the issue at hand, except indirectly. The issue at hand is this: where were you at eleven-forty last evening?"

"At eleven-forty? I was in bed, of course."

"You were not," my uncle said sharply. "Elsie saw you going downstairs at five minutes of eleven, fully dressed."

Elsie was the family maid, and much too nosy for her own good. She was also the only person who lived on this small estate except for me, Uncle Walter, and Aunt Pearl. I frowned and said, "I remember now. I went for a walk."

"At eleven P.M.?"

"I couldn't sleep and I thought the fresh air might help."

"Where did you go on this walk?"

"Oh, here and there. Just walking, you know."

"Did you leave the grounds?"

"Not that I recall."

"Did you go out by the old carriage house?"

"No," I lied.

My uncle was making an obvious effort to conceal his impatience. "You were out by the old carriage house, weren't you?"

"I've already said I wasn't."

"I saw you there, Harold. At least, I'm fairly certain I did. You were lurking in the oleander bushes."

"I do not lurk in bushes," I lied.

"*Somebody* was lurking in the bushes, and it couldn't have been anyone but you. Elsie and Aunt Pearl were both here in the house."

"May I ask a question?"

"What is it?"

"What were *you* doing out by the old carriage house at eleven-forty last night?"

Uncle Walter's face had begun to take on the unpleasant color of raw calf's liver. "What I was doing there is of no consequence. I want to know why you were there, and what you might have seen and heard."

"Was there something to see and hear, Uncle?"

"No, of course not. I just want to know—look here, Harold, what did you see and hear from those bushes?"

"I wasn't *in* them in the first place, so I couldn't have seen or heard anything, could I?"

Uncle Walter stood and began to pace the room, his hands folded behind his back. He looked like a pompous old lawyer, which is precisely what he was. Finally he came over to stand in front of my chair, glaring down at me. "You were not out by the carriage house at eleven-forty last night? You did not see anything and you did not hear anything at any time during your alleged walk?"

"No," I lied.

"I have no recourse but to accept your word, then. Actually it doesn't matter whether you were there or not, in one sense, because you refuse to admit it. I trust you will continue to refuse to admit it, to me and to anyone else."

"I don't believe I follow that, Uncle."

"You don't have to follow it. Very well, Harold, that's all."

I stood and left the library and went out to the sun porch at the rear of the house. When I was certain neither Elsie nor Aunt Pearl was about, I slipped out and hurried through the landscaped grounds to the old carriage house. The oleander bushes, where I had been lurking at eleven-forty the previous night, after following Uncle Walter from the house—I *had* gone for a short walk, and had noticed him sneaking out—were located along the southern wall of the building. I passed along parallel to them and around to the back, to the approximate spot where my uncle had stood talking to the man whom he had met there. They had spoken in low tones, of course, but in the summer stillness I had been able to hear every word. I had also been able to hear the muffled report that had abruptly terminated their conversation.

Now, what, I wondered, glancing around, *did Uncle Walter do with the body?*

The gunshot had startled me somewhat, and I had involuntarily rustled the bushes and therefore been forced to run when my uncle came to investigate. I had then hidden behind one of the privet hedges until I was certain he did not intend to search for me. Minutes later I slipped around by the carriage house again; but I had not been able to locate my uncle. So I returned to the privet hedge and waited, and twenty-five minutes later Uncle Walter had appeared and gone back to the house.

A half-hour or so is really not very much time in which to hide a dead man, so I found the body quite easily. It was concealed among several tall eucalyptus trees some sixty yards from the carriage house, covered with leaves and strips of bark. A rather unimaginative hiding place, to be sure, although it was no doubt intended to be temporary. Uncle Walter had given no prior consideration to body disposal, and so had hidden the corpse here until he could think of something more permanent to do with it.

I uncovered the dead man and studied him for a moment. He was small and slender, with sharp features and close-set eyes. In the same way my uncle looked exactly like what he was, so did this person look like what *he* was, or had been—a criminal, naturally. In his case, a blackmailer. And not at all a clever or cautious one, to have allowed Uncle Walter to talk him into the time and place of last night's rendezvous. What excuse had my uncle given him for the unconventionality of it all? Well, no matter. The man really had been quite stupid to have accepted such terms under any circumstances, and was now quite dead as a result.

Yet Uncle Walter was equally as stupid: first, to have put himself in a position where he could be blackmailed; and second, to have perpetrated a carelessly planned homicide on his own property. My uncle, however, was impulsive. He also had a predilection for beautiful blonde show girls, about which my Aunt Pearl knew nothing, and about which I also had known nothing until overhearing last evening's conversation. This was the reason he had been blackmailed. He had committed murder because the extortionist wanted more money than he had been getting for his continued silence—Uncle Walter was a notoriously tightfisted man.

It took me the better part of two hours to move the body. I am not particularly strong, and even though the dead man was small and light, it was a physical struggle to which I am not accustomed. At last, however, I had secreted the blackmailer's remains in what I considered to be quite a clever hiding place— one that was not even on my uncle's property.

Across the dry creek which formed the rear boundary line was a grove of trees, well into which I found a large decaying log, all that was left of a long-dead tree felled by insects or disease. At first glance it seemed to be solid, but upon inspection I discovered that it was hollow. I dragged the body to the log and managed to stuff it inside; then I covered all traces of the entombment.

Satisfied, I returned unobserved to the house, had a bath, and spent the remainder of the day reading in my room.

Uncle Walter was apoplectic. "What did you do with it?" he shouted at me. "What did you *do* with it?"

I looked at him innocently across his desk. It was just past eight the following morning, and he had summoned me from my room with furious poundings on the door. I was still in my robe and slippers.

"What did I do with what?" I asked.

"You know what!"

"I'm afraid I don't, Uncle."

"I know it was you, Harold, just as I knew all along it was you in the oleander bushes two nights ago. So you heard and saw everything, did you? Well, go ahead—admit it."

"I have nothing to admit."

He slapped the desk top with the palm of one hand. "Why did you move it? That's what I fail to comprehend."

"The conversation seems to be going around in circles," I said. "I really don't know what you're talking about, Uncle."

"Of course you know what I'm talking about! Harold—what did you do with it?"

"With what?"

"You know—" He caught himself, and his face was an interesting color bordering on mauve. "Why do you persist in lying to me? What are you up to?"

"I'm not up to anything," I lied.

"Harold . . ."

"If you're finished with me, I would like to get dressed."

"Yes, get dressed. And then you're coming with me."

"Where are we going?"

"Out to look for it. I want you along."

"What are we going to look for?"

He glared at me. "I'll find it," he said. "You can't have moved it far. I *will* find it, Harold!"

Of course he didn't.

I knocked on the library door late that evening and stepped inside. Uncle Walter was sitting at his desk, holding his head as if it pained him greatly; his face was gray, and I saw that there were heavy pouches under his eyes. The time, it seemed, was right.

When he saw me, the gray pallor modulated into crimson. He certainly did change color often, like a chameleon. "You," he said. "You!"

"Are you feeling all right, Uncle? You don't look very well."

"If you weren't a relative of mine, if you weren't—oh, what's the use? Harold, just tell me what you did with it. I just want to know that it's . . . safe. Do you understand?"

"Not really," I said. I looked at him steadily. "But I have the feeling that whatever it is you were looking for today *is* safe."

He brightened. "Are you sure?"

"One can never be sure about anything, can one?"

"What does that mean?"

I sat down and said, "You know, Uncle, I've been thinking. My monthly allowance is really rather small, and I wonder if you could see your way clear to raising it."

"So that's it."

"What's it?"

"What you're up to, why you keep lying to me and why you moved the . . . *it*. All I've done is trade one blackmailer for another, and my own nephew at that!"

"Blackmailer?" I managed to look shocked. "What a terrible thing to say, Uncle. I'm only asking for an increase in my monthly allowance. That's not the same thing at all, is it?"

He calmed down. "No," he said. "No, it isn't. Of course not. Very well, then, you shall have your increase. Now, where is it?"

"Where is what?" I asked.

"Now look here—"

"I still don't know what it is you're talking about," I said. "But then, if I weren't to get my increase—or if I were to get it and it should suddenly be revoked—I could find out what is going on. I could talk to Aunt Pearl, or even to the police . . ."

My uncle sighed resignedly. "You've made your point, Harold. I suppose the only important thing is that . . . *it* is safe, and you've already told me that much, haven't you? Well, how much of an increase do you want?"

"Triple the present sum, I think."

"One hundred and fifty dollars a month?"

"Yes."

"What are you going to do with that much money? You're only eleven years old!"

"I'll think of something, Uncle. I'm very clever, you know."

He closed his eyes. "All right, consider your allowance tripled, but you're never to request a single penny more. Not a single penny, Harold."

"Oh, I won't—not a single penny," I lied, and smiled inwardly. Unlike most everyone else of my age, I knew exactly what I was going to be when I grew up. . . .

BUTTERMILK

When Tarrant came home from the office, Fran was in the kitchen drinking a glass of buttermilk.

She greeted him perfunctorily as he entered, turning her face up for his kiss. But Tarrant didn't kiss her. Her upper lip was mustached with a thin, yellowish residue. *Lord,* he thought. He sat heavily on one of the kitchen chairs and rubbed his neck with an already damp pocket handkerchief.

"Why do you have to drink that stuff?" he asked.

"What stuff?"

"What stuff do you think?"

"Buttermilk? I like it."

"Well, I don't."

"It's just the thing in this heat."

Tarrant stood abruptly, went to the sink and turned on the cold water tap. It ran tepid. He cursed and shut it off again. Behind him Fran said, "You look flushed tonight."

"It's ninety-five, for God's sake!"

"You don't have to snap at me. I *know* it's ninety-five."

"You know," Tarrant said. "You know." He returned to the table.

"What would you like to eat?" Fran asked.

"Nothing. I'm not hungry."

"You'd better eat something. The Bensons and the Waverlys will be here at seven for bridge."

"Christ, not tonight!"

"Now, Stan, don't start in."

"It's too hot for company."

"It'll cool off later on."

"The hell it will. Cancel them, can't you? I'm not in the mood for bridge and polite chit-chat. I want to relax."

"I won't cancel it," Fran said peevishly. "You know how active Ida Benson and Jean Waverly are in the country club. If we want to get that membership—"

"To hell with the damn membership!"

"Stan, what's the *matter* with you tonight?"

"I don't like the Bensons or the Waverlys," Tarrant said, "that's what the matter is. They're boors, the lot of them."

"They happen to be very important people around here. Maybe it doesn't matter to you, but their friendship means a great deal to me and I'm not calling off the bridge game. Now stop acting like a child."

Tarrant glared at her for a moment, and then stood again. "I'm going outside for a while," he said.

On the patio, he sat in one of the lawn chairs beneath the gumberry tree. The white flagstones reflected the sun like a mirror; he closed his eyes. *My head feels like it's going to explode,* he thought. *Rat race at the office today, work backlogged, everybody chattering like a bunch of wind-up squirrels. Then the freeway traffic, horns braying, brakes screaming. Stop and go, stop and go. And this heat. Two months now, two months with no relief in sight . . .*

"Hey-o, Stan," a voice called.

Tarrant opened his eyes. Across the drive to his right was a waist-high privet hedge separating his property from that of his neighbor, Tom Nichols. Nichols was standing at the hedge, a bright blue baseball cap pulled down on his forehead. In one hand he held a tumbler filled with ice and clear liquid.

"Evening, Tom."

"Hot enough for you, boy?"

Tarrant's lips pulled in against his teeth. *You damned fool,*

*why do you have to keep asking that same trite question? Every
time I see you, it's the same stupid goddamn question.*

"Gin and tonic," Nichols said, raising the tumbler. "Want
a belt to cool off?"

Tarrant shook his head.

"Look like you could use one, boy."

"Not right now, thanks."

"Suit yourself. What time you want to leave in the morning?"

"What?"

"Tomorrow's Saturday. Golf day, remember?"

"I don't think I'll be playing tomorrow."

"Why not?"

"It's going to be hot again."

"Hell, we haven't missed a Saturday in two years."

Tarrant's temples began to pound. "What difference does
that make? There some kind of law that says we have to play
golf every Saturday morning? Is that what life is all about, banging a little white ball around every Saturday morning?"

Nichols said, frowning, "I thought you enjoyed the game."

"It's a great game. Just a wonderful frigging game."

"Well, if that's the way you feel—"

"Does it really matter to you how I feel?"

Nichols started away in a huff. Then he paused and looked
back across the hedge at Tarrant. "What the hell got into you all
of a sudden, Stan?"

Tarrant didn't answer. He rose from the lawn chair and
went back inside the house. Fran was shredding cabbage into a
colander, making cole slaw. "We'll eat in twenty minutes," she
said. "You'd better shower and get ready."

Tarrant went on into their bedroom. From his dresser he
took a thin cotton shirt and a pair of summer slacks, carried
them into the bathroom, stripped off his suit and sodden under-
wear, and then turned on the cold water in the shower.

After ten minutes under the spray, he began to feel a little
better. The pain in his temples had subsided. He toweled himself dry, dressed, ran a comb through his hair, and walked out
to the kitchen.

A large, beaded pitcher of buttermilk sat on the table.

Anger flared inside him. *Damn it, Fran,* he thought, *I told you about that stuff. Didn't I tell you about that stuff?* He turned on his heel, crossed the air-conditioned living room—air conditioner *still* wasn't working right—and sank into a chair and stared through the window at the street outside. Beautiful Shady Port: a sweltering sea of heat.

Fran came in. "Everything's on the table," she said.

"I told you before, I'm not hungry."

"Well, you have to eat."

"Why? Why do I have to eat?"

"I've had a hard day, Stan. You're not making it any easier."

"*You've* had a hard day? What about me? What about my day?"

"Oh, God, I don't want to argue."

"Who the hell is arguing?"

"What's the use?" Fran said, exasperated. "There's just no point in talking to you when you're like this." She retreated to the kitchen and slammed the door.

Tarrant sat and stared out the window a while longer. Then he got up and switched on the TV. The screen lit up immediately, but there was no picture; the set emitted a swelling hum that seemed to set up an answering vibration inside his head. He drove the palm of his hand against the Off button.

"Fran!" he shouted.

"What is it?"

"Come in here!"

She opened the kitchen door and looked in.

"What's the matter with this thing?" Tarrant demanded.

"The television? I don't know. It won't play."

"Why didn't you call a repairman?"

"I was going to, but I had so many other things to do today, it slipped my mind."

"Oh, that's fine, that's just great. What do I do for some relaxation this weekend?"

"Read a book or something," she said, and put the door between them again.

Tarrant ran his hands through his hair, then wiped them across the front of his shirt. His temples were throbbing again. *Why doesn't this headache go away?* Once more he sat down and looked out through the window.

Time passed. Tarrant sat motionless, breathing through his mouth. Fran came in after a while and began setting up the card table and laying out snacks. She said nothing to him.

The doorbell rang at exactly seven. Fran appeared from the bedroom; she had changed into a fashionable summer frock and fluffed her hair and applied makeup. She said to Tarrant, "They're here. Try to be civil, will you? This is important to me."

"To you," he said. "To you."

"Stan, please!"

"All right," he said.

Fran admitted the Bensons and the Waverlys. Tarrant shook hands with each of them and smiled until his jaws ached. *I don't want them here*, he thought the whole while. *I don't want anything to do with them, they're boors, they're snobs. I just want this headache to go away, and some rain, and some peace.*

"A scorcher today, wasn't it, Stan," Frank Benson said.

"Yes, a scorcher."

"Damnedest heat wave in the history of the state."

"Yes."

"Did you catch Barker's speech tonight, Stan?" Brian Waverly asked.

"Barker?"

"Sam Barker. You're backing him for assemblyman, aren't you? Every right-thinking person in the community is."

"Oh," Tarrant said. "Barker. Yes."

"Did you catch his speech on TV tonight?"

"No, our set isn't working."

"Too bad," Waverly said. "Fine speech."

"Damned fine speech," Benson agreed.

I don't care about Barker's speech, Tarrant thought. *I don't care one goddamn little bit about Barker or his goddamn speech.*

But he smiled and nodded and took the women's wraps and put them away in the hall closet. The pain in his head was furious.

The evening went badly. He and Fran were paired against the Bensons in the first rubber, the Waverlys kibitzing, and he could not keep his mind on his own cards, much less the bidding around the table. He played stupidly, sweating in spite of the air conditioning, ignoring Fran's annoyed glances.

They lost the rubber, of course, and the Waverlys took their places. Tarrant went into the kitchen and drank a glass of lukewarm water from the tap. After a few seconds Fran came in.

"What's *wrong* with you tonight?" she snapped. "You played like a novice and you bit poor Mrs. Benson's head off twice for no reason. Why can't you act decently tonight, of all nights? Don't you care about my feelings at all?"

Tarrant didn't respond. He opened the screen door and walked out onto the dark patio. It was quiet there; summer insects and the distant hum of an electric drill in somebody's workshop were the only sounds.

The temperature had dropped slightly, but the air was still choked with humidity. Tarrant lifted his face to the sky, drawing the heavy air into his lungs, his thoughts random and dreamlike. He held that position for more than a minute—until the gentle sucking sound reached his ears.

He jerked around and stared through the screen door. Fran was standing at the sink, head tilted back, eyes closed. Her expression in the bright light of the kitchen was ecstatic—hideously, obscenely ecstatic.

She was drinking a glass of buttermilk.

Tarrant's fingers knotted into fists, the nails digging into the flesh of his palms. Sweat flowed on his body; he had difficulty breathing. The pain in his head raged out of control. He trembled, trembled—

And suddenly the trembling stopped. Suddenly he was calm.

Through the screen he watched Fran as she smacked her lips over the last of the buttermilk, then rinsed the glass and went to the door to the living room. When she was gone he crossed the patio to the garage. It took him less than two minutes to remove his hunting rifle and a box of cartridges from the storage cabinet. Deliberately, he loaded the rifle. Then he put the rest of the cartridges in his pocket, left the garage, and reentered the kitchen.

The smell of buttermilk was overpowering . . .

MAN GOES BERSERK,
KILLS SIX PEOPLE

A Shady Port man went berserk last night and shot his wife, four guests, and a police officer to death with a hunting rifle. During the two-hour reign of terror, some fifty shots were exchanged before police SWAT team marksmen succeeded in mortally wounding Stanley L. Tarrant, 36.

Described by friends and neighbors as a quiet, easygoing person, Tarrant had no history of violent behavior. Authorities were at a loss to explain what triggered his murderous rampage. . . .

RETIREMENT

L ehman was relaxing on the balcony of his mountain cabin, smoking his pipe and watching the graceful silver thread of the river that curled through the redwoods in the valley below, when the knocking sounded at the front door.

The sudden intrusion made him frown. He hadn't been expecting anyone this afternoon, and almost no one dropped by without calling first, because he had made it known that he didn't like unexpected visitors. He considered staying where he was, ignoring the summons, but whoever it was was persistent. At length, he got up and went through the cabin and yanked the door open.

The man standing on the porch wore a toothy smile, a fancy new hairpiece, and a fifteen-hundred-dollar suit. His name was Dave Pardo. He'd come alone, Lehman saw, which was even more of a surprise than his coming at all. The big Cadillac limo parked next to Lehman's jeep was empty.

Pardo said, "Long time no see, Hal. What's it been? Four, five years?"

"Six," Lehman said.

"You look good—fit as ever."

"I keep myself in shape."

"All right if I come in, talk a while?"

Lehman stood aside to let Pardo enter, then closed the

door. Pardo glanced around at the rustic furnishings, the framed hunting prints on the unvarnished redwood walls. "Nice place you got here," he said. "Nice little hideaway."

"What's on your mind, Dave? You didn't come all the way up here just to say hello."

"No, you're right," Pardo said. "I need a favor."

Lehman relit his pipe, got it drawing evenly before he said, "I figured it was something like that."

"Fact is, I'm in a spot. I wouldn't ask you, there was anybody else I could trust."

"I'm out of the business," Lehman said. "Retired six years now. I'm getting old, Dave. Sixty-four my next birthday."

"Sixty-four's not old."

Lehman didn't say anything.

Pardo said, "We were pretty good friends once. I did favors for *you*, remember? Plenty of favors."

"I remember."

"I'm not asking you to do this for nothing," Pardo said. "Your usual fee, plus five as a bonus. Hell, make it ten."

"Money doesn't mean that much to me any more."

"Hal, listen—"

"I'm retired and I want to stay retired. I got enough put away to live comfortably. And this cabin here, these mountains—I never been any place I liked better. I don't travel any more, I don't go anywhere except four miles down to the village for groceries once a week. I don't *want* to go anywhere, not even for one day. Peace and quiet, that's all I'm interested in. You understand?"

"Sure, sure. But this spot I'm in, it's a bad one. There's a power struggle going on, heads rolling left and right, people switching sides. That's why I can't trust anybody."

Lehman's pipe had gone out again. He paused to touch another match to the bowl.

"It's between Nick Gault and me," Pardo said.

"I figured. Nick's the favor you want?"

"Yeah. Nick."

"He and I were friends once, too, you know."

"Sure, I know. But I told you, I'm desperate. I got nobody

else to turn to. Besides, you worked for anybody had your price in the old days. You never let personal feelings stand in the way."

"This isn't the old days."

"You could get to him, Hal. Easy. The way things are now, you're about the only one who can."

Lehman smoked and said nothing.

Pardo said, "Give it some thought, will you? At least do that much for me."

". . . All right, that much."

"Good. Good."

"How about a drink, Dave? You look like you could use one."

"Yeah, I could."

"Still bourbon-and-water?"

"Right."

Lehman crossed into the kitchenette, mixed a bourbon-and-water, and brought it back to Pardo. "Aren't you having one?" Pardo asked him.

"Little early for me. You want to come out on the balcony, take a look at my view? Nice out there this time of day. Good place to talk business."

Pardo's eyes brightened. "Then you'll do it?"

"Maybe. Come on."

They went out onto the balcony. Lehman asked, "Some view, isn't it?"

"Nice. Nice, Hal."

"It's one of the reasons I fell in love with this place, first time I saw it. You can see for miles from up here."

Lehman moved over to the far railing. Pardo joined him, looked over and down, and said, "Jesus, there's nothing but empty air down there."

"Five-hundred-foot drop," Lehman said. "You can't tell from in front, on account of all the trees, but this cabin's built right on the edge of the mountain."

"Yeah. Listen, about Nick—"

Lehman clapped him on the back, said, "Relax, Dave, enjoy the view," and let his hand remain on Pardo's shoulder.

Pardo lifted his glass, started to drink from it. He was standing with his thighs touching the top bar of the railing.

Lehman backed off a step, slid his hand down into the middle of Pardo's back, and shoved hard.

Pardo's arms flailed as he pitched forward. The glass flew from his hand, arced outward into space. An instant later, with an assist from the railing, Pardo followed it—over and down.

He fell in long, twisting turns, screaming the whole way. But there was no one to hear him except Lehman, and the sound of screaming had never bothered him in the slightest.

Lehman stood looking down until Pardo disappeared into the sea of greens and browns far below. Then he went inside to the telephone, took a card from his wallet and dialed the long-distance number written on it.

A low, wary voice said, "Hello?"

"Nick?"

"Yeah. Who's this?"

"Hal Lehman."

"Hal! You change your mind about my proposition?"

"As a matter of fact," Lehman said, "I did."

"Hey, that's good to hear. But how come? Last time we talked, you made a thing about not leaving that retirement place of yours even for one day."

"I don't have to leave," Lehman said. "The job's already done."

"What?"

"I'll explain when you bring my fee and the bonus you mentioned. You might send a removal team at some point too. No hurry, though. No hurry at all."

ONE OF THOSE DAYS

R oehampton Estates was one of those residential districts where the homes are of redwood or stone and glass, the yards are rustically landscaped, and the streets wind and curl and double back on themselves through wooded acreage. In a phrase, Roehampton Estates was middle-class affluence.

I parked my rental car in front of 244 Tamarack Drive a few minutes before eleven of a pleasant spring morning. Stepped out, straightening my tie, and stood for a moment looking at the chunk of lacquered redwood suspended on gold chains between two redwood posts at the foot of the drive. *The Curwoods*—and below that, *Peggy and Glen*—had been etched into the wood, and the words had then been painted with a gilt that would probably glow in the dark. I smiled. Good old Glen, I thought.

I followed the drive to a path and the path to an arbored porch grown thickly with honeysuckle. The house was low and made of redwood, with a fieldstone facade—nice looking and well kept up. Next to the door was a plaque similar to the one by the drive, but much smaller, and under that was the doorbell. Twenty seconds after I pushed the bell the door opened and a woman looked out.

She was about thirty, tall and slender, wearing a bulky orange sweater and black flared slacks. Honey-blonde hair curled under at the nape of her neck. Very attractive lady. Ingenuous blue eyes looked at me questioningly.

"Yes?"

"Peggy? Peggy Curwood?"

"Yes?"

"You're even prettier than I expected."

"I beg your pardon?"

I laughed. "Is Glen home?"

"No, he's at work."

"Sure he is," I said. "It's the middle of the week, right? I don't keep regular hours myself and sometimes I forget that others do."

"Are you a friend of my husband's?"

"You might say that," I told her, grinning. "Glen and I have known each other for more years than either of us cares to remember. I haven't seen him since . . . oh, way before the two of you were married."

Her eyes widened. "You're not . . . Larry? Larry Byers?"

"None other than," I said.

"Well, for—! Well, we thought you were in South America, in Maracaibo! I mean, Glen said the last he'd heard a couple of years ago, you were down there on some of kind of wildcat oil deal."

"So I was. Right up until last week."

She touched her hair in that self-conscious way women have, looking at me with color in her cheeks and her head cocked a little to one side. "I just can't believe it," she said. "Larry Byers! Glen's told me a lot about you."

"All of it good, I hope."

"Well, not *all* good."

"That's Glen for you. I'm not sure if I ought to be flattered or insulted."

"Flattered, by all means," Peggy said. "How did you find out where we live? You and Larry haven't been in touch in so long . . ."

"Oh, I've got connections."

She had a nice laugh. "Are you back in California to stay now? Or just visiting, or what?"

"Fund-raising, you might say. Arranging finances for a venture in Saudi Arabia."

"Oil again?"

"Uh-huh."

"What happened in Venezuela?"

"Politics," I said.

"Oh, I'm sorry."

I shrugged philosophically. "It's a hard world sometimes."

"Well, you *can* stay for a while, can't you? You don't have to rush off? I'll phone Glen—"

"I'm free and clear the rest of the day," I said. "But instead of you phoning him, why don't I just wait until he gets home and surprise him face to face? That is, if you wouldn't mind."

"Of course I wouldn't, Mr. Byers—"

"Larry."

"Peggy."

"Now that that's settled," I said, "you don't suppose I could talk you into a cup of coffee, do you?"

She put a hand to her mouth. "Well, will you look at me! I'm sorry, Larry, please come in. I didn't mean to make you stand out there all this time like a brush salesman or something."

We went into the living room with a beamed ceiling and a big fieldstone fireplace. The furniture was newish, tasteful, on the expensive side. Ornate glass-doored cabinets contained what looked to be genuine jade figurines and other gew-gaws.

"You know," Peggy said, "Glen just won't *believe* you're back in California. He thought when you turned down that professional baseball contract to go globe-trotting for oil, he'd never see you again."

"He probably wouldn't have if I hadn't found out he married this nice blonde lady who also happens to be a terrific cook. I haven't had a good home-cooked steak dinner in years."

She laughed again. "Steak later, coffee now. I put some fresh on just before you came. How do you take it?"

"With cream, no sugar."

"I won't be a minute. Make yourself comfortable."

I wandered around the room, listening to her make domestic noises in the kitchen. After a couple of minutes she came back with two cups of coffee and handed me one. It was good coffee.

"Nice place you have here," I said. "Glen must be doing pretty well these days."

"Yes, he is. A home like this is what we've always wanted, so as soon as we could afford it, we bought it."

"Is the rest of the place as impressive as this room?"

"Would you like to take the guided tour?"

"That I would."

She conducted me through the house. In addition to the living room and kitchen, there was a dining room, three bedrooms, a den, a family room, two and a half baths, and a garage workshop. The master bedroom impressed me the most; it was full of all sorts of interesting furniture and things.

When we were back in the living room, Peggy said, "Now then. Suppose you sit down and tell me all about South America."

"I'll do that very thing. But first, why don't I run down to that shopping center I noticed and pick up some wine and three fat steaks for supper?"

She started to say something, but I put up a staying hand. "No arguments, now," I said. "I insist." And I started for the door.

Peggy lifted the bottom of her bulky sweater and reached underneath. What was in her hand when it reappeared stopped me in my tracks. It was a little pearl-handled automatic.

"That's far enough," she said coolly.

"Hey! Hey, Peggy, what's the idea?"

"You know what the idea is."

"No, no I don't—"

"Let me see your wallet."

"What for?"

"Put it on the coffee table. Right now."

I didn't have much choice; the little automatic was steady in her hand. I put my wallet on the table, and she picked it up and flipped the card section open to look at my driver's license.

Then she set the wallet down again and said, "Now empty your pockets, Mr. Reardon. All of them."

No choice in that, either. The jig, as they say, was up.

Her eyes were glacial as she watched me transfer what was in my pockets to the table. "Four of my best jade pieces," she said. "And my emerald pin and birthstone ring. And the fifty-dollar bill from my dresser. Well, I thought so. You slipped all of these things into your pockets while I made coffee and while I showed you the house."

I sighed and said nothing.

"Sit down on the couch," she said. "Put your hands in your lap where I can see them."

I did as I was told. "Okay, Mrs. Curwood. But tell me this: How did you know?"

"The real Larry Byers was never offered a professional base-ball contract. He never even played baseball."

"You set me up?"

"Let's just say I had a good idea what your game was."

"But how? I thought I followed your lead on this Byers long-lost pretty well. How did you figure what kind of con I was putting on you?"

She moved across to her telephone. "I'm very close to my husband's work," she said.

"Huh?"

She dialed a number with her free hand. After a moment, watching me and smiling a little, she said into the receiver, "Yes—I'd like to speak to Captain Glen Curwood, please. Of the bunco squad."

I closed my eyes.

It was one of *those* days.

DON'T SPEND IT ALL
IN ONE PLACE

Harry was slicing lemons behind the bar when the kid
came in and told him it was a stickup.

Carefully, Harry put down the saw knife he'd been using
and wiped his hands on his apron. He looked at the kid standing
in front of the cocktail slot, his hands in the pocket of his thin
cotton jacket, his white face pinched and sweating.

"I don't see any gun," Harry said.

"I've got one, all right." But there was no conviction in the
kid's voice.

"You better show it to me," Harry said, "and you better do
it quick. Because if you ain't got one, I'm going to come around
and kick you out of here on your ass."

The kid tried to stare Harry down. He had funny eyes,
bright and murky at the same time. But Harry didn't flinch;
there wasn't much that he was afraid of.

"All right," Harry said after a few seconds, and he started
over to where the flap was up at the near end of the bar.

The kid turned and ran.

Harry watched him run out through the door and off down
the street. Then he grinned to himself and went back to slicing
lemons.

A little while later one of his regular customers, a retired shoemaker named Irv, came in. Irv sat at the bar and ordered a beer. Harry poured it for him.

"Little commotion down the street," Irv said.

"That so? What happened?"

"Kid held up old man Dowd at the liquor store."

"What kid?"

"How do I know what kid? Some kid, that's all."

"They catch him?"

"Not yet."

"How much did he get?"

"Fifty bucks," Irv said. "Big deal."

Harry started to laugh.

"What so funny?" Irv asked him.

Harry told him what had happened earlier.

Irv drank some of his beer. "Must have been the same kid."

"Sure," Harry said. He was still laughing. "I'll bet he scared the shorts off of old man Dowd. And he didn't even have a gun."

"Not everybody's big and brave like you, Harry."

"No," Harry said, "and that's a fact."

Harry had a nice crowd that night, but it thinned out shortly after ten. By ten-thirty, the place was empty.

He didn't hear the front door open. He was washing glasses in the stainless-steel sink and the water splashing made a lot of noise. So he wasn't aware anyone had come in until he looked up and saw the kid with the white face standing there in front of him.

A slow grin stretched Harry's mouth. "Well, well," he said.

The kid didn't say anything. He had both hands in the pocket of his cotton jacket, as he had that afternoon. His funny eyes were even brighter and more murky now.

"I see you had a little better luck down the street today," Harry said.

"That's right," the kid said in his high-pitched voice. He was watching Harry intently.

"What'd it do? Give you enough guts to come back and try me again?"

"Not exactly."

"I hear you got fifty bucks off old man Dowd," Harry said. He started to laugh again. "Don't spend it all in one place."

"But I already did," the kid said. "I spent it all in one place, all right."

"That so?"

"I spent it on this," the kid said.

He took the gun from his jacket pocket and shot Harry three times in the chest. Harry didn't have time to stop laughing before he died.

The kid was sitting on the floor, cradling the gun in both arms, crooning to it, when the beat cop came running in a minute later.

CACHE AND CARRY
A "Nameless Detective" / Sharon McCone Story

(With Marcia Muller)

"**H** ello?"

"'Wolf'? It's Sharon McCone."

"Well! Been a while, Sharon. How are you?"

"I've been better. Are you busy?"

"No, no, I just got home. What's up?"

"I've got a problem and I thought you might be able to help."

"If I can. Professional problem?"

"The kind you've run into before."

"Oh?"

"One of those things that *seem* impossible but that you know has to have a simple explanation."

". . ."

"'Wolf,' are you there?"

"I'm here. The poor man's Sir Henry Merrivale."

"Who's Sir Henry Merrivale?"

"Never mind. Tell me your tale of woe."

"Well, one of All Souls' clients is a small outfit in the Outer Mission called Neighborhood Check Cashing. You know, one of those places that cashes third-party or social-security checks for local residents who don't have bank accounts of their own or easy access to a bank. We did some legal work for them a year or so ago, when they first opened for business."

"Somebody rip them off?"

"Yes. For two thousand dollars."

"Uh-huh. When?"

"Sometime this morning."

"Why did you and All Souls get called in on a police matter?"

"The police were called first but they couldn't come up with any answers. So Jack Harvey, Neighborhood's owner and manager, contacted me. But I haven't come up with any answers either."

"Go ahead, I'm listening."

"There's no way anyone could have gotten the two thousand dollars out of Neighborhood's office. And yet, if the money is still hidden somewhere on the premises, the police couldn't find it and neither could I."

"Mmm."

"Only one of two people could have taken it—unless Jack Harvey himself is responsible, and I don't believe that. If I knew which one, I might have an idea of what happened to the money. Or vice versa. But I don't have a clue either way."

"Let's have the details."

"Well, cash is delivered twice a week—Mondays and Thursdays—by armored car at the start of the day's business. It's usually five thousand dollars, unless Jack requests more or less. Today it was exactly five thousand."

"Not a big operation, then."

"No. Jack's also an independent insurance broker; the employees help him out in that end of the business too."

"His employees are the two who could have stolen the money?"

"Yes. Art DeWitt, the bookkeeper, and Maria Chavez, the cashier. DeWitt's twenty-five, single, lives in Daly City. He's studying business administration nights at City College. Chavez is nineteen, lives with her family in the Mission. She's planning to get married next summer. They both seem to check out as solid citizens."

"But you say one of them has to be guilty. Why?"

"Opportunity. Let me tell you what happened this morning. The cash was delivered as usual, and Maria Chavez entered the amount in her daily journal, then put half the money in the till and half in the safe. Business for the first hour and a half was light; only one person came in to cash a small check: Jack Harvey's cousin, whom he vouches for."

"So Chavez couldn't have passed the money to him or another accomplice."

"No. At about ten-thirty a local realtor showed up wanting to cash a fairly large check: thirty-five hundred dollars. Harvey doesn't usually like to do that, because Neighborhood runs short before the next cash delivery. Besides, the fee for cashing a large check is the same as for a small one; he stands to lose on large transactions. But the realtor is a good friend, so he okayed it. When Chavez went to cash the check, there was only five hundred dollars in the till."

"Did DeWitt also have access to the till?"

"Yes."

"Any way either of them could have slipped out of the office for even a few seconds?"

"No. Harvey's desk is by the back door and he was sitting there the entire time."

"What about through the front?"

"The office is separated from the customer area by one of those double Plexiglas security partitions and a locked security door. The door operates by means of a buzzer at Harvey's desk. He didn't buzz anybody in or out."

"Could the two thousand have been removed between the time the police searched and you were called in?"

"No way. When the police couldn't find it in the office, they body-searched DeWitt and had a matron do the same with Chavez. The money wasn't on either of them. Then, after the cops left, Jack told his employees they couldn't take anything away from the office except Chavez's purse and DeWitt's briefcase, both of which he searched again, personally."

"Do either DeWitt or Chavez have a key to the office?"

"No."

"Which means the missing money is still there."

"Evidently. But *where*, 'Wolf'?"

"Describe the office to me."

"One room, with an attached lavatory that doubles as a supply closet. Table, with a desktop copier, postage scale, postage meter. A big Mosler safe; only Harvey has the combination. Three desks: Jack's, next to the back door; DeWitt's in the middle; Chavez's next to the counter behind the partition, where the till is. Desks have standard stuff on them—adding machines, a typewriter on Chavez's, family photos, stack trays, staplers, pen sets. Everything you'd expect to find."

"Anything you *wouldn't* expect to find?"

"Not unless you count some lurid romance novels that Chavez likes to read on her lunch break."

"Did anything unusual happen this morning, before the shortage was discovered?"

"Not really. The toilet backed up and ruined a bunch of supplies, but Jack says that's happened three or four times before. Old plumbing."

"Uh-huh."

"You see why I'm frustrated? There just doesn't seem to be any clever hidey-hole in that office. And Harvey's already starting to tear his hair. Chavez and DeWitt resent the atmosphere of suspicion; they're nervous, too, and have both threatened to quit. Harvey doesn't want to lose the one that isn't guilty, anymore than he wants to lose his two thousand dollars."

"How extensive was the search you and the police made?"

"About as extensive as you can get."

"Desks gone over top to bottom, drawers taken out?"

"Yes."

"Underside of the legs checked?"

"Yes."

"Same thing with all the chairs?"

"To the point of removing cushions and seat backs."

"The toilet backing up—any chance that could be connected?"

"I don't see how. Harvey and I both looked it over pretty carefully. The sink and the rest of the plumbing, too."

"What about the toilet paper roll?"

"I checked it. Negative."

"The extra supplies?"

"Negative."

"Chavez's romance novels—between the pages?"

"I thought of that. Negative."

"Personal belongings?"

"All negative. Including Jack Harvey's. I went through his on the idea that DeWitt or Chavez might have thought to use him as a carrier."

"The office equipment?"

"Checked and rechecked. Copier, negative. Chavez's typewriter, negative. Postage meter and scale, negative. Four adding machines, negative. Stack trays—"

"Wait a minute, Sharon. *Four* adding machines?"

"That's right."

"Why four, with only three people?"

"DeWitt's office machine jammed and he had to bring his own from home."

"When did that happen?"

"It jammed two days ago. He brought his own yesterday."

"Suspicious coincidence, don't you think?"

"I did at first. But I checked both machines, inside and out. Negative."

"Did either DeWitt or Chavez bring anything else to the office in recent days that they haven't brought before?"

"Jack says no."

"Then we're back to DeWitt's home adding machine."

"'Wolf,' I told you—"

"What kind is it? Computer type, or the old-fashioned kind that runs a tape?"

"The old-fashioned kind."

"Did you run a tape on it? Or on the office machine that's supposed to be jammed?"

". . . No. No, I didn't."

"Maybe you should. Both machines are still in the office, right?"

"Yes."

"Why don't you have another look at them? Run tapes on

both, see if the office model really is jammed—or if maybe it's DeWitt's home model that doesn't work the way it should."

"And if it's the home model, have it taken apart piece by piece."

"Right."

"I'll call Harvey and have him meet me at Neighborhood right away."

"Let me know, huh? Either way?"

"You bet I will."

"'Wolf,' hi. It's Sharon."

"You sound chipper. Good news?"

"Yes, thanks to you. You were right about the adding machines. I ran a tape on DeWitt's office model and it worked fine. But the one he brought from home didn't, for a damned good reason."

"Which is?"

"Its tape roll was a dummy. Hollow, made of metal and wound with just enough paper tape to make it look like the real thing. So real neither the police nor I thought to remove and examine it before. The missing money was inside."

"So DeWitt must have been planning the theft for some time."

"That's what he confessed to the police a few minutes ago. He made the dummy roll in his workshop at home; took him a couple of weeks. It was in his home machine when he brought that in yesterday. This morning he slipped the roll out and put it into his pocket. While Maria Chavez was in the lavatory and Jack Harvey was occupied on the phone, he lifted the money from the till and pocketed that too. He went into the john after Maria came out and hid the money in the dummy roll. Then, back at his desk, he put the fake roll into his own machine, which he intended to take home with him this evening. It was his bad luck—and Jack's good luck—that the realtor came in with such a large check to cash."

"I suppose he intended to doctor the books to cover the theft."

"So he said. You know, 'Wolf,' it's too bad DeWitt didn't apply his creative talents to some legitimate enterprise. His cache-and-carry scheme was really pretty clever."

"What kind of scheme?"

"Cache and carry. C-a-c-h-e."

". . ."

"Was that a groan I heard?"

"McCone, if you're turning into a rogue detective, call somebody else next time you come up against an impossible problem. Call Sir Henry Merrivale."

"What do you mean, a rogue detective?"

"The worst kind there is. A punslinger."

THE KILLING

Martin Coe was a monolithic individual, with whisky-veined features and eyes as warm as frozen Alaskan tundra. In the month I had known him, he had never openly displayed emotion of any kind—until this very minute. Now, he leaned forward across the table, staring at me with incredulity. "What did you say?"

"How would you like it," I repeated, "if your wife were suddenly to die?"

He glanced around as if he were afraid someone had overheard us; but except for ourselves, two barmen, and three elderly men at a table across the room, the lounge of the Warm Springs Country Club was empty. Coe put his gaze back on me.

"Just what are you suggesting, Foster?"

"I was merely speculating."

"I . . . don't care for that sort of speculation."

"Don't you?" I asked him. "If Sondra were dead, you'd have control of her money. And of course, you'd be free to marry Angela."

Coe's mouth dropped open.

"Oh, yes, I know about Angela," I said. "A lovely young woman. So much more desirable than Sondra."

He continued to stare at me for several seconds; then,

jerkily, he raised his glass and drank half of his bourbon-and-water in a single swallow: He was trying to regain control of himself and of the situation, but I had the ball now and I intended to keep it.

I said, "Frail, middle-aged women are forever dying, you know. Accidents, heart seizures, suicide—there are hundreds of causes. Or should I say ways and means?"

Coe seemed to be having difficulty breathing. "Who are you, Foster? You're not the financial consultant you claim to be. And you didn't just happen to strike up a conversation with me four weeks ago."

"Right on both counts," I said, and smiled.

"Well? Who *are* you?"

I shrugged. "Let's just say I'm an eliminator of problems, a remover of burdens."

"A killer for hire. A professional assassin." His tone of voice said more than the words; it said that instead of being appalled or outraged, he was interested. Very interested.

"I don't care for either of those terms," I said, "but I suppose they're accurate enough."

"How did you get into a private country club like this? You can't be a member!"

I laughed. "No, but I have friends who are. When I'm not working I lead a rather normal upper-class existence."

"Am I to understand you're offering me your . . . services?"

"You may presume so, yes."

We watched each other for a time. Then Coe said, "You know what I ought to do, don't you?"

"What's that?"

"Turn you in to the police."

"Is that what you *intend* to do?"

"No," he said, his eyes fixed on mine.

"I didn't think so. Of course, if you did call the police, I would simply deny everything. I have no criminal record, an impeccable background, and a high credit rating. Your word against mine, you see?"

It was Coe's turn to smile now, but there was no humor in

the cold wastes of his eyes. "You must have researched me pretty carefully," he said.

"Oh, I did."

"How did you get my name as a potential client?"

"I have friends here, as I said."

"Scouts, is that it?"

"If you like."

He took out a thin, expensive panatela, snipped off the end with a pair of gold clippers, lighted it with a thin gold lighter. Through a cloud of fragrant smoke he asked, "How much?"

"I like a man who gets right down to business," I said. "Ten thousand. Half in advance, half after completion of the contract."

"I'll have to consider it," Coe said. He was his old self now: calm, assured, coldly calculating. "I never make hasty decisions."

"Take your time."

"Tomorrow night, here, at nine?"

"Fine," I said. "If your answer is yes, bring the five thousand in cash, small bills—and a complete floor plan of your house."

My second drink and Martin Coe arrived simultaneously at nine the following evening. When the waiter drifted away with Coe's order for a bourbon-and-water, I said, "Right on time. To the minute, in fact."

"I make it a policy to be punctual for appointments."

"An admirable trait."

"I also make it a policy never to hedge when I've made up my mind." He patted the breast pocket of his suit coat. "Five thousand dollars, I believe you said."

"I did. You can give it to me a little later, in private. Did you bring the floor plan?"

"Yes. In the envelope with the money."

"Excellent."

He leaned forward. "When will you do it?"

"Whenever you prefer."

"This coming Thursday night."

"The sooner, the better, eh?"

"Yes. Any time after eleven. Sondra is always asleep by eleven. And I'll be here from eight o'clock on, attending our monthly board meeting and socializing afterward, as I customarily do."

I nodded. "You'll make sure your wife is alone in the house?"

"Of course. Thursday is the houseman's regular day off, and I can arrange to have the cook away for the evening without arousing suspicion."

"What about the dogs?" I asked.

"You know about them, too, do you?"

"Naturally."

"I'll see that they don't give you any trouble. Anything else?"

"Yes. Leave a door open for me."

"Wouldn't it be better to break in?"

"It would if I were going to make it look as though she surprised a burglar."

"But you're not?"

"No," I said. "Did you know that one out of every five falls in the home proves fatal?"

Coe smiled icily. "That's an interesting statistic."

"Isn't it?"

"There's a service porch at the rear," he said. "You'll see just where when you look at the floor plan. I'll leave that door open."

I nodded again and matched his smile with one of my own.

A few minutes before midnight on Thursday, I parked my car in a copse of bay and pepper trees near the east boundary wall of Coe's estate. I pulled on a pair of thin, pliable gloves, then climbed the wall and dropped down on the other side.

Moving cautiously, I made my way across the grounds. There was no sign of the three vicious Dobermans that normally ran free. Ahead, the house—a bulky two-story Colonial—loomed dark and silent against the night sky, no lights showing anywhere.

I located the service porch, and when I tried the door it opened under my hand. I slipped inside, stood listening for a few seconds. Silence.

Mentally, I again studied the floor plan Coe had given me. Then I took the pencil flashlight from my pocket, shielded the beam with my left hand as I switched it on, and moved through the back rooms to the vaulted gloom of the entrance hall. I paused there, at the foot of a curving staircase, to listen again. It might only have been my imagination but I thought I could hear, from somewhere above, the faint rasp of a woman's snoring.

Pleasant dreams, Mrs. Coe, I thought, smiling. And I turned away from the staircase to enter Martin Coe's private study.

It took me less than fifteen minutes to locate and open his wall safe, one of those vault types with a recessed dial. Inside, I found seven thousand dollars in cash, better than fifteen thousand in negotiable bonds, and another ten thousand or so in diamond jewelry.

Three minutes after I had slipped all of these items into my overcoat pockets, I was once again moving quickly across the empty grounds. And wishing as I went that I could see Martin Coe's face when he came home from the club to find his wife still alive and his safe cleaned out. The cold ruthlessness of the man had rankled me from the beginning; it would be a pleasure watching him deal with having been both robbed and flimflammed.

One can't have everything, though. I would have to settle for the satisfaction of a job well done and well paid for—a job worthy of the talents of one of the best confidence men in the business.

You can steal anything from anybody with a little patience and the proper approach. My father had told me that just before he retired to the French Riviera in 1966, after thirty years of successfully practicing what he preached.

It's a shame that more children don't listen to their fathers' advice in these trying times. . . .

BLACK WIND

It was one of those freezing late-November nights, just before the winter snows, when a funny east wind comes howling down out of the mountains and across Woodbine Lake a quarter mile from the village. The sound that wind makes is something hellish, full of screams and wailings that can raise the hackles on your neck if you're not used to it. In the old days the Indians who used to live around here called it a "black wind"; they believed that it carried the voices of evil spirits, and that if you listened to it long enough it could drive you mad.

Well, there are a lot of superstitions in our part of upstate New York; nobody pays much mind to them in this modern age. Or if they do, they won't admit it even to themselves. The fact is, though, that when the black wind blows the local folks stay pretty close to home and the village, like as not, is deserted after dusk.

That was the way it was on this night. I hadn't had a customer in my diner in more than an hour, since just before seven o'clock, and I had about decided to close up early and go on home. To a glass of brandy and a good hot fire.

I was pouring myself a last cup of coffee when the headlights swung into the diner's parking lot.

They whipped in fast, off the county highway, and I heard the squeal of brakes on the gravel just out front. Kids, I thought, because that was the way a lot of them drove, even around here—fast and a little reckless. But it wasn't kids. It turned out instead to be a man and a woman in their late thirties, strangers, both of them bundled up in winter coats and mufflers, the woman carrying a big fancy alligator purse.

The wind came in with them, shrieking and swirling. I could feel the numbing chill of it even in the few seconds the door was open; it cuts through you like the blade of a knife, that wind, right straight to the bone.

The man clumped immediately to where I was behind the counter, letting the woman close the door. He was handsome in a suave, barbered city way; but his face was closed up into a mask of controlled rage.

"Coffee," he said. The word came out in a voice that matched his expression—hard and angry, like a threat.

"Sure thing. Two coffees."

"One coffee," he said. "Let her order her own."

The woman had come up on his left, but not close to him—one stool between them. She was nice-looking in the same kind of made-up, city way. Or she would have been if her face wasn't pinched up worse than his; the skin across her cheekbones was stretched so tight it seemed ready to split. Her eyes glistened like a pair of wet stones and didn't blink at all.

"Black coffee," she said to me.

I looked at her, at him, and I started to feel a little uneasy. There was a kind of savage tension between them, thick and crackling; I could feel it like static electricity. I wet my lips, not saying anything, and reached behind me for the coffee pot and two mugs.

The man said, "I'll have a ham-and-cheese sandwich on rye bread. No mustard, no mayonnaise; just butter. Make it to go."

"Yes, sir. How about you, ma'am?"

"Tuna fish on white," she said thinly. She had close-cropped blonde hair, wind-tangled under a loose scarf; she kept brushing at it with an agitated hand. "I'll eat it here."

"No, she won't," the man said to me. "Make it to go, just like mine."

She threw him an ugly look. "I want to eat here."

"Fine," he said—to me again; it was as if she wasn't there. "But I'm leaving in five minutes, as soon as I drink my coffee. I want that ham-and-cheese ready by then."

"Yes, sir."

I finished pouring out the coffee and set the two mugs on the counter. The man took his, swung around, and stomped over to one of the tables. He sat down and stared at the door, blowing into the mug, using it to warm his hands.

"All right," the woman said, "all right, all right. All right." Four times like that, all to herself. Her eyes had cold little lights in them now, like spots of foxfire.

I said hesitantly, "Ma'am? You still want the tuna sandwich to eat here?"

She blinked then, for the first time, and focused on me. "No. To hell with it. I don't want anything to eat." She caught up her mug and took it to another of the tables, two away from the one he was sitting at.

I went down to the sandwich board and got out two pieces of rye bread and spread them with butter. The stillness in there had a strained feel, made almost eerie by the constant wailing outside. I could feel myself getting more jittery as the seconds passed.

While I sliced ham I watched the two of them at the tables—him still staring at the door, drinking his coffee in quick angry sips; her facing the other way, her hands fisted in her lap, the steam from her cup spiraling up around her face. Well-off married couple from New York City, I thought: they were both wearing the same type of expensive wedding ring. On their way to a weekend in the mountains, maybe, or up to Canada for a few days. And they'd had a hell of a fight over something, the way married people do on long tiring drives; that was all there was to it.

Except that that *wasn't* all there was to it.

I've owned this diner thirty years and I've seen a lot of folks come and go in that time; a lot of tourists from the city, with all sorts of marital problems. But I'd never seen any like these two. That tension between them wasn't anything fresh-born, wasn't just the brief and meaningless aftermath of a squabble. No, there was real hatred on both sides—the kind that builds and builds, seething, over long bitter weeks or months or even years. The kind that's liable to explode some day.

Well, it wasn't really any of my business. Not unless the blowup happened in here, it wasn't, and that wasn't likely. Or so I kept telling myself. But I was a little worried just the same. On a night like this, with that damned black wind blowing and playing hell with people's nerves, anything could happen. Anything at all.

I finished making the sandwich, cut it in half, and plastic-bagged it. Just as I slid it into a paper sack, there was a loud banging noise from across the room that made me jump half a foot; it sounded like a pistol shot. But it had only been the man slamming his empty mug down on the table.

I took a breath, let it out silently. He scraped back his chair as I did that, stood up, and jammed his hands into his coat pockets. Without looking at her, he said to the woman, "You pay for the food," and started past her table toward the rest-rooms in the rear.

She said, "Why the hell should I pay for it?"

He paused and glared back at her. "You've got all the money."

"I've got all the money? Oh, that's a laugh. *I've* got all the money!"

"Go on, keep it up." Then in a louder voice, as if he wanted to make sure I heard, he said, "Bitch." And stalked away from her.

She watched him until he was gone inside the corridor leading to the restrooms; she was as rigid as a chunk of wood. She sat that way for another five or six seconds, until the wind gusted outside, thudded against the door and the window like something trying to break in. Jerkily she got to her feet and came over to where I was at the sandwich board. Those cold lights still glowed in her eyes.

"Is his sandwich ready?"

I nodded and made myself smile. "Will that be all, ma'am?"

"No. I've changed my mind. I want something to eat too."
She leaned forward and stared at the glass pastry container on the back counter. "What kind of pie is that?"

"Cinnamon apple."

"I'll have a piece of it."

"Okay—sure. Just one?"

"Yes. Just one."

I turned back there, got the pie out, cut a slice, and wrapped it in waxed paper. When I came around with it she was rummaging in her purse, getting her wallet out. Back in the restroom area, I heard the man's hard, heavy steps; in the next second he appeared. And headed straight for the door.

The woman said, "How much do I owe you?"

I put the pie into the paper sack with the sandwich, and the sack on the counter. "That'll be three-eighty."

The man opened the door; the wind came shrieking in, eddying drafts of icy air. He went right on out, not even glancing at the woman or me, and slammed the door shut behind him.

She laid a five-dollar bill on the counter. Caught up the sack, pivoted, and started for the door.

"Ma'am?" I said. "You've got change coming."

She must have heard me, but she didn't look back and she didn't slow up. The pair of headlights came on out front, slicing pale wedges from the darkness; through the front window I could see the evergreens at the far edge of the lot, thick swaying shadows bent almost double by the wind. The shrieking rose again for two or three seconds, then fell back to a muted whine; she was gone.

I had never been gladder or more relieved to see customers go. I let out another breath, picked up the fiver, and moved over to the cash register. Outside, above the thrumming and wailing, the car engine revved up to a roar and there was the ratcheting noise of tires spinning on gravel. The headlights shot around and probed out toward the county highway.

Time now to close up and go home, all right; I wanted a glass of brandy and a good hot fire more than ever. I went around to the tables they'd used, to gather up the coffee cups.

But as much as I wanted to forget the two of them, I couldn't seem to get them out of my mind. Especially the woman.

I kept seeing those eyes of hers, cold and hateful like the wind, as if there was a black wind blowing inside her, too, and she'd been listening to it too long. I kept seeing her lean forward across the counter and stare at the pastry container. And I kept seeing her rummage in that big alligator purse when I turned around with the slice of pie. Something funny about the way she'd been doing that. As if she hadn't just been getting her wallet out to pay me. As if she'd been—

Oh my God, I thought.

I ran back behind the counter. Then I ran out again to the door, threw it open, and stumbled onto the gravel lot. But they were long gone; the night was a solid ebony wall.

I didn't know what to do. What could I do? Maybe she'd done what I suspicioned, and maybe she hadn't; I couldn't be sure because I don't keep an inventory on the slots of utensils behind the sandwich board. And I didn't know who they were or where they were going. I didn't even know what kind of car they were riding in.

I kept on standing there, chills racing up and down my back, listening to that black wind scream and scream around me. Feeling the cold sharp edge of it cut into my bare flesh, cut straight to the bone.

Just like the blade of a knife . . .

A CASE FOR QUIET

(With Jeffrey M. Wallmann)

The ivy-covered Kings Head Hotel sat stern and austere on the edge of little-traveled Ickley Moors in England's North Country. Constructed in the Elizabethan manner of red brick that had faded and eroded over the three centuries it had been standing, the hotel wore its garland of shredded fog like an expensive if somewhat dowdy fur wrap, and looked upon the bleak and barren moors with haughty aloofness.

Inside, beyond a small reception lobby, was a massive, rather antiquarian lounge. A deep inglenook fireplace dominated most of one wall; on its hearth logs were kept burning as long as there were guests about. The furniture was dark and heavy, composed mostly of wing chairs and long couches with ornamentally carved frames and legs.

On this night, as on most nights, the chairs and couches were occupied by some dozen ladies and gentlemen of varying ages beyond that of threescore. They sat in a silence that, to an outsider, might have seemed almost funereal—the men reading the London *Times* or the Manchester *Guardian* with careful scrutiny, drinking brandy and soda or very old Scotch; the women crocheting antimacassars and doilies or knitting argyles while they sipped cream sherry or tea laced liberally with milk and sugar. They spoke to one another rarely, and then only in whispers. An elderly waiter named Peters circulated among the guests now and then to refill glasses and empty the heavy pewter ashtrays of cigar ash and pipe dottle.

The gentle crackle of the fire in the inglenook was the only sound when the stranger made his appearance at a quarter past ten.

The stranger was a big, florid-faced man in a bulky tweed overcoat, silk muffler, and expensive driving gloves. He came into the reception lobby with a flourish, letting the thick oaken door slam behind him, and stood for a moment blowing his breath noisily through his opened mouth. Then, having spotted the bar inside the lounge, he nodded once to old Hathaway, the night clerk, and strode purposefully through the archway.

"Scotch on the rocks," he demanded of Michaels, the barman, who was manufacturing a brandy-and-soda.

"Sir?" Michaels said, looking up. He was a somewhat younger, spryer version of Peters.

"Scotch on the rocks," the stranger repeated. "And hurry it up, would you?"

"Yes, sir."

Michaels finished mixing the brandy-and-soda and placed it on the silver serving tray that Peters held waiting. Then he turned to the rows of bottles and glasses on the backbar.

The stranger took off his driving gloves. "Where's the nearest garage?" he demanded.

"Garage, sir?"

"These damned roads of yours have done something to the steering on my car. I can't go any farther until a mechanic checks it out."

"The only mechanic hereabouts is Jerome Bosley, sir," Michaels said. "He mainly repairs tractors."

"Tractors?"

"Yes, sir." Michaels carefully placed a serviette before the stranger, then centered a crystal tumbler on the napkin. He made certain the Kings Head crest on both faced the newcomer. "And a lorry now and then. But he's gone into Bridlington to visit his mum and won't be back until tomorrow evening. I'm afraid there's no one else for forty miles, sir."

"Oh, that's fine, just fine," the stranger said with heavy sarcasm. "And what am I supposed to do in the meantime?"

"I wouldn't know, sir," Michaels said. He poured a generous dollop of Scotch into the tumbler and stepped back.

The stranger scowled. "The rocks," he said.

"Sir?"

"Damn it, man, the rocks, the rocks!" The stranger pointed accusingly at his drink. "You forgot the ice. You don't expect me to drink it *warm*, do you?"

"No, sir. Of course not, sir. Peters, would you. . . ?"

Peters bowed and moved away slowly through the lounge and across the darkened dining room beyond. The stranger watched his retreating form for a moment, then turned to survey the remainder of the lounge. Its occupants studiedly ignored him.

The stranger made a derisive sound and swung back to Michaels, thumping his gloves on the polished surface of the bar. Then, in what to him was an undertone, he said to himself, "An archaeologist's dream—a tomb full of old fossils."

This comment stiffened the backbone of Michaels, produced a harsh intake of breath from Colonel (Ret.) Gloucester-Smith, and caused the widow Pemblington to drop a stitch. Other than that, the lounge was reminiscent of a forest glade on a windless day.

The stranger said, "I have to make an important call. Where's your telephone?"

"There is no telephone, sir."

"What's that?"

"We have no telephone here."

"Nonsense! Every hotel has a phone!"

"Not the Kings Head, sir. Not any longer. We had ours taken out some time ago."

"What the devil for?"

"Our guests have no use for them," Michaels said. "They've a nasty habit of ringing in the late hours. Very disturbing."

The stranger stared at him in exasperation. "I don't suppose there's anyplace I can send a wire?"

"No, sir. Not at this time of night."

"Damn it, man, I have to contact my business associates in London and tell them where I am. They have no idea I was driving up to Manchester today; won't have the faintest suspicion of where I've gone."

"I'm sorry, sir."

"Damned well ought to be," the stranger muttered. He looked up as Peters returned with a bowl containing four ice cubes. "Well, it's about time. I thought maybe you got lost."

Some of the guests had now taken notice. There was a raising of eyes over the top edges of the *Times* and the *Guardian*, a lowering of unfinished antimacassars and doilies and argyles. Sir Pruitt, sitting in the corner near the disconnected phonograph, had sipped just enough brandy to sit up and glower at the stranger before sinking back out of sight behind his chair's wing.

If the stranger felt the gazes on him, he gave no indication. Impatiently he watched as Peters lowered two ice cubes into his Scotch with a pair of sugar tongs; then he swirled the liquid with his index finger and lifted the glass. "Well, here's mud in your eye!" he said and drained the Scotch in one swallow. He smacked his lips, put the glass down, and demanded a refill.

Michaels poured.

"Got anything to eat around here?" the stranger asked.

"The dining room is closed, sir."

"I can see that. What about sandwiches, or some cheese and crackers?"

"I'm afraid not, sir."

"Peanuts, then? Pretzels? Onion rings?"

"I shall see, sir," Michaels said.

After some searching, he located a half-empty box of arrowroot biscuits. He shook some of the biscuits into a silver serving dish and placed the dish before the stranger.

"What're these things?"

"Biscuits, sir. We serve them at teatime, occasionally."

"Biscuits?" The stranger picked one up, nibbled it, made a face, and said, "*Chalk*, you mean!"

"I believe they are all we have at the moment, sir."

The stranger mumbled something incoherent and ate another biscuit. He chewed with a harsh grating intensity that caused the widow Pemblington to drop another stitch.

His mouth still full of biscuit, the stranger said, "You have any rooms available here, or do I have to sleep in my car tonight?"

"We have accommodations, sir."

"Well, well, don't tell me." The stranger turned toward the archway and shouted, "Clerk! Hey, clerk!"

Several of the guests started at this outburst. There was a scuttling sound in the reception lobby and Hathaway appeared. "Sir?"

The stranger pitched him a leather keycase. Hathaway failed to raise his arms in time to catch it, and the case made a loud jangling noise as it hit the floor. The old fellow bent over slowly to retrieve it, one hand braced on his knee for support.

"Take my bags out of the orange Porsche outside and check me in, will you? Name's Rasmussen, Harold J. Rasmussen."

Hathaway was having difficulty regaining an upright position. "For the night only, sir?"

"I damned well hope so. But who knows what's wrong with my car? I could be here *days*, God forbid." He popped another biscuit into his mouth. "Make that a room with a bath—and there'd better be some hot water to go with it."

"Yes, sir," Hathaway said. He took his leave.

The stranger turned back to the bar. "I hope he doesn't have a heart attack or something, carrying my bags." He seemed to think such a prospect was uproariously funny; his laugh was sharp and loud, almost a bark.

After a time he stopped laughing, wiped his eyes, blew his nose into a silk handkerchief, and said to Michaels, "How about some music?"

"Sir?"

"Music. You hard of hearing? If I'm going to be stuck in a place like this tonight, I might as well enjoy myself. So come on, let's liven up this mausoleum."

He had finally managed to collect the undivided attention of each of the guests. His words were like a sudden chill wind through that proverbial forest glade. An almost imperceptible rustling, like that of disturbed leaves, could be heard throughout the lounge.

Colonel (Ret.) Gloucester-Smith sighed softly and rose from his chair. He glanced around the room, sighed again, then crossed to the bar in a stiff military stride.

"Who're you?" Rasmussen demanded.

"Colonel Gloucester-Smith, Retired, at your service. I wonder, sir, if you would care to join me in a drink."

"What's that? You offering to buy a round, Corporal?"

"*Colonel*," Gloucester-Smith corrected, wincing. "Yes, my good man, I am so offering. Local hospitality, you know."

"Well, that's damned decent of you, Corporal."

"Indeed," Gloucester-Smith said. He looked at Michaels. "Some of the vintage blend for our guest, I believe."

"Very good, sir." Michaels withdrew a short, amber-colored bottle from beneath the bar and poured a generous dollop over the melting ice cubes in Rasmussen's glass.

"Aren't you having any, Corporal?"

"Brandy is my tipple and I've a full snifter."

"Your loss," Rasmussen told him. "Nothing like good Scotch. Well, cheers, old boy." He lifted the glass, sniffed, nodded approvingly, and tossed off half the drink. He smacked his lips, nodded again, and finished it. "Not bad, Corporal, not bad at all. It—"

Rasmussen's eyes suddenly bulged wide, and his mouth opened and a strangled sound came from his lips. His right hand clutched his throat. Then, abruptly, he toppled over onto the carpet, twitched once, and lay still.

The room was very quiet. Colonel Gloucester-Smith knelt beside the stranger and felt his wrist. Then he rose and motioned to Peters and to Michaels. The two servants lifted Rasmussen's inert form and carried it through the darkened dining room, through the kitchen and out the rear door and away onto the fog-shrouded moors.

In the still and silent lounge, circumspect hands resumed their chores and the only sound was the crackling of the fire in the inglenook. No one spoke until Colonel Gloucester-Smith returned once more to his chair.

Cecil Whitehead, on his immediate right, leaned forward. "How many does that make now, Colonel?"

"Six, I believe."

"I do hope there won't be any more," Whitehead whispered. "I so enjoy this lovely quiet."

"Quite," Colonel Gloucester-Smith whispered back, and folded his copy of the London *Times* carefully so the newsprint would not rustle.

WHODUNIT

The last person on earth lay dead in a room, a victim of foul play.